BEYOND THE PARALLEL

ROBIN BRANDE

BEYOND THE PARALLEL
Parallelogram Quartet, Book 4
By Robin Brande

Published by Ryer Publishing
www.ryerpublishing.com
Anniversary Edition © 2026 Robin Brande
www.robinbrande.com
All rights reserved.
Cover art by Joseph Gough, Simonkr, and Steve Allen/Dreamstime
Hikmak Studios, Adi Arianto, Likanis_flares, vetortradition,
Rizkreativ, Icons8, DGJ, goodprintsshop, Sketchily, Sinaelgicon, and
Marie Dautel/Canva
Cover design by Ryer Publishing, based on original design by Robin
Ludwig/gobookcoverdesign.com
Ebook ISBN: 978-1-946627-15-5
Paperback ISBN: 978-1-952383-24-3
Hardback ISBN: 978-1-952383-71-7

ALSO BY ROBIN BRANDE

YOUNG ADULT STANDALONES

Evolution, Me & Other Freaks of Nature

Doggirl

Fat Cat

Replay

Young Adult Series

Young Adult Self-Help

Psychic Cozy Mysteries
A Mind for Mysteries
The Secret Juror
The Truth Chamber

Fantasy & Science Fiction
Dove Season Series
Heart of the Future
The Love of a Good Dog
The Miraculous Unknown
Life with the Afterlife

And Many More

See the complete
list of books at

RobinBrande.com

BEYOND THE PARALLEL

par·al·lel·o·gram /par-*uh*-lel-*uh*-gram/ *noun*: a four-sided figure having both pairs of opposite sides parallel to each other.

par·al·lel·o·gram: communication between parallel worlds

"If we all worked on the assumption that what is accepted as true really is true, then there would be little hope for advance." ~Orville Wright, American Inventor and Aviation Pioneer

1

———

W*alk*, I have to keep telling myself. *Don't run.*

But the urge is so strong.

"Halli Markham!" Sarah shouts from the distance, and she's already racing toward me. Across this vast, polished lobby, toward the girl she thinks I am.

Walk, don't run. Stay calm. Stay in control.

I know this scene. I've been here before. It's Monday. I'm in London. I've just spent the day touring Halli's parents' headquarters, and now Sarah and Daniel are here to meet me.

I don't have much time.

"And Red!" Sarah cries, hugging me first, then the dog. "How are you, you handsome boy?" Red wags his tail so hard he might achieve liftoff.

I look past Sarah to where Daniel is still making his

slow, steady way. He's limping a little, just like last time.

So far everything is like last time.

Which means by tomorrow night I'll be screaming. My head will feel like it's been split in two. I'll be rushed to the hospital, pumped full of drugs, unable to think or get away.

A week later, I'll be dead.

I want it so badly: to run to Daniel now, to throw my arms around him, hold him hard, and whisper urgently in his ear, *"It's me. It's Audie. Halli is trapped inside my body, back in my universe. This is me in here. We have to hurry. I need your help. We don't have much time."*

But I can't. I know that. Because telling him the truth right now—this day, this exact moment—started a whole chain reaction before, a chain that ended in pain and suffering and death, and I can't afford for the any of those things to happen this time. I can't take even one step down that same path. I have to do it all differently—*everything*.

My life depends on it.

2

I t's tricky, traveling across time and space.
Especially when you're not really sure how you did it.

"How are you?" Daniel asks, giving me a friendly, platonic hug.

"Great!" I could say. *"Although I've only been alive for about five minutes so far, so let me get back to you on that."*

Because the truth is, I'm not really sure myself.

It's all coming at me pretty fast: the sudden sunshine through the windows, the echoing noise of the lobby, people calling to me, talking to me, wanting things from me—when just a moment ago I was somewhere dark and peaceful and warm, all by myself, and in the moment before that I remember being *furious*—

I kneel down next to Red and pretend I really need

to pet him right away. Anything to buy myself a few extra seconds so I can think through my next move.

"My manners!" Sarah says, seeming to notice for the first time the other people standing around me. "Sarah Everett," she tells the group, "and this is my brother, Daniel." She shakes hands with Mr. Chilton, the man in charge of the London facility. Says something complimentary about his tie. Then she turns and smiles for the camera. "I suspect there's a person behind those."

The guy holding what look like big square binoculars lowers them to enjoy the sight of Sarah with his bare eyes. He offers his hand. "Bryan Stewart."

Bryan. The history reporter Halli's parents saddled me with for this trip. The Bryan Stewart who hounded me so hard, looking for the next great scoop on the famous Halli Markham, he ended up being the main reason why I was rushed to the hospital where I spent the last remaining week of my life. No thanks, Bryan. Not this time. I'm going to have to figure out what to do about you.

Sarah turns to the final member of our little party. "Jake Demetrios," he says, smiling politely, but not exactly with as much enthusiasm as Bryan.

Jake. That one ... is a little more complicated. In love with Halli most of his life, sort of made me fall in love with him for a little while, and now ... well, I'm going to have to get away from him, too. I need to have total freedom to do the things I need to do if I'm going to come out of this whole situation alive this time.

"Where's your cousin?" Sarah asks me. "Is she here?"

"Couldn't make it." I flash a look at Daniel that I know he'll understand. He's quick. And he, unlike Sarah, knows there is no cousin. He knows Audie is a visitor from a parallel universe. He just doesn't know he's looking at me right now.

But he can guess that the cluster of other people around us might be curious why his sister is asking about some cousin Halli Markham doesn't have.

"We don't mean to interrupt if you still have work to do," Daniel says in his polite British way.

"Of course we mean to interrupt!" Sarah says. "Halli Markham, we are here to steal you away. We have grand plans for you this afternoon, and then I hope you know you'll be staying with us for as long as you're here. You can share my unreasonably tiny bedroom in our parents' unreasonably—"

"—*tiny house*," I could finish for her, but I don't.

Instead I just smile. "That sounds great."

"Splendid!" Sarah says. She looks at Bryan and Jake and I know what's coming, I'm just not fast enough to catch her at the start. "And of course your fr—"

No, my "friends" aren't welcome to come along. Not this time. That won't work for me at all.

"Hey, Jake, Bryan—can I talk to you two for a sec?" I have no idea what I'll say, I just know I need to break up this party as soon as possible. "Let me just finish this up," I tell Sarah and Daniel. "Then I'll be all yours."

"Will that be all, Miss Markham?" Mr. Chilton asks me.

"Yes. Thank you." He looks happy to be released. As I recall, I asked him a lot of questions about the science behind one of Halli's parents' inventions. Mr. Chilton didn't seem to like that.

I draw Jake and Bryan a little ways off to the side. "Listen," I say. "I have a favor to ask both of you."

I feel a strange vibration against my leg. I look down and it's Red. It's Red leaning against me and growling low in his throat. Growling, it appears, at Jake.

Jake can take the hint. Even though Bryan is right next to me, Jake backs up and stands a few feet away.

"Red, it's okay." But the growl gets deeper. I reach down to pet his head, but that doesn't comfort him at all. He just keeps snarling at Jake, warning him away.

Which makes no sense whatsoever. The two of them were best buddies a few days ago, back on Halli's parents' island. Jake must have thrown the stick for Red at least five hundred times. That creates a certain bond.

But I don't have time to sort it out. I have a deal to make.

"Look," I tell Bryan, "I haven't seen my friends for a long time." Kind of a lie, since they were visiting me in the hospital just a day or two ago. "I'd like to hang out with them for a while, you know? Relax for a couple of days. Without ..." I gesture at his camera. "That."

Bryan doesn't look happy. Halli's parents promised him full access to me. He's supposed to get the exclusive story on Halli's new venture, finally becoming involved in her parents' business empire.

"But I'll make it worth it to you," I say. The idea occurs to me in a flash, and I know in my gut it's right. "If you leave me alone for a few days and just let me rest and relax, I'll give you something no one else is going to get."

"I'm listening," Bryan says.

I glance at Jake. From his safe distance away, he's listening, too.

I take a deep breath, like this is hard for me.

It's not.

"You know how private I've been about Ginny's death?" I start. And it's true: Halli doesn't even like to talk to me about her grandmother's death. Even a year later it still feels too raw. But in that brief time that Halli and I shared a brain together—*my* brain, in my former body, just a short time ago—I saw enough footage in her memories to be able to piece together a pretty believable story.

Maybe a day ago I never would have considered using Halli this way—using her private memories to buy myself some time. But that was before I understood exactly how Halli has treated my own life. She didn't worry about messing up everything I've worked so hard to put into place. She felt perfectly fine quitting school, quitting my job, running off in the middle of the night with some guy she just met—okay, a parallel version of Daniel, but still, it's not like she really knew him—and just leaving without even bothering to write my poor mom a note. I begged her. I pleaded with her. But Halli didn't care. She said she had to do what she had to do.

Well, so do I.

"I'll give you a full hour," I tell Bryan. "Maybe even up to two. I'll share with you how my life has been this past year without Ginny. I'll tell you some of my favorite childhood memories of her. Would you like that?"

Bryan smiles. I've got him. And he thinks he's got me. "Monologue, or can I ask you questions?"

"Um …" That's a little tricky, since I don't exactly know every part of Halli's history. But do I know enough to fake it? "Tell you what," I say, "you can ask, and I reserve the right not to answer. You'll edit out any questions I don't feel comfortable answering. Deal?"

"Deal." Bryan shakes my hand.

One down.

"Jake," I say.

Red growls again, just at the mere word. Jake takes another step back.

"What should I tell your parents?" he asks.

Okay, well, that's a relief. I thought he'd put up more of a fight about me not wanting him around. Last time he was pretty possessive—especially whenever Daniel was in the picture, like right now.

But Jake is right: I'm going to have to come up with a story for Halli's parents. They might not care about their daughter, but they do care about the image she projects. I found that out a few days ago when Halli's mother chewed me out for all my "attention-seeking" behavior like being rushed to the hospital. She was probably furious when I died—think of the publicity.

"Tell them whatever you want," I say, sounding like Halli, but meaning it myself. "It's none of their business what I do. I've been on my own a long time. I don't have to clear things with them."

Besides, I'm well aware that Halli's parents can check up on me anytime they want just by looking at the tracking information sent out by the microchip beneath Halli's collarbone. So telling them where I am or where I'm going is pointless. It's *why* I'm doing what I'm doing that is entirely my secret.

"Of course, Miss Markham," Jake says, way too formally for a guy I know I was making out with just a little while ago, every time Mr. Chilton left the room.

But it's good Jake is keeping everything looking professional. Last time, Sarah guessed right away that Jake and I had something going on. And since I made the mistake of telling Daniel last time that it was really me in here, he wasn't happy at all to find out I'd been kissing another guy—even if I was kissing him with Halli's lips, not mine. And then Bryan the reporter put the pieces together himself and forced Jake and me to confess, and then everything kept going haywire after that.

So if Jake wants to pretend he just works for Halli's parents and has no personal relationship with me, I'm all for it.

"I'll need my clothes delivered to Sarah's house," I remember to tell him. Last time I had to go back to the hotel first, which led to more kissing, and then that whole confrontation with Bryan ... "The driver can get the address when he drops me off."

"Of course, Miss Markham," Jake says again. "I'll go speak to the driver now, if you're ready to go. He can take you and your friends."

Good. So far changing things up this time is a lot easier than I thought it would be.

"And me," Jake adds.

3

"*N*o, *you don't say that,*" I want to tell Jake. That wasn't how it was last time.

Last time I stayed at Sarah and Daniel's house by myself. Daniel and I talked through the night while I caught him up on everything that had happened to me in the past few days: waking up in Halli's body, having to pretend to be her during that whole bizarre weekend at her parents' island, and yes, even as much explanation as I felt comfortable giving him for why he'd seen me, the girl he thought was his girlfriend, kissing Jake. Not the best part of the evening.

What *was* the best part was finally having someone I could talk to about all of it. Someone I could be honest with. And also someone with enough science background to try to help me puzzle through the physics of how it all happened. It's not like we came to some great conclusion—if we had, I wouldn't be back here right now, playing out this whole scene again—but it was just … nice. Nice having him there for me. Nice being with him again.

Which is why I realized it was him I really wanted, not Jake. No matter how charming Jake can be. Which is very charming when he wants.

But right now? Trying to horn in on my private time with Daniel and Sarah? Not so charming. Especially since it's their parents that I need to talk to most.

"You can't come," I tell Jake. "I just want to be with my friends by myself."

"I'm afraid I have to come," he says. "You know the rules."

"The *rules*?" I can't believe he just said that to me. To Halli Markham. Halli Markham doesn't abide by anyone's rules.

"Miss Markham, please," he says, taking half a step forward. Red immediately growls him back to his place.

Jake casts a glance over at Bryan, who is now off chatting with Sarah and Daniel.

"Halli," Jake says, keeping his voice low. "You know that won't work. I have to stay with you. They're checking on me."

I can guess who *they* are. And I know how they're checking: Jake has a microchip, too. Everyone here does. Halli's parents must have the password to Jake's tracking information. Great.

But why should I care about that? I'm here for one thing, and that's to save my own life. I won't let Halli's parents or Jake or anyone else interfere with that.

"I'm going to my friends' house by myself," I tell him. "You're not invited. I don't care what my parents' *rules* are. They're not in charge of me and neither are you."

I almost feel like backing that up with a growl of my own.

"Of course, Miss Markham," Jake answers. Then he smiles, more to himself than me. "I told them you wouldn't like it."

"I don't. You were right."

I'm starting to get the hang of this, being Halli. She says what she wants. She does what she wants. There's nothing like seeing her take over my life and discard the people and things she didn't like to teach me how to do it myself.

Truth is, it feels good. It feels strong.

"I understand," Jake says. "Listen, I appreciate you letting me stick around as long as I did. Thank you. It was an honor to finally meet you. I wouldn't trade that for anything. I'll go give the driver your instructions.

Thank you, Miss Markham. It's been a pleasure." He tries to take a step forward again and offer me his hand, but Red puts a stop to that. Instead Jake just gives me a solemn nod, then turns and walks away.

It's all too … easy.

And something doesn't feel quite right. What he said sounded so final. I suspect in a way it is.

"What will they do?" I call after him.

"Don't worry about it," he says back.

"No, Jake, wait."

He pauses, and so do I. Because right now I have a decision to make. If I don't ask, I won't know. And that's probably for the best.

But then I won't know.

"Are we ready?" Sarah asks, seeing that my conversation with Jake is over. "I'm *famished*. We're taking you to the loveliest café, where they serve the most mammoth cinnamon buns, and they have scones so sublime they will make you weep—"

"Just a second," I tell her. "Red, stay." The dog looks at me, seems to accept the command, but I can see that he's still tense. He doesn't want me going off on my own—not to go talk to *him*.

I catch up to Jake. "Just tell me."

He shrugs. "You can guess."

"They'll fire you."

"It's all right," he says. "I can find work someplace else."

"But where will you live?" Jake and his whole family work for Halli's parents and live on their private island. If he's out of a job, he's probably out of a home, too.

Am I really going to do that to him?

"Halli, I meant what I said," Jake tells me. "It was worth it. Why do you think I took the apprenticeship with your father in the first place? I could have looked for work someplace else."

"But you wanted to meet me." He already confessed that to me last time, so I assume he did it this time, too.

Jake nods. "And I did. And it was great." He smiles and offers me his hand again. Without my guard dog here, I can shake it.

"I'll be fine," Jake says. "Thanks for everything. I'm going to go talk to the driver now."

He heads toward the door outside.

Aaaarrrrgggg ...

"Hold on," I tell him.

I jog back to the others. Sarah is laughing at something Bryan the reporter just said.

She threads her arm through his. "Do you know he's just been telling me the most fascinating stories of all the people he's interviewed? Of course you and your grandmother are top of the top, but do you know he actually met Spirelli?"

"Yeah, that's great. Hey, Daniel, can I talk to you for a second?"

"Certainly."

I lead him over to where Red is still obediently sitting in a stay.

"I have a situation."

"Right," Daniel answers, immediately serious. That's what I like about him—so entirely reliable.

"There are things I need to talk to you about," I say. "Audie things." Now he's really paying attention. "I don't want Jake to hear any of it, for obvious reasons."

"Understood," Daniel says. He's well aware that he is the only person in this universe—at this stage, at least — who knows about Halli and me. Eventually, last time, I told his parents and a few other people, and that didn't end up so well.

"So I don't want him coming with us," I continue, "but my parents will fire him if he doesn't. Is there someplace close to your house where he can stay, but not *too* close?"

"There's an inn. Not far."

"Will that work?" What I really want to know is whether the tracking will show that Jake is with me, but I can't come right out and ask it. Halli would probably already know the answer. I need Daniel to believe I'm her.

"I think so," he says.

"Okay."

I have no idea if I'm doing the right thing. Maybe I'm doing exactly the wrong thing. I could be rid of

Jake Demetrios right now. Let him go fend for himself while I do the same.

That's what the real Halli would do.

Jake pushes through the glass doors and calls that the car is ready.

I'm on my own here. Every decision is mine.

"Okay," I answer. "Let's go."

4

"No, but you *must* come!" Sarah says, holding tightly to Bryan's arm. "What could possibly be more enchanting than sitting in a café with me and thrilling me with more of your stories while I gaze adoringly into your eyes?"

Sarah is just teasing him, the way I've seen her flirt with guys before, but there clearly is a lot of adoration there—it's just coming from the other direction. Bryan looks miserable about having to leave us. Good. He caused me a lot of pain. And if he's only just realizing he made a bad deal with me by agreeing to disappear for a few days, that's his problem, not mine. I have no pity for him.

"Off we go," I tell Sarah and the others. Jake doesn't even try to sit in the back with us—Red has made it clear he's not welcome. So he sits up front next to the driver while Sarah and Daniel and the dog and I load into the back.

And there I am, in the reflection of the car window: Halli Markham, in the flesh, no question about it. That's her long, thick hair. Her broad shoulders and muscular frame. Her.

I may never look like myself again. Maybe it's time to accept that.

My old, original body doesn't want me anymore. It threw me out, like a body rejecting an organ transplant. I could feel myself being squeezed. Pushed. I wasn't welcome anymore.

Or maybe it wasn't entirely my body's choice. Halli had a part to play. She wanted one thing, I wanted another, and ultimately the stronger of us won.

I was too weak for my own body to want me anymore. It preferred a better owner. How's that for a bitter truth?

Sarah reaches across the seat to clutch my hand. "Halli Markham, how lovely to have you back with us. Although I do wish you'd brought your cousin along! Poor Dan here is utterly forlorn. Aren't you, Daniel?"

"Forlorn," he agrees, humoring her.

"Don't pretend you're unaffected," his sister says. "I could tell many a tale of how you've been moping about the house this past week, pining for a certain someone."

Daniel ignores her. "Any chance she'll come?" he asks me.

I hesitate, then shake my head. It won't do either of us any good for me to pretend otherwise.

"Shame," he says.

"Yeah," I agree. I glance down before I can fall into the trap of gazing too intently into his eyes. *Look, it's me in here! Can't you see?* This isn't a game. Knowing who I am only leads to trouble.

I clear my throat and give Red a solid scratch behind the ear. "Okay, so change of plans: we're not going to a café right now—" I hold up my hand before Sarah can object. "—because I'd rather go straight to your house. I've been listening to that man Mr. Chilton drone on all day, and I have a headache like you wouldn't believe. I'm hoping your very tiny house has at least one decent-sized bathtub," which I know it does, "so I can soak for a little while. I'm afraid I won't be very good company until I do."

Now it's Sarah who looks forlorn. "Oh. All right, then … only … I may have invited a few friends …"

I remember. Two very nice girls from Sarah's school. But those hours I spent at the café that afternoon ended up being a huge waste of time. Plus the whole thing wasn't exactly relaxing. Daniel was still in shock from me telling him who I really was, and he and Jake were already brewing up the rivalry that would eventually end in my death. If Jake hadn't been so jealous, he never would have tried to follow Daniel and me the next day. Then Sarah led him and Bryan right to us, and everything went wrong from there.

So I can think of a lot better things to do with my time right now than to go back to that café. I'd rather find someplace where I can be alone and finally have the chance to think.

"I promise I'll meet your friends some other time," I tell Sarah, even though I have no intention of doing that. This isn't a vacation. I'm not here to socialize and play.

While Sarah gives the driver the address to her house, then makes a quick comm call to her friends telling them we won't be there, I hold a quiet conversation with Daniel.

"Audie really wanted to come."

"I understand," he says. "We knew … it might be difficult."

Back when he first met me, the only impediments were time zone and whether Halli and I could sync up so I could travel over to this universe. Those were the easy days.

"How is she?" he asks.

"She's fine. She … misses you." It's a risk, but I have to say it. He's right here and I need to say it. I just make sure I'm not actually looking at him right now.

"You said you had other things to talk to me about."

"I do," I say. "We will."

Then Sarah is done, and so are we.

Their neighborhood is nice, very English, and I've been here before. What I didn't notice before was the inn. No surprise, since there are no signs out front or any other indication that's what it is.

"Should we invite him for supper?" Sarah asks as the driver pulls up in front.

"No," I answer. "He'll be fine."

I lower the window just enough to hear what Jake has to say. Red growls so loudly I can barely make it out.

"Tomorrow!" Jake finally shouts.

"Maybe," I shout back, then I raise the window again. I don't mind saving his job and keeping him from being homeless, but that's as far as my charity goes. And I especially don't plan on having him tag along on the excursion I intend to take tomorrow.

"Wait here," Sarah tells me when the car pulls up in front of her house. "My parents don't know you're staying over yet—you're meant to be a surprise. They think they're not meeting you until the party."

The party. Right. Sarah and Daniel's father's birthday. Last time I missed it because I was in the hospital. And there was a bit of extra cleanup ahead of the party thanks to poor Red flipping out and tearing their house apart because I wasn't with him.

I'll have to make it up to all of them this time.

"Come on, Dan," Sarah says. "You and I go in first.

I'll wave to you when it's time," she tells me. Then the two of them exit the car and head up the walkway into their narrow, two-story house.

I'm suddenly exhausted. I've been thinking so hard and performing so hard for the past hour or so, it's finally all catching up with me. I'm glad I came up with the excuse of a hot bath. I need a good long stretch of quality time with myself to try to get a grip on all of this.

Sarah is waving to me from the doorway. Inside that house are the two people who hold the key to what I need to know. I need to decide what to say—how much to say. And how much of it I want to Daniel to know ahead of time. I'm going to need his help. But he has to think he's helping Halli, not me.

My head is pounding. That part of my excuse to Sarah wasn't a lie.

Now she's standing on her porch, jumping up and down and waving wildly because she thinks I don't see her. It's sweet how enthusiastic she is about Halli. And how nice she's always been to me. I obviously have my own problems to deal with here, but there's no reason I can't be a good sport with her while I'm at it.

"Come on," I tell the dog. "Show time."

5

"She said I have the makings of a true explorer," Sarah tells her parents. She laughs right along with them. "She did! Tell them, Halli Markham."

"I must have," I admit, although I have no memory of it. Maybe the real Halli told her that while we were all together in the Alps.

"Explorers don't need sums and calculations," Sarah argues. Apparently there's been some discussion about her performance in school. "All they need is a stalwart heart and an excellent sense of direction. Tell them it's so, Halli Markham."

"Those will get you far," I say. Although I'm pretty sure Halli has needed math throughout the years as part of her navigation and planning.

But it's so much fun to watch Sarah and Daniel with their parents, I'll go along with whatever anyone says.

We've been enjoying a late afternoon snack of tea and toast. "I would have loved to serve you something *proper*," their mother, Francie Everett, told me as she set out the jars of jam while simultaneously giving her children the stink eye, "but no one told me we'd have a guest. Not to mention such a famous one."

"Sarah's idea," Daniel had answered, holding up his hands in surrender.

"She enjoys being treated like a regular, average, boring person—isn't that true, Halli Markham?"

"Absolutely true," I agreed. I've had a taste of Halli's fame, and I didn't like it one bit. "Besides," I told Francie, "this is better than anything I could have had in a café."

"Liars are always welcome at my table, of course," Francie said, "but one of us will still have to go to the market if I'm to serve you anything for supper except leftover soup and more toast. And I assume your companion would enjoy some food as well."

She reached down and scratched Red behind one of his ears. The dog gave a thump of his tail. It was true, I didn't seem to have any food for him. It was nice of Francie to think of it.

"I'll be happy to reimburse you," I told Francie and her husband, Sam Wheeler. Although I wasn't sure how

I would do that. I know Halli has lots and lots of money, but I have no idea how to access it.

"Don't be daft," Sarah scolded me. "You're our guest."

"I'll go to the market later," Sam offered at the time.

But right now, he's still too busy discussing Sarah's ambition to become an explorer.

"What about the histories?" he asks me. "I imagine anyone traveling the world needs to know who the people are and where they came from. Not to mention understanding a few languages—*French*, for example." He gives Sarah a significant look, which I take to mean she's failing in that class, too.

"Oh, pish posh," Sarah says, waving her hand dismissively. "You know nothing of the great explorers. The only history I'll need is to reread all of Halli's and her grandmother's journals. As for languages, I'll rely on the oldest form of human communication."

"Grunting?" Daniel suggests.

"How very droll," Sarah answers. "No, for your information, I have been practicing signs." She demonstrates by pinching her fingers together and bringing them up to her mouth.

"Kiss me?" Francie suggests.

"Precisely," Sarah jokes back. "And this one?" She wraps her arms around her torso and pretends to shiver.

"Hug me?" her father guesses.

"Yes," Sarah says. "So you can see I shall have all the love and protection I need out in the greater world. Halli Markham would be a fool not to take me on as an apprentice."

Sarah pops a last piece of toast into her mouth and rises from the table. "Now if you'll excuse me, I must go run Miss Markham a bath. My mistress is weary from the day, and although she's far too polite to say so, she finds her present company especially wearisome. Your bath will be ready in just a few minutes, Miss. I hope you enjoy the scent of lavender."

"Thank you." I smile at Sarah and she gives me a little bow. Then she leaves me alone with the three people I need to talk to most.

It was nice relaxing for a little bit and just enjoying the company. But I have to seize the opportunities as they come.

Liars are always welcome at my table ...

"So ... speaking of school," I say, "I've been thinking about applying to Oxford."

It's the only information I have to go on. When Daniel visited me in the hospital a few days ago, he told me that he and his parents had just met with a professor at Oxford and described everything that had happened to me—from the whole traveling between universes thing to the piercing headaches that kept me trapped in a hospital. The professor told them he'd seen a case like that before.

What? How? When? But Daniel said it was too complicated, and I needed to hear the professor's story for myself.

Which was fine, in theory, except I ran out of life before I could do it.

Just like the professor warned them might happen. He said my condition could deteriorate. He said I could die.

And since he was right about that, I need to hear the rest of what he has to say. As soon as possible—tomorrow.

"Oxford?" Daniel says, obviously surprised. "Not that you wouldn't excel there," he hurries to add, since I'm sure he doesn't want to offend Halli, "but … I didn't realize you were interested in formal education."

He's right, of course. The real Halli has absolutely zero interest in school. She proved that within the first hour of having to sit through one of my classes and pretend to be me. She could barely wait to escape.

"I wasn't before," I say. "But now with Ginny gone … I just thought it might be a good direction to take next. You know, a new challenge."

"It would certainly be that," Francie says. "Oxford. Very competitive place, you know?"

"I know." I almost laugh. The fact that I'm sitting in their kitchen right now is a direct result of trying to get into another competitive college, Columbia University. That seems like a lifetime ago.

Technically, considering where and who I am right now, it really was another lifetime.

"What would you want to study?" Francie asks me.

"Science of some sort."

Now Daniel looks really shocked.

"A friend of mine got me interested in it," I say, giving him a significant look.

"Oh." He smiles at me in return. He knows I'm talking about Audie, but his mother assumes I'm referring to him.

"You've told her about your studies?" Francie asks him. "Well done," she tells me. "You should feel very flattered. Daniel rarely tells anyone what he's been working on—"

"She wouldn't be interested, Mum."

"Of course I would," I say, and it's true. But Francie is right: I've noticed that Daniel always seems to deflect attention away from himself anytime we start talking about his schooling. He told me he knows a little about science and about plants, but that's it. And Sarah said he's interested in something called "neurobotany," but then I think Daniel changed the subject.

"So tell me," I say. "I want to know."

"I'll bore you with it some other time," he answers. "Now, what about you and Oxford? Does that mean you'd move here?"

"I don't know, I suppose so."

"How soon?" Daniel asks.

See, this is why I needed a bath first. I should have worked out all of the elements of my lie before I tried it out on people.

"I'm not really sure," I say. I don't know why Daniel is pushing me so hard. He should know Halli's life is complicated.

But looking at his expression—this combination of both eagerness and caution—I think maybe I get it:

He's asking because of me. Audie. And the pleasure of that realization brings a nice warm flush to my face.

The way it worked before, I could visit Halli wherever she was—the Alps, Colorado, wherever. Which meant that if she ever went to London, I could visit Daniel, too. It was why he looked so disappointed this afternoon when he asked me if Audie was here, too, and I said no. He probably assumed I'd come along.

I love that he cares about that. But I can't let him see how happy that makes me. I have to act like it's no big deal.

"Hate to be the bearer of bad news," Sam tells me, "but there's no guarantee they'll accept you. As Francie said, it's highly competitive. Simply deciding you want to go there isn't enough."

"Right," I say, getting back to business. "I know that. But Ginny told me if I ever wanted to go, I should talk to this professor friend of hers there. She said he could help me get in." I hope that sounds plausible. Ginny Markham was famous all over the world. She probably knew a professor or two.

"Who is it?" Sam asks.

"See, that's the thing," I say. "I don't know his name. She told me this a long time ago. I was hoping maybe you guys could help me find out who he is."

"It's possible," Francie says. "Sam went there for a time."

"And elsewhere for a time," Sam adds wryly. I'm sure there's a story there. "What college is he in, do you know?"

"I don't know." I remember that Oxford is broken up into a bunch of different colleges with very British-sounding names, but I have no idea what they're called or which ones belong to which subjects.

Francie laughs lightly. "You're not giving us much to go on. Do you know anything about him at all?"

"Yes, I do. He's very old—ancient," I say, using Daniel's description of him. "He's practically deaf."

"That could describe fifty percent of the faculty," Sam says. "What is his field? What does he specialize in? Classics, languages, mathematics …"

How am I supposed to explain it? *He's someone who knows what happens to you when you switch bodies with someone in a different universe.* "It's sort of …"

"Ready!" Sarah calls down from upstairs.

"Just a minute!" *Think of something, Audie.* "It would

be … some kind of unusual science. Something about …" I glance at Daniel. He's watching me, very still. He's probably wondering if I'm going to tell his parents Audie's and my secret. *As little as I can.* "Something about physics. Or maybe … parallel universes." There. I said it. Daniel looks only mildly surprised.

Francie and Sam both process that. "Binty?" Sam asks his wife.

"No, Binty is more of the supersciences," Francie says. "Do you mean fringe science?" she asks me.

"Yes," I answer. "Maybe. What would that be?"

"The philosophical sciences," Francie says. "Theories rather than practice."

"Maybe," I say. "Sure."

"It's Venn," Daniel says with great confidence.

"Venn?" his father repeats with a chuckle. "Haven't seen him in decades. Is he still alive, then?"

"Professor Lacksmith mentioned him the other day," Daniel says. "It sounded as if they met fairly recently."

"But he'd be over a hundred by now, wouldn't he?" Sam asks.

Ancient, just like Daniel said.

"Well, one way to find out," Francie answers. She gets up from the table and retrieves a small tablet from the kitchen counter. She sits back down and starts swiping and poking at the screen.

"I'm not a magician!" Sarah calls down the stairs. "I

cannot return cold to heat! If you want me to draw you another bath, I will, but this one smells so heavenly!"

Be a good sport.

"Coming! I'll be back in a little while," I tell Daniel and his parents. "But if you can find out anything about this Venn guy—if you think he's the right one …"

"*Doctor* Venn," Sam corrects me. "Wasn't I brought up for that once myself?"

"Prickly, is he?" Francie asks.

"I imagine he has to be careful," Sam says. "Professors in his line—not much respect from his colleagues. Probably made even his wife call him doctor."

It reminds me of the things other physicists said about Professor Whitfield back in my world. The way they made fun of him and lied about the success of his experiments, just because what he discovered threatened their nice, neat view of the scientific world.

Dr. Venn is sounding more and more like the right person.

"I don't mean to be a pest," Sarah calls down. "But the bubbles!"

"Oh, for goodness sake, *I'll* go take the bath," Francie mutters.

"Mum, it's the hardest she's worked in months," Daniel says. "Give her credit."

"My hearing is exceptional, thank you!" Sarah calls.

I can't help but laugh. Even in the midst of all this.

"Please find out what you can," I ask Daniel. "I'll be back in a while. Come on, Red."

Sarah isn't the only pest. There's something that's been nagging at my brain—something that's off. Something important.

Now it's time to finally give it my attention.

6

You weren't supposed to say that.

I sink into the scent: not just lavender, but vanilla, too. Sarah was right: heavenly. The dog stretches out on the rug beside the tub. Peace has descended on the land.

He wasn't supposed to say that.

It's tricky, traveling across space and time.

Especially when things have already changed on their own before you even got here.

I sort of noticed it in the moment, but then there was so much else going on. The formality: it wasn't just an act for the other people, it was real. There was no secret eye contact, no *"Wait until we're alone again—I'm going to kiss you straight out of your mind"* kinds of looks. The way Jake was acting toward me was true.

There's nothing going on between us this time. Our past together was already different before I showed up today.

And I didn't do a thing to make that happen.

Same with Red's reaction to him: crazy different. Last time, Jake completely endeared himself to Red by the end of the first day, throwing a stick for him over and over and over while Red chased it into the freezing ocean. Unless Jake secretly kicked Red this afternoon while I wasn't looking, their relationship was already different by the time I got here.

So what does that mean?

That's the point: it's not enough to see it, I have to understand the *why* behind it.

For all I know, my whole survival might rely on some very subtle *why*s.

Because if I just keep going along, making decisions and choices based on only partial clues or evidence I'm in too much of a hurry to notice, I might end up right where I was last time, leaving this life way too early before I have a chance to reclaim the life I really want.

I sink all the way underwater. Let myself float. Block out the world for as long as I can.

What do I know? That's the most important question right now. Not just what do I think or believe, but what do I actually *know?*

My physics teacher Mr. Dobosh said something in class once that really stuck with me: about how all these great scientists in the past—the real pioneers who were willing to risk their careers and sometimes even their lives in pursuit of the truth—had to learn to *recognize* truth in the first place. They had to be willing to free their minds from what everyone else told them was true—that the heavens revolved around the earth, for example, or that a particular disease was caused by rats, or whatever someone's parents or society or other scientists had said—and instead go on this journey of discovery where they looked at everything fresh again. Asked questions. Assumed nothing.

I suppose you could say that's how I've ended up exactly where I am right now. Some physicists, including Mr. Dobosh, don't believe parallel universes exist. I thought they might. So I set out to experiment with that, and here I am.

I come up for air and announce to the dog, "I'm a pioneer." He thumps his tail on the rug. "Yeah, I know. *Big deal. Figure it out.*" I sink under the water again and blow some bubbles. I'm sure Einstein used to do that, too.

So, Audie Masters, what do you know is true?

1. This is not my original body.
2. This is not my original universe.

I know those two things for sure.

3. The last time I checked, Halli Markham was inhabiting my original body in my former universe. I briefly shared that body, so I know that much is true.

4. I know that I have been in Halli's body in this universe one time before this. I have specific memories of that life, starting with waking up in her body in her bedroom in Colorado, and ending with me dying in a hospital bed—

Stop. Do I really know that for sure? That I died? Did I really see it or experience it?

Well, not exactly. I sort of left that movie early. I remember feeling tremendous pain and then deciding I didn't want that anymore. Next thing I knew, I was floating for a while, feeling very peaceful and pleasant again, and then I found my old body sleeping in my old bedroom. What a happy discovery that was. But then it all ended up in that fight with Halli, and then she pushed me out—

Stop. Do you really know that?

I felt a push.

Can you say with one hundred percent certainty that Halli is the one who did that? That she's the reason you left?

Okay, no, not a hundred percent. So that one goes in the *Maybe* pile, along with the dying. Maybe those two things happened, but a true scientist wouldn't assume. So I won't.

So where does that leave me?

I know *where* I am, I know *who* I am … and that's about it. I don't know what's going on with Halli right now or with my old body and my old world, because if things have already changed here, maybe they've changed there, too. I have no way of knowing. I'd have to guess.

There's a gentle knock at the bathroom door. "Halli, we found him," Daniel says, keeping his voice low. "I thought you'd like to know."

"Yeah, I did. Thanks."

"And your driver brought your luggage," he adds. "I'll leave it outside the door."

"Thanks, Daniel. I appreciate it."

I splash downward one more time, just to dunk my whole self in oblivion one last time. But I'm not here to lounge around in a tub for a while, no matter how much I'd love to.

I climb out and dry off and wrap the towel around me. Then I open the door and retrieve my duffel.

There's a note on top, written on stationery from the inn where we dropped off Jake.

I have a message from your parents. Please come see me whenever it's convenient. Jake

It will never be convenient to deal with Halli's parents. I shove the note to the bottom of the duffel and change into a pair of jeans and some thick socks and a long-sleeved T-shirt.

As I comb out my long wet hair, I study my reflection in the mirror. I remember watching one of Halli's memories where she was still trying to get used to living inside my body. She stood in front of my bathroom mirror at home, brushing my teeth. She leaned in close to look herself in the eyes. And wondered if she could see herself looking back.

So who are we? Who am I? Last time, Professor Whitfield called me Halli 2. He said Halli 1 was gone forever—killed in that avalanche I tried to save her from.

So I suppose when Halli took over my body, she became Audie 2.

And now I'm Halli 3.

I don't want that. I don't want to be Halli at all.

Audie 3. A new creature. That's who I am this time.

Although no one gets to know that but me. Everything bad that happened last time started because I revealed who I was. That's a mistake I won't repeat.

I kneel down next to Red. I hug him around his thick, furry neck and whisper, "You think I'm Halli, don't you?" He thumps his tail and licks my lavender and vanilla cheek.

It's time to go contact Dr. Venn. And make sure he knows I'm Halli, too.

7

"HALLI MARKHAM," Francie shouts for the third time, still trying to make Dr. Venn understand. "VIRGINIA MARKHAM'S GRAND-DAUGHTER. DO YOU REMEMBER VIRGINIA?"

"Who?" He has an American accent. Somehow I thought he'd be British.

"VIRGINIA MARKHAM," Francie tries again. "SHE WAS A FAMOUS EXPLORER. YOU WERE HER FRIEND?"

I don't know why I thought this lie would work.

It's just Francie and Daniel and me in the kitchen right now. Sarah and Sam are at the market. Sam thought it might be best if he weren't around for the call, just in case Dr. Venn remembered him.

Francie laughed at that. "It was ages ago! You look completely different now. For one thing, you had hair."

"He'll remember me," Sam assured her. "I was *legendary.*"

He gave her a wink and then shuffled Sarah out the door. She said she had some shopping of her own to do.

It took Francie a while to make contact. The woman who answered the comm seemed reluctant to bother Dr. Venn. But finally his ancient, holographic, 3D head hovered over Francie's tablet on the table. Dr. Venn was in the house.

His head is very round, mostly bald, with just a few clumps of wispy white hair growing out of the sides. He has a white beard, neatly trimmed. He wears glasses, but still squints. If he's wearing hearing aids, they don't work. From the look of time-worn face, I can believe he really is over a hundred.

"I'M HERE WITH VIRGINIA'S GRANDDAUGH-TER, HALLI," Francie is shouting. "SHE WOULD LIKE TO MEET WITH YOU."

"Who?"

Francie coughs and rubs at her throat. "Maybe one of you can try," she murmurs to Daniel and me. "This is exhausting."

Daniel scoots his chair closer. "DR. VENN, MY NAME IS DANIEL EVERETT. I'M A PUPIL OF PROFESSOR LACKSMITH'S."

"Lacksmith?" He heard that. "How is that old yorker?"

I shoot Daniel a look of surprise. I remember him showing me his own biography once, and it said he had won some award for "yorking." I asked him what it was, but he wouldn't tell me.

Oh, but that was me—Audie. He never had that conversation with Halli. I quickly douse my curiosity.

"HE'S FINE, SIR," Daniel shouts. "HE SENDS HIS REGARDS."

Francie gives her son a hidden thumbs up.

Liars are always welcome at my table.

"MY FRIEND HALLI WOULD LIKE TO MEET WITH YOU, SIR."

"Meet with me?" Daniel's lower voice must be at the right register. Dr. Venn seems to hear him fine.

"YES, SIR. SHE'D LIKE TO APPLY TO OXFORD. SHE WANTS TO SPEAK WITH YOU FIRST."

"No, no … she needs to go to Admissions."

It's time for me to take a stab at it.

"I WANT TO MEET WITH YOU FIRST BECAUSE I'M VERY INTERESTED IN YOUR FIELD OF STUDY."

"What's that?"

"YOUR FIELD OF STUDY. I HAVE SOME QUESTIONS FOR YOU."

Dr. Venn scowls at that. Actually scowls.

"PLEASE, SIR, I REALLY NEED TO TALK TO YOU."

"Young lady, you must have me confused with someone else—"

"NO, SIR, IT'S YOU I NEED TO TALK TO."

But suddenly the thought hits me: what if he's right? Maybe he isn't the professor Daniel and his parents met with. Maybe I'm just wasting my time.

In which case I need to get rid of this hovering head and go find the right one.

There's only one way to find out. It's risky, because it reveals more than I want to, but I don't really see another choice. I have to know.

"DR. VENN," I shout, "IT'S URGENT. HEADACHES. DEATH. PARALLEL UNIVERSES. THERE ISN'T MUCH TIME."

Dr. Venn's holographic image jerks for a moment, blurs out of focus. When it steadies again, he's staring right at me, eyes squinting into mine. The mouth above his trim white beard looks very tight and small.

What can I do but stare back? And give him a slight nod.

"Tomorrow," he says. "Ten o'clock. Be on time. I nap at noon. And bring the yorker," he adds, jerking his head toward Daniel.

Then Dr. Venn's head swirls back into nothing. He's ended the call.

I slouch back into my seat. Francie was right: that was exhausting.

"What was that all about?" she asks me. "Parallel universes? Death?"

Francie is a very open-minded person. So is her husband. They both own a history studio that uses people with extrasensory abilities to tell the stories behind archaeological artifacts. When Daniel told them the truth about me last time, they were happy to help me. They introduced me to a woman who was able to tell me what really happened when I threw myself into that avalanche. And she introduced me to her daughter, who helped me to contact Halli.

And by the end of the day, I was screaming in agony. I was rushed to the hospital and never came out.

Not an experience I intend to repeat. No matter how helpful Francie and her husband might want to be.

So I laugh at Francie's question. "I have no idea what it means. It's just something Ginny told me to say if the professor gave me a hard time about trying to meet him."

"You really don't know?" she asks.

"Not at all."

"Hm. Curious," she says. "In any case, it's done. My vocal chords will recover one day. That man really does need an amplifier."

When Sarah and Sam return from the store, Sarah

presents me with a gift. She's uncharacteristically shy about it.

"I saw it a few days ago, and I thought you might like it."

I pull it out of the bag.

And burst out laughing.

"No," she says, looking slightly hurt. "It's sincere."

"I know, Sarah. And I love it. Thank you." I stand up and give her a hug.

It's a sleep shirt. Made of soft lavender T-shirt material. On the front is a picture of a sweet, well-groomed little poodle wearing a pink gemstone collar. She's lying on her plump cushion, sleeping with a little smile on her doggie lips.

Above her is a thought balloon showing what she's dreaming of: a ragged-looking mutt in a noble-looking pose, fur swept back and teeth gritted against a fierce driving storm.

Underneath is a caption: *Princess dreams of adventure.*

"That's me," Sarah says. "And you."

Oh, Sarah. Just ask Halli: adventure isn't always as much fun as you think it is. I saw plenty of it in Halli's memories: the fear, the pain, the constant uncertainty.

But also, I have to admit, a certain pride in overcoming all those things. Why is Halli stronger than I am? Because she's been through more. I've spent my life holed up in my room reading physics books. Halli has been out in the world.

Correction: Audie 1 spent her life that way. I've had adventures of my own since then. I've known fear and pain and uncertainty myself. And I suppose you could say I've overcome some of that.

Audie 3 is a new creature. A long-haired girl with her teeth gritted as she braces against the storm.

I carefully fold up the shirt and slip it back into its bag. "Thank you, Sarah. I'll wear it every night. It's perfect." I give her one more hug.

And now it's time to face the storm and grit my teeth some more. I'm going to have to go talk to Jake.

8

"This place is nice," I say when Jake comes downstairs to meet me in the lobby of the inn. It's night now, chilly outside, and I'm wearing one of Daniel's coats since I didn't seem to pack one of my own. It's too big on me, but Sarah's and Francie's were too small. I'm sure they'd fit the real me, but Halli's back and shoulders are broader. Plus Daniel's coat has the advantage of having a collar that smells like him.

"Yes, it's very nice here," Jake agrees, smiling at the lady behind the front desk. As he leads me into the sitting area in the next room, he murmurs, "If you like flowers. Thousands and thousands of flowers."

The inn is pretty flowery. Not only the many vases full of fresh cuttings resting on every available flat surface, but also the tiny blue flowers on all the upholstered furniture. It looks like the kind of place where somebody's grandmother might live. I think it looks sweet.

"Come on, it's better than the last place," I point out. I was staying in Halli's parents' London flat, in what was obviously their special Rose Room. Roses everywhere: on the furniture, the dishes, the curtains, the bedspreads, the tablecloths, even fresh roses crowded into the bathtub. A little rose goes a long way. Someone should tell them.

"Other than the yippy dogs, I thought it was good," Jake says.

"What yippy dogs?"

"Henry and Wallace?" Jake suddenly looks around. "You didn't bring Red."

"No, he's in the entryway with Sarah." I enlisted her to walk over with me so she could watch the dog. I didn't want to leave him at their house, just in case he might have another bout of separation anxiety and decide he needed to destroy everything in sight. And I didn't want to bring him inside the inn with me, then have to shout to Jake from a safe distance away while Red growled in disapproval.

"Thank you," Jake says. "I appreciate it. So … you're probably going to want to do this upstairs."

"Do what?"

He gestures toward the tablet in his hand. "She wants to talk to you."

I feel like growling in disapproval myself. *She* can only be Halli's mother.

My real mother always hates it when I say I hate someone, so let's just say I strongly, strongly, *strongly* dislike Halli's mother. She's a cold, mean, bossy woman. She and my own mother might look a lot alike, but the two of them are totally different. I used to think Halli was always so rude for how she treated her mother during their comm calls, but once I spent a little time with the woman myself, I understood completely.

"Do we know the topic?" I ask, not even bothering to cover up how annoyed I am.

"Our meeting today with Mr. Chilton." Jake says. "Apparently you were too 'inquisitive.'"

I can feel my blood starting to simmer. "Aren't I supposed to be asking questions? Isn't that what I came here for? Ginny left me forty-nine percent of this company. I'm almost half owner. I'd like to know what it is we *do*."

"Whoa," Jake says with a light chuckle, holding up his hand in surrender. "I'm just the messenger here."

I take a breath and try to calm down. I'm surprised I'm so worked up anyway. This isn't *my* company or *my* 49 percent. Coming to London to tour the headquarters here was just an excuse I cooked up last time so I could find Daniel and get his help trying to solve the mystery of what happened to Halli and me.

"I'm sorry," I say, blowing out a breath. "You're right."

"Look," Jake says, "you know they don't like this—any part of it. They've been doing whatever they wanted to for the past seventeen years. Your grandmother never really interfered. And now you're here asking one of their employees about chemical processes and technical specs—of course it's going to make them nervous."

I study his face for a moment. Who is he? Whose side is he on? I remember thinking those same things when I first met him.

And I'm still wondering.

Last time, he gave me a lot of inside information. Things I'm sure Halli never knew. Things about her parents, her grandmother, the company—and also plenty of inside information about Jake's feelings for Halli. He'd been waiting for her for a long time. And then I showed up, and one thing led to another …

Anyway. Different life now, different situation.

But if he still wants to help the girl he thinks is Halli, why wouldn't I take advantage of that?

"I don't want to talk to my mother," I say. "Just tell her you delivered the message and I promised to settle down."

Way down. I'm not interested in their company at all this time. I won't be bothering Mr. Chilton ever again.

"I would," Jake says, "but I can't. You and I never had this conversation. I'm just here to shadow you, Miss Markham."

"And report back to them?"

"Theoretically," Jake says.

We both look at each other for a moment while I take that in.

"Fine," I say with a groan. "You win. Take me to my doom."

9

"*Other than the yippy dogs ... Henry and Wallace ...*"

As I follow Jake up the carpeted wooden staircase to his room, I play those words over in my head. I don't know any yippy dogs named Henry and Wallace. Jake thinks I do.

They don't belong to Halli's parents—I'm sure of that. They made it very clear that they wished I hadn't brought Red with me to their island—let alone let him stay with me inside their mansion and come with me to meals and meetings. They'd be the last people to own yippy dogs. Dogs like that need lots of attention and love. That disqualifies Halli's parents right away.

And I never saw any dogs, yippy or otherwise, in the building where their flat is. Once again, Red was the sole canine ambassador. But that doesn't mean there weren't some down the hall or on another floor, and maybe I met them this time around.

Only one way to find out.

"Henry and Wallace ... what cute little guys they were, huh?"

Jake snorts. "Red didn't think so. Of course, he doesn't think I am, either."

"Yeah, he's a funny one sometimes." *Red is his own dog*, Halli told me once. She would know better than any of us. "I assume you went with the driver to pick up my duffel this afternoon? Or did you just give him the note to put inside it?"

"No, I went. I had to pick up my things, too."

"Right." So we were staying someplace together again. Someplace with yippy dogs.

"Did you ... see Henry and Wallace?" I try to sound as casual as possible, even though every question feels so obvious I'm sure he's going to get suspicious.

"Right there on their favorite lap. Mrs. Scott wanted to know if we're coming back. I told her I didn't know."

Mrs. Scott. Wow.

My mind is whirling. That's a pretty major change. But a very, very welcome one. Mrs. Scott is definitely an ally.

Last time, I met her at the company board meeting on the island. She's the one who warned me that Halli's parents were trying to steal the company away from Halli. Mrs. Scott lives here in London, and she said I could fly back with her after the meeting and stay with her as long as I wanted. We were supposed to leave the next morning. But that evening, Halli's parents had her escorted off the island and flown back to London right away. She was gone by dinner time.

It wasn't the last time I saw her, though. She came to visit me in the hospital, too. We were in the middle of discussing Halli's parents again when Jake showed up and basically kicked Mrs. Scott out. He said Halli's parents didn't want me to have any visitors—that I was too weak and it was harmful. Mrs. Scott and I could both guess that they just didn't want her talking to me, but then I had to go and prove Jake's point by having a massive coughing fit. I never saw Mrs. Scott again.

But now, this time, I stayed with her before I moved to Sarah and Daniel's? That's a really incredible piece of news.

Something I'll have to process later after I'm done dealing with Halli's mother.

"Halli," she says in that tight voice of hers. Her head hovers over Jake's tablet on top of the quaint little wooden desk in his room. "I've been trying to contact you since this afternoon. Why haven't you answered your comm?"

I didn't have a tablet of my own last time, and I don't seem to have one now. Which is fine, since I don't know how to work them anyway. "How can I help you, Regina?" I ask in a bored voice.

"You can help me by not taking up any more of my employees' time. I told Mr. Chilton you'd only be there for an hour or so this morning. Instead you wasted his entire day."

"Really? Because I'm pretty sure I only wasted *forty-nine percent* of his day," I shoot back, and I can see that I've scored a hit. Halli's mother's face looks even more pinched than usual.

I remember when I first witnessed a few of the comms between Halli and her mother. Her mother used to at least pretend to be nice. But that was back when Halli's parents still thought they could get her to do what they wanted and sign over her shares in the company to them.

Those days are over.

"I don't know how many more locations of our company you plan to visit," Halli's mother says, "but I'm warning you right now, I don't want to hear about a repeat of today. Our Chief Operating Officers aren't going to take valuable time away from their work to explain chemistry and hydroengineering to some uneducated girl who's been living like a wild thing out in the woods for most of her life."

Now my blood is on full boil.

I'm just about to argue with her about how she and Halli's father are the ones who abandoned me when I was just an infant and let me be raised by a grandmother who took me all over the world with her because she *loved* me; and how the expeditions Ginny and I went on from the time I was small were amazing and dangerous and would have scared anyone else out of their wits; and how I might not be formally educated, but I can speak dozens of languages, I know how to survive in impossible conditions, I can fix broken bones and deal with infected wounds, I saved Ginny's life at least one time that I know of and probably more; and I might be "uneducated," but at least I know how to treat people decently, which obviously isn't a skill Halli's mother picked up at any of her fancy schools—

And suddenly it hits me: Halli's mother has just handed me the perfect gift.

Thank you, Regina. I might not have thought of it otherwise.

I take a few breaths to calm myself down. Then I try to sound as rational and neutral as possible.

"I don't want to fight with you," I say. "I'm sorry if I took up too much of Mr. Chilton's time today. I didn't mean to. It's just that once he started telling me about some of the products you and …" I don't know how to refer to Halli's father. She calls both her parents by their first names, but the man is too scary for that. "… you two invented, I couldn't stop asking questions. I really want to understand more. Ginny never told me all the things you two have done."

I steal a glance at Jake out of the corner of my eye.

I'm laying it on pretty thick here, and I wonder how it sounds. He's looking at me with a mixture of both amusement and fascination. I keep going.

"So it got me to thinking," I continue. "You're right about what you said: I am uneducated. I was always too busy following Ginny around to ever want to go to school. But now that she's gone, I was thinking … Oxford."

"Oxford?" Halli's mother repeats with a laugh. "I don't think so."

Calm, stay calm …

I smile. Even though I want to swat my hand through the holographic face in front of me.

"Ginny knew some people there," I say. "I'm going to go talk to some of them tomorrow."

"That's ridiculous," Halli's mother tells me. "You'll never get in. If you think that simply being famous is enough—"

I don't bother to let her finish. Mr. Chilton isn't the only one who doesn't like to waste time. "The only way to find out is to try. It's late, Regina. I have to get to bed."

I get up from where I'm sitting and stride from the room. Since I don't know how to turn off Jake's tablet, it's the best exit I can make.

I keep on going down the stairs. Then, knowing he'll probably follow me, I wait in the lobby. It takes him a few minutes to catch up. Halli's mother must have had more than a few things to say to him—no doubt including some instructions for what he's supposed to do about me now.

"Are you really going there tomorrow?" he asks.

"Yes."

"I'll let the driver know. What time should we pick you up?" Jake smiles politely, knowing I heard the "we."

"I have to meet with someone at ten."

"We'll pick you up at eight."

I narrow my eyes at him, but there's really no point in arguing. I was never going to be able to sneak to Oxford without anyone knowing, and at least this way I've already announced my excuse.

"You're not coming to my meeting," I say.

"That's fine."

"You'll have to find something else to do all day."

"Also fine. I told you before, Halli, I knew you wouldn't like any of this. I appreciate you letting me keep my job for a while longer."

"Hmm." I turn and head toward the entryway where Sarah and Red are still waiting. "Oh, and don't forget I'll be bringing Red."

"How could I? Good night, Miss Markham." He gives me a quick bow, just like the doorman used to whenever I went in and out of Halli's parents' mansion. He always acted like he was just there to do as he was told.

I'm not buying it with Jake.

"So, what did you two just talk about?" I ask him. "You were up there for a long time."

"She doesn't think you have even the slightest chance of getting into Oxford or any other school. She thinks you're a barbarian."

"*What?*" I answer with a laugh. I don't think anyone's ever called me that. I almost like the sound of it. "And what did you say?"

"I told her she was right. You don't even wear shoes most of the time, and I'm pretty sure you can't read."

"You're not very grateful," I point out.

"I am," he says. "And I'm also very loyal." He bows again. "See you in the morning, Miss Markham."

10

I t's funny how you can start to believe your own lies.

For half of the walk home with Sarah and Red, I've been fuming over what Halli's mother said. *Of course I can get into Oxford if I want! I'm smarter than she thinks. She doesn't know anything about me!*

And then I come to my senses. I'm not trying to get into Oxford. I just want to meet the professor that Daniel and his parents talked to. I'm trying to go home. I don't want to go to a parallel university.

"I wish I could go with you and Daniel tomorrow."

"Yeah, me too," I lie. I was happy when their parents said Daniel could miss school but Sarah couldn't.

"I could have watched Red again or done *something* for you."

"I appreciate you helping me out tonight."

"Red's my little love, aren't you, sweet one?" She reaches down to pat his side. Red looks up at her with a panting kind of smile. I'm glad to be here with them this time so I can spare her the betrayal of her little love ripping apart her house.

"It's strange how he's made up his mind that your friend Jake is actually a five-headed dragon sent here to destroy us all."

That's as good a description as any. I've been on the receiving end of that dog's ferociousness. The first time I popped into Halli's world, Red acted like he'd tear me apart. I might not have been a five-headed dragon, but I probably qualified as a space alien.

"Red has his opinions," I say. "But he obviously loves you."

"You do, don't you, handsome boy?"

The dog pants and wags.

"Speaking of handsome boys," Sarah says, "what do you have to say about our Mr. Jake? Apart from the dragon heads?"

"He's ... okay, I guess."

"Oh, very high praise, indeed," Sarah says. "I'll reserve the wedding chapel immediately."

"I'm not interested."

"No," she says, "I meant for me."

"I thought you liked Bryan."

"Yes, well, Bryan isn't here, is he?"

No, but he sure wanted to be.

Sarah threads her arm through mine as we continue walking along. "I know you must think me the most terrible flirt. This bloke one day, the next one another … but how do you know which is the right one if you don't chat them all up?"

I can't deny the wisdom of that.

"The truth is," she goes on, "I've never had a proper boyfriend."

"You haven't? I find that very hard to believe."

"Well, tell me, Halli Markham: how would you describe a proper boyfriend?"

I give that a little bit of thought. "Someone who only wants to go out with you …"

"Never had it. Check."

"Someone who's nice to you and treats you well …"

"Mm, sort of had once, but not lately. Next?"

"Someone who *you* like and treat well and is the only person you want to go out with …"

"Once, and that ended very badly."

"How many boyfriends have you had?" I ask.

"Were you not listening? None, by your definition. By *my* definition, I've endured two broken hearts, one enraged liver, several sprains to my pride, and at least half a dozen complete and utter failures of emotion. So judge me if you must, but until I find what I believe to be a proper boyfriend, I will continue my fervent search."

"You really have a way with words."

"Don't I?" Sarah agrees. "Pity no one appreciates the sharp tongue of a substandard student anymore. I'd be as high up in the academic rankings as our fair Daniel."

Which reminds me: "What's yorking?" I ask her.

Sarah laughs her bright, tinkling laugh. "Oh, a very proud day that was. He won first place, don't you know?"

"Yes, but what *is* it?"

"You should ask Daniel. If he considers you a *true* friend, he'll tell you. He's very shy, my brother—not everyone can see that. Your cousin did. She didn't try to rush things. It's why they've made such a sweet match."

It's true I didn't try to rush things. Daniel was a lot faster than I was. I was still thinking it was a really bad idea to fall for some guy in a parallel universe who I might never see again, when Daniel planted that heart-stopping kiss on me.

Plus, to be honest, for a while in the beginning I was still nursing my thirteen-year crush on Will, the parallel version of Jake over in my world. I had to get past that before I could even look at another guy.

And even then, even though I already liked Daniel so much, I still let myself get swept away by Jake.

I made a lot of mistakes last time. I'm not going to repeat a single one of them.

"You should definitely chat it up with Jake," I tell Sarah. "You might like him."

You like him over in my universe. The versions of Sarah and Jake over there have been dating for a year. Although that might not be true anymore, now that she's caught him kissing the Halli version of me.

Wait, has that happened yet? Or is that still in the future?

Sarah pauses in front of their house. "Is there any chance your cousin might join us after all?"

"What? Oh, no ... I don't think so."

"Such a pity," Sarah says. "He might not be showing it now, but poor Daniel has been positively morose ever since we came back. He misses Audie terribly."

I gather the coat around me as if it's Daniel's arms in the sleeves, not mine. "Really? How do you know?"

"'*Audie said this, Audie said that ... Oh, did I tell you about the time Audie and I ...'* My parents have heard her name so many times, it's as if they've already met her. But it's sweet, you know? I've never seen my brother with a girl for longer than ten minutes."

"Really? Why not?"

"Who knows?" Sarah answers. "I've tried to introduce him to girls from my school loads of times, but he always claims they're too silly or too boring. Very high standards, that one. So you can imagine my relief when he actually found a girl all on his own. He falls and sprains his ankle, and *magic!* There she is."

It was sort of magical. I won't deny it. And not only because I traveled across parallel universes to be there.

"But he was still so slow about it," Sarah says. "Day after day, clearly smitten, but what of it? I finally had to push him, poor lad."

Yes, and thank you. I remember it exactly: Sarah was teasing her brother, reminding him we only had two days left together on our trip, and he should get on with it and do something about it. "Champion idea," he said as soon as we were alone. Then he planted a kiss on me that had me practically melting into my boots. Maybe he hasn't had much experience, if Sarah is right, but he sure knew what he was doing that day.

Sarah hugs herself and hops in place. "But enough of all this—it's freezing out here, Halli Markham."

Not to me. I'm feeling toasty and warm.

But Daniel is inside that house, and even though I can't rush to his arms and declare, *"I'm here! It's me!"* I'd still rather be in the same room with him than out here just talking about him.

Besides, I have a big day tomorrow. Maybe the biggest, if everything goes right.

It's not every day you learn how to save your own life.

11

"What made you so sure it was Dr. Venn yesterday?" I ask Daniel. "How do you even know about him?"

We're sitting at his kitchen table, waiting for the car to arrive. Everyone else has gone off to school or work. I've been sipping tea and picking at the same blueberry scone for the last half hour. I don't seem to have much of an appetite.

It took me a while to dress, too. My options were pretty limited. Jeans and a clean flannel shirt are as good as it's going to get. And Halli's hiking boots, since I didn't bring anything else.

Barbarian.

I thought of all the clothes in Halli's size hanging in that enormous closet back at her parents' mansion.

Couldn't I have packed at least one outfit from there? Even just a sweater and nicer pants and shoes that haven't been hiking through dirt and snow?

But then I had to get a grip on myself. Halli Markham wouldn't care what she wore to go talk to some ancient professor. And it was just nerves making me care, anyway. Dr. Venn didn't seem like the kind of person to notice anyone's outfit. Considering how much he squinted, maybe he wouldn't even be able to see it.

"I have a tutor who's on faculty at Cambridge," Daniel says in answer to my question.

"Professor Lacksmith."

"Yes. I don't know if you're aware, but there's a bit of a rivalry between Oxford and Cambridge. Competition for new discoveries, number of awards, distinguished faculty—that sort of thing."

"There are colleges like that in …" I almost say, *my world*, but catch myself in time. "… America, too."

"So you know it can be a friendly competition as well. Scholars sharing ideas and collaborating."

"Sure," I say. "So have Lacksmith and Venn collaborated on something?"

"No, theirs is a different sort of connection," Daniel says. "More of an affinity. You have to understand: some fields are highly respected. Others are not. My tutor and Dr. Venn belong to the latter."

"What's their field?" I ask.

"It's called the Philosophical Sciences. They develop theories, some of which may never be susceptible of testing." He shakes his head. "I'm sorry, let me put it more plainly—"

"No, I understand," I say. *Audie understands.* "It's like theoretical physics. There are a lot of ideas that are based on just the math of what might be possible, but there's no practical way to actually test them in the real world. Quantum physics is full of theories like that. The idea of parallel universes was one of those. Until …you know, Audie set out to prove it."

Daniel gives me a strange look for a second. But then he goes on. "Doctors Venn and Lacksmith have shared their ideas with one another over the years, and sometimes one or the other will devise experiments to test their particular theories. Professor Lacksmith has told us about some of them. So when you were describing an Oxford professor who might be involved in fringe science, as my mother called it, I thought of Dr. Venn. And now it's my turn."

"Excuse me?"

"Headaches? Death? Parallel universes? 'There isn't much time'? What's going on, Halli? Are you or Audie in some kind of danger?"

I've been waiting for it. Daniel isn't stupid. Nor deaf. I've been waiting for him to ask me since last night.

But we haven't been alone until now. The house

really is tiny—Sarah wasn't kidding—and it seems like everyone is always within earshot.

And while I've been waiting for the question, I've been trying out answers on myself, testing whether I think I would believe them if I were Daniel.

Because what does he know about what's happened so far in this version of our history? The last time he saw Halli before yesterday, they hiked out of the Alps together and said goodbye at a train station. She looked perfectly healthy then. So did I, when he said goodbye to me at the top of the trail. No one was having any headaches, no one was in trouble—so what was I talking about?

Liars are always welcome at my table ...

"It's something Professor Whitfield told Audie," I say. "He was doing research, and he found some reference in some obscure medical journal about a patient who had these excruciating headaches and claimed they were from traveling back and forth to a parallel universe."

"Well done, Professor," Daniel says with a smile. "Although I'm not keen on either of you having excruciating headaches."

"Yeah, no kidding," I say. "So the professor wants to do some additional testing on Audie while the two of us are communicating to make sure there's nothing odd going on with her brain."

"I don't like the sound of that."

"We don't, either. That's why I offered to help in any way I can. It turns out the doctor in that medical journal consulted with some professor at Oxford, and between them they figured out the solution."

"Which was?" Daniel asks.

"Not in the published paper, unfortunately."

Daniel groans. I'm happy for the brief break. He's been asking exactly the kinds of questions that he should, but I can't say I've been ready for all of them. This whole interrogation is making me sweat.

"So anyway," I say, plunging ahead, "we know it's a long shot, but Professor Whitfield wanted me to see if maybe I can find that professor over in this universe."

"Why didn't he just contact him over in yours?"

"He died a few years ago." An easy lie. I was ready for that one.

Daniel leans his head into his hands for a moment and tries to process everything I've just told him. I'm processing it, too, aware of all the many holes in my story and all the ways Daniel can trip me up if he keeps asking too many questions.

"I have no idea if this Dr. Venn guy is the right one," I say. "This whole idea may be pointless and a waste of time. But I have to do whatever I can—it's for Audie, you know?"

"Yes, of course—of *course*," Daniel agrees, and that seems to stop him from any further analysis. "Obviously I'll help you in whatever way you need."

"Good." I breathe out a sigh. "Thank you." I'm tempted to reach over and squeeze his hand, but I don't think Halli would do that. They got to know each other pretty well up in the mountains since Halli was taking care of his ankle every day, but I'm not really sure how close they were.

I can think of one way to find out.

"My turn," I tell him. "What's yorking?"

"Pardon?"

"Why did Dr. Venn call you and Professor Lacksmith 'yorkers'? What does that mean?"

"Well … technically," he says, "a yorker is one way of delivering the ball in cricket."

"Cricket?" That wasn't what I was expecting. "Do you and Professor Lacksmith play cricket?"

"No … I'm afraid this is a long story, and look—the car has arrived. Shall we?"

He gets up from the table with a satisfied sort of smirk, and I shake my head to let him know he hasn't gotten away with it. "We'll come back to this," I tell him.

"I'm certain we will."

As he and Red and I head down the walkway toward the street, I just can't let it go. "So you don't play cricket, but you still won something for yorking?"

"As I said," he answers, "it's a long story."

"Perfect. We have a long ride to Oxford."

"I'll tell you one day," he says. "I promise."

Somehow I don't believe him. Although I bet Audie could have gotten it out of him by now.

"Good morning, Miss," the driver says as he opens the door for us. Jake waits until Red has hopped into the back seat before he lowers his window to say hello. Coward. Red would rip only a little hole in his face.

"I'm sorry, I don't know your name," I say to the driver. I'm willing to be strangers with someone I've only met once or twice, but now it's become uncomfortable. This man was my driver last time I was Halli, too, so I've seen him about six times by now.

"It's Wilkinson, Miss. Happy to be of service." He closes the door after Daniel and Red and me, then returns to the front seat where he presses a button, starts up the car, and goes back to drinking his tea with one hand and holding his tablet to read the news with the other. He doesn't even bother looking up at the street as the car pulls out and drives on.

I still can't get used to that, visually. It makes my stomach feel a little queasy. It just strikes me in my gut as wrong.

I see Jake put a button-shaped item inside his ear. He points to it.

I shrug, because I have no idea what he wants.

Daniel flips up a lid on the door closest to him and removes two buttons just like it. He hands one to me and inserts the other one in his ear.

"I talked to your mother again this morning," Jake

says. I can hear his voice coming through the earpiece. Red can't hear it, though, and continues sleeping peacefully next to me with his head resting across my lap.

I try not to tense up for his sake.

"Yes?" I say.

"Dr. Markham suggested that your time would be better spent moving on to the next facility you want to tour. She recommends the one in Finland. She isn't paying for her pilot and the jet to sit around idle while you indulge some fantasy about being admitted to Oxford just because your grandmother said you could. This is the real world, and spoiled celebrity rich girls don't get everything they want. Miss."

Jake smiles innocently. I think he's waiting for the steam to start pouring out of my ears.

"That's what she said?"

"I may have shortened it a bit," he admits.

I hear a sound to my right and turn to find Daniel trying hard not to laugh. I glower at both of them.

I calmly take the button out of my ear and hand it back to Daniel. He removes his, too.

I still haven't said anything. Right now I don't trust myself with words.

"Halli?" Daniel says quietly.

I calmly pet the dog.

"You're not alone. No one likes that woman."

I let out a trapped breath. He's probably right. And it does make me feel better.

"The thing is," I tell him and remind myself, "I'm not even trying to get into Oxford. That's just the excuse. But she makes me so crazy, I just want to prove her wrong. Right now I've never wanted anything *more* than to get into Oxford."

As I finish saying it, I can't help but laugh. Daniel is laughing, too.

And whether Halli would do it or not, I reach over and clasp his hand. "Thanks, Daniel. I really appreciate everything you do."

Daniel's gaze softens. He looks at me with a tender kind of smile.

What am I doing? I jerk my hand away and turn to look out the window. It doesn't matter how much I want it—I can't take even a step down that old road. I actually sit on the offending hand so it won't do that again.

"Halli?" Daniel says. "Is everything all right?"

"Mm-hm." *As long as I don't look at you or touch you or think about you too much.*

Audie 1 had it easy. Audie 3 has work to do.

12

"Miss Markham, if I might say so," Wilkinson says as he opens the car door for me, "I believe in you. Far as I've seen, you can do anything you put your hand to."

I don't know how to react at first, but then I realize he heard Jake's part of the conversation in the car about all the horrible things Halli's mother said about me.

"Thank you, Wilkinson. I really appreciate that."

And I do. So much, in fact, I can feel myself starting to tear up. Although I think that has more to do with the fact that we're here now, and I'm about to find out my fate.

I could see from a distance the domes and spires and the tops of buildings that look like castle turrets. I thought the Columbia campus looked beautiful in pictures. But *this* place.

There's something about being someplace really old. You feel it. You feel the people that came here before you. The scholars and teachers who walked these streets. The fantastic minds gathered together in one place, starting hundreds of years ago. The scientific discoveries and the literature—

"Watch it!" a bicyclist shouts as he nearly runs me over. I forgot that I need to look the opposite way here before crossing a street: right, left, right.

"What time will you be done?" Jake asks me. He's crossed the street with Daniel and me, but he knows he's not invited any further. The deal is he can be in Oxford for the sake of his tracking, but he has to leave me alone.

"I have no idea," I tell him. Dr. Venn said he has to nap at noon, but I don't know if that means he'll give me more time this afternoon. "Let's say five o'clock for now. If it's any earlier …"

Jake hands me a small metallic card. "Page me."

I accept it as if I know what to do.

Daniel points to the closest clock tower. Quarter to ten.

"We should hurry," he says.

My heart agrees. It's already starting to pound.

What if Dr. Venn isn't the right professor? What if he is?

What's he going to say about my chances for survival when the last time it didn't work out so well?

"Through here," Daniel says, cutting through an archway into a courtyard carpeted with yellow leaves. There are trees everywhere, showing off the last of their autumn colors. There are benches under most of them where people can sit to study or talk or just look out on the beauty and enjoy it.

"Over here," Daniel says, leading toward a different path.

Halli loves her maps, but I'm relying on Daniel for this one. "He's in a dark corner of a minor college," he told me this morning. "That says something of his prestige."

Suddenly Daniel comes to a halt. "There he is."

That's Dr. Venn, all right—I recognize the head. As for the rest of him …

It's hard not to gawp. But nobody else seems to give him a second glance. They must be used to the sight of Dr. Venn rolling along the path. Encased in something that makes him look like a giant purple robot.

"Easy, boy." Red doesn't like that thing at all. A low, dangerous growl vibrates in his chest. I put my hand on his head to steady him.

The machine is like a wheelchair, only it's tall, and holds Dr. Venn in an upright position. The purple casing around his arms and legs undulates every few seconds and looks like a bread machine kneading dough. The purple casing along his back is doing it, too.

It reminds me of the cuffs the nurses put around my legs while I was in the hospital. They felt like they were filled with gel, and they covered my legs from the ankles to the thighs. Every few seconds the cuffs would pulsate and squeeze different parts of my leg, one section at a time. It felt strange but also relaxing, and I'm sure it was to help my circulation after being stuck on my back for so long.

I suppose a hundred-year-old man might need a little help with his circulation, too.

I keep thinking we should probably go up to him and introduce ourselves, but I can't bring myself to do it. I just stand here and watch him make his slow progress toward the building where we were headed.

"Let's wait," Daniel murmurs, as if reading my mind. Or maybe he's feeling intimidated, too.

Suddenly I'm aware of the dog. Knowing how unreasonable he is around Jake, I'm not so sure I can trust him around a man who looks like a robot. That has to be at least as bad as a five-headed dragon.

I wish I brought Sarah after all. She could have entertained the dog.

I kneel down in front of him. "Red, I'm begging you. Please, please be nice to Dr. Venn. Please. I mean it."

The dog wags his tail and licks my nose. I'm not really sure we communicated.

"If there's a problem, I'll take him outside," Daniel promises. "Don't worry. Shall we go?"

Dr. Venn has made the turn and seems to be moving toward his far dark corner. If we walk slowly we should get there about the same time.

"Daniel …"

"I know." He reaches down and holds my hand. An unexpected and very kind gesture. I don't care what I told myself before—I need this. I weave my fingers through his, but don't dare look at him. I'm starting to feel choked up again.

"Knowledge is better than ignorance," he reminds me. "If there's something he can tell us that will help you and Audie …"

I nod. "Right."

When I still haven't moved, Daniel gives my hand a squeeze.

"Be normal," I instruct the dog. And the three of us set off in search of some knowledge.

13

"Well! Who do we have here?"

A huge smile splits Dr. Venn's face as he holds out his arms to Red.

Daniel and I exchange a look. This is not the man we met in 3D yesterday.

Red approaches with his body in full wag. Dr. Venn already compressed his tall purple contraption down into a chair before we got in here. Now he detaches his arms from the cuffs of it, then reaches into a box on his desk. He hands Red two small dog biscuits.

"I have a schnauzer friend who goes on walkabout every day," Dr. Venn tells us. "He visits me in the afternoon for tea and biscuits. What is this fine fellow's name?"

"Red," I say.

"Hmm?"

"RED," I shout.

Daniel holds out his hand. "DR. VENN, I'M DANIEL EVERETT AND THIS IS—"

Dr. Venn holds up an index finger. "Wait. Sit." He points to the two chairs in front of his desk.

Daniel and I sit down. Dr. Venn roots around in a pile of debris at the edge of his desk, and pulls out a trapezoidal device about the size of a dinner plate.

Meanwhile, Red is looking up at him expectantly.

"Yes, of course," Dr. Venn answers cheerfully. He runs a gnarled hand over Red's head. Then he fishes out another biscuit and feeds it to his new friend.

I secretly poke Daniel in the leg. He secretly pokes me back.

"Are we still supposed to wait?" I mutter to him.

"I think so," he whispers.

Dr. Venn opens a drawer of his desk and pulls out a big silver microphone. "Sometimes old technology is still the best technology. Plug that in," he tells Daniel, pointing to our side of the trapezoid. Next he retrieves a set of huge earphones, pulls them over his head, and holds out the cord to me. "It's too small," he explains, holding up his arthritic hands. "If you please." He points to a hole on his side of the unit.

"Speak," Dr. Venn tells Daniel.

"SIR, I'M—"

Dr. Venn's hands fly to his ears. "Not so loud! I can hear you now. Please, your regular voice."

What a relief. I thought we were going to have to shout the entire day.

"I'm Daniel Everett and this is Halli Markham."

"Are you Lacksmith's student, too?" he asks me.

Daniel passes me the microphone. "No, sir." My hand is shaking a little, I notice.

"I apologize for yesterday," Dr. Venn says. "I get calls sometimes. People who … don't wish me well. I've learned to be very cautious."

And mean, I think, but I don't say it.

"But if Lacksmith sent you …"

"To be honest, sir," Daniel says, taking the microphone back, "he didn't send me. I know of your work because of him, and I believe you might be able to help us."

"Help you." It's a statement, not a question. And Dr. Venn doesn't exactly look thrilled. "What is it you think I do, young man?"

"I believe you're a philosophical physicist, sir."

"And what do you think that is?" Dr. Venn asks.

"As contrasted with a mechanical physicist," Daniel says. "I believe you pursue questions that may not have answers in the physical universe as we understand it at the present moment."

Dr. Venn considers that for a moment. "Fair enough.

I've heard longer descriptions that are more accurate, and of course there are the shorter ones like 'freak science' and 'useless' and 'fantasy physics' and 'fringe' …"

I'm glad Francie only called it *fringe* to me and didn't mention that in front of Dr. Venn.

"And you," he says, turning to me. "Halli of the headaches, death, and parallel universes."

"Yes, sir."

I don't bother repeating the lie that my grandmother knew him. We're past that now.

"Forgive an old man his paranoia," he tells us, "but I have to ask: has anyone put you up to this? Lacksmith, Curtis—anyone?"

"No, sir," Daniel says. "I don't know any Curtis, but the answer is still no. We are here entirely on our own behalf."

"Excuse my paranoia, too, Dr. Venn," I say, "but I have to make sure you're the right person to talk to. If you're not, we won't waste your time or our own."

"Fair enough," he says.

I take a breath. I spent a lot of time as I lay awake last night, thinking about how to put this. I don't want to alarm Daniel, but I have to give Dr. Venn enough information to go on.

I decided the best thing to do was to describe the same kind of scenario Daniel and his parents would have when they met with Dr. Venn the first time.

"Suppose someone came to you," I say, "and told you

a friend of theirs had discovered a parallel universe. She even found a version of herself over there. And the two of them learned how to travel back and forth to each other's worlds."

Dr. Venn is studying me with a very intense look. Maybe the fact that he hasn't already shouted, *"What?"* and thrown us out of his office is answer enough—that he's the right man. But I have to be sure.

"Everything is fine for a while," I continue, "but then … things start to go wrong."

"Wrong, how?" Daniel asks me.

I can't look at him. I have to keep going. "And one of them starts to have these really violent headaches. So bad that she ends up in the hospital. So these friends of hers come to you and ask you if you can help her. Would you … believe them?"

"Oh, yes," Dr. Venn answers without any hesitation at all.

"Has something happened to Audie?" Daniel asks. "Halli, answer me."

"No, it happened to me," I say. A good solid half-truth.

"Are you all right?" he asks.

Dr. Venn can only hear my side of it through the microphone, but anyone can see that Daniel is agitated. Dr. Venn barks at him, "Quiet! Let her finish!"

There's the Dr. Venn we met yesterday.

I can feel my hand shaking again. "Would you know

what to tell them?" I ask him. "Would you know how to help?"

"I might," he says. "I'd need all the facts."

All the facts. Right.

I hate to do this, but I have to. "Daniel, I promise I'll tell you more later, but right now I have to talk to Dr. Venn in private. Can you go out—"

"No," he says. "Absolutely not. I'm the one you need to speak to privately. Dr. Venn, will you excuse us for a few minutes?"

Then without waiting for an answer, Daniel gets up and leaves.

I'm a little speechless. "I'm sorry, sir, he's not usually like that."

Dr. Venn looks irritated. "Tell me the rest, now."

"Just … can you wait a second? I'll be right back."

I turn back at the door. Red looks perfectly content lying at the base of Dr. Venn's chair. I slip out before he notices.

Daniel is waiting for me in the courtyard. "Come with me."

"I really need to get back," I tell him. "This isn't anything personal. I just think Dr. Venn would be more comfortable—"

"Don't lie," Daniel says. "Stop lying."

He pulls me into a deserted alcove and backs me against the wall. "Stop me if we've never done this before."

Then he takes my face gently between his hands and kisses the living daylights out of me.

I'm too shocked to do anything but take it at first. But then I wrap my arms around him and give as good as I'm getting.

We pull back, panting, and look at each other. "You don't ever have to lie to me, Audie."

"How did you know?"

"Little things added together. I can give you a list later. But right now I need you to go back in there and tell him who you really are and tell us both what's happened to you. How bad is it?"

"It's … bad."

Daniel grabs my hand and starts pulling me back the way we came. "Then let's do something about it," he says. "Now."

So we return. And I sit down and pick up the microphone and tell them both everything.

Daniel is leaning forward in his chair with his head cradled between his hands. He's been getting more distressed the longer I've talked.

But Dr. Venn …

Opposite.

The old man I met when I first walked in here looks younger and more alive by the second. And for every groan of Daniel's, I watch Dr. Venn's face light up in a smile.

Finally, when I get toward the end of it where I'm

fighting with Halli and can feel myself being squeezed out of my old body, and meanwhile my other body here is either dead or dying, and I'm left with no place else to go—that's when Dr. Venn looks really happy. He almost looks ready to applaud.

"And then I came back," I finish. "Yesterday afternoon. Right in the middle of a scene I've already been through. But I've been really careful. I haven't let myself repeat anything I did the first time. Including telling you," I say to Daniel. "So … I'm sorry about that. But I thought it was the smart thing to do."

"It probably was," Daniel admits.

"Maybe, maybe not," Dr. Venn says. "It's hard to know. So many different permutations—go left, go right, say this, don't say that—it's maddening, isn't it?"

I nod. He really gets it.

Dr. Venn closes his eyes for a moment and smiles in a very calm, satisfied way. I watch while the purple casing of his chair squeezes and pulsates around him. Then Dr. Venn lets out a contented sigh, opens his eyes, and fixes me with a gaze that's bright and alive.

"I want to thank you, young lady. From the bottom of my heart. You've just made an old man very happy."

"I sort of noticed that," I answer, feeling a little awkward. "But why?"

"Because I finally understand why I've needed to live so long. It was so I could meet you today. You see, all this time I thought I was the only one."

14

"The split happened in 1946," Dr. Venn says. "I didn't know it at the time. I found out later, the way you did—suddenly I was there. I met him."

"Hold on," I say. "Hold on." My mouth is dry and my heart is racing. I'm having a very hard time processing this.

Daniel asks what I would have if I could come up with the words. "You're saying there's a parallel you."

"*Was*," Dr. Venn corrects him. "Sadly, gone for many years. In much the way Audie has described. Which is obviously why I tried to warn her."

I swallow past what feels like a huge rock lodged in my throat. My voice comes out strangled and raw. "How … how did he die? Exactly?"

"Brain aneurism. No family history, of course, why would there be? I could have told people what happened, but no doctor in the world—either world—would have believed the truth."

Now it's my turn to lean forward in my chair and cradle my head in my hands. I feel dizzy. And scared.

It's all too real. I knew it was real, but now it must be. This respectable old man has confirmed it.

You'd think I'd feel relieved. Reassured. Safe, even. Instead I feel like I'm going to throw up.

"What do you two know of World War II?" Dr. Venn asks us.

"The Last War," Daniel says.

"Not in my world," I manage.

Dr. Venn points a gnarled finger at us both. "Exactly. That's where you'll find the split. It was after the bombs. Hiroshima and Nagasaki. You know about those."

"The bombs that ended the war," Daniel says.

Dr. Venn nods. "I was one of the physicists who invented those bombs."

This is getting more surreal by the minute. I lift my head. Sit back up. Listen to him like I'm listening to a movie.

"There were a lot of us," he says, "some in America, some here in Britain. You have to understand how we felt about our work. Young men were dying every minute, it seemed, of every single day. No one wanted to sleep. We didn't take time with our families. We didn't want to talk, unless it was about the work. You had this feeling that if you just put in another minute, another hour, maybe you could be the one who helped end the war. How could you sleep when you had that kind of responsibility?"

"You were in Los Alamos?" I ask.

"Some of the time. Sometimes here at Oxford, meeting with my colleagues on the project. All very secretive, all very necessary. It was a horrible war—they all are.

"The bombs were in August, 1945. Terrible, terrible … you can't imagine the suffering and the devastation. You've seen photographs, I imagine."

Daniel and I both nod.

"They don't even begin to match the horror of it. All those children. The burning, the bodies. Whole families incinerated. People just like you and me, going about their day, not soldiers, just people."

Dr. Venn looks off to the side and squints, not at us, but maybe at the memory.

"And I was part of that."

"You helped end the war," I say. "Just like you wanted."

"The price was too high," he answers. "We all knew that. Or at least most of us did. And that was the beginning of the Manhattan Pact."

"The Manhattan *Pact*?" I say. I've heard of the

Manhattan Project—that was the code name given to the top-secret development of the atomic bomb. But I've never heard of a pact.

"It began with a few of us physicists," Dr. Venn says. "Grumblings, really. Nightmares. All around us, people from the project were turning to drink. Wild parties. Celebrations night after night for weeks at a time to try to mask how they really felt. When really they were dying inside. I saw it, some of my colleagues saw it. So we started talking to each other. And eventually ... you know this part of it, don't you, young man? They've taught you in school."

"You agreed to a boycott," Daniel answers.

"Yes. You tell her. I've already talked too much."

Dr. Venn closes his eyes and rests in his chair while Daniel takes over.

"There was a worldwide strike by scientists in every discipline. Not just physics, but medicine. Engineering. Aviation. Anything that required scientific training or a degree."

"What do you mean, a strike?" I ask. "For how long?" I can't imagine doctors refusing to treat patients for more than a day or two.

"Permanently," Daniel answers. "In one specific category: none of them would ever agree to use their knowledge for anything related to war."

Wow. I let that sink in for a moment. "Did that work?"

"It's still working," Dr. Venn mumbles. His eyes are still closed. "I'm sorry, children, I need … to sleep."

The man looks exhausted.

"Is there anything we can get you, sir?" Daniel asks. "Do you need help with anything?"

Dr. Venn lifts an arm just a few inches off his chair. "Help me back in."

Daniel and I reconnect the cuffs around Dr. Venn's arms. We're just finishing when the old man starts to snore.

"We should eat," Daniel whispers to me. I nod. I carefully remove the headphones from Dr. Venn's head and lay them on his desk.

Red seems reluctant to leave the professor's side. It's sweet and surprising. Red really is his own dog. But after a little more whispered coaxing from me, he gets up and follows us out.

Right into a swarm of reporters.

"Halli Markham! Who's the new man in your life?"

"You got a name, son? Where'd you meet Miss Markham? How long you been seeing each other?"

"Miss Markham! Why are you at Oxford? Are you going to enroll here?"

"Why are you meeting with Edgar Venn?"

Cameras jostling, all trying to get the best shot. A cluster of square binoculars all aimed at my face.

And at the edge of the crowd, Jake. Next to him, with his camera trained on me too, is Bryan.

Red snarls at the whole mess of them. I couldn't agree with him more.

15

I ignore the rest of the history reporters and go straight for Bryan.

"We had a deal," I say.

"I didn't start this," he answers. "I just followed the chatter."

I look around at the crowd that's gathered: not just the reporters, but students and even some distinguished faculty.

"Where can we go?" I ask Daniel.

"I know a place," says Jake.

He leads us down a leaf-strewn walkway to where my new friend Wilkinson awaits with the car. Jake gets in front, Bryan climbs in back. I have no choice but to share the back seat with him.

"No comment," I say as soon as we're all settled. Wilkinson pulls out into light traffic. History reporters scramble to their vans and motorcycles and however else they arrived. Of course they're not just going to give up.

I notice that Wilkinson is actually steering the car this time. Obviously this is no time for autopilot.

"You might as well tell me," Bryan says, looking very pleased with himself. He's right—he didn't create this situation. But he's obviously very happy to profit from it. "If we don't get the truth out there quickly, the rest of them will keep digging." He shrugs. "Or make something up."

If there's any bright spot, it's that at least I've already practiced my excuse.

"I've decided to follow my parents into the sciences," I say. Halli's mother is a hydroengineer and her father is a chemist. Why wouldn't Halli take an interest?

Other than the fact that she has absolutely no interest in it at all. But that's not Bryan's business.

"Why talk to Venn?" Bryan asks. "He's hardly where the serious student would go."

"Why do you say that?" I ask.

Bryan scoffs. "You haven't done your homework."

And he probably did his just in the time he was waiting for me to come out of Dr. Venn's office. Bryan is from America just like Jake and me. There's no reason he would have had any prior knowledge about some Oxford science professor.

Wilkinson stops at an intersection, and someone bangs on the passenger side window. Red leaps across Daniel and me to bark bloody murder at the offender. Wilkinson speeds on.

That's when I notice Bryan doesn't have his camera going at the moment. This is just a conversation.

Another chance to make a deal.

"Dr. Venn was a friend of Ginny's," I say. "If you really feel it's important, I'll include it in my memoirs when I sit down with you."

Bryan considers that.

And rejects it.

"All my competitors out there," he says, pointing, "already have enough footage to air right now. 'Halli Markham and her mystery man.' By the way," he tells Daniel, "you won't be a mystery for long. They'll be sending teams to your house by tonight."

Just like last time. Bothering Sarah, harassing Daniel, hounding their friends—no, thank you.

"How do I make it stop?" I ask, feeling pretty certain he already knows. It's fair to say Bryan has the upper hand this time.

"Exclusive," Bryan answers with a self-congratulatory smile. "A sit-down with both of you. Right now."

"No way," I say.

Bryan shrugs. "Then I can't help you."

"Right. Because I'm sure you want to help me."

"Saying what?" Daniel asks him. "How much?"

"No, Daniel, don't bother."

I've been here before, living Halli's life in the spotlight. Daniel was part of it, too—he just doesn't know it. It was one of the times when I most wished I were just plain, anonymous me.

The car has stopped. I look around, but have no idea where we are. There are shops nearby, people walking and biking and driving, but that doesn't tell me much.

Jake gets out of the car and disappears into one of the shops.

One of the history reporter's vans pulls up. Then one of the cars. And the motorcycle.

Jake comes out of the shop holding a big paper bag. Then he stops right where he is.

"What's he doing?" I ask.

He's waiting, is what he's doing. Waiting for the history reporters to circle around him.

I can't hear what he's saying, but he's smiling in a really friendly way. He shakes his head at one of the questions and points at the car.

Then he comes over to my side and makes a motion like I should lower the window.

Mindful of the already wound-up Red, I crack it just a little.

"You might want to come out here, Miss Markham." He's using that formal, polite manner from yesterday—what I realize now is his public face. "You too, Bryan. Daniel, I suggest you wait in the car with the dog. Although you're welcome to listen, of course."

"I don't think that's a good idea," I tell him. "Why would I want to go talk to those people?"

Jake smiles and mumbles, "Trust me."

So I get out of the car. Tell Red to stay. Close the door and let Bryan come out on his own side. Then the two of us follow Jake back to where the crowd of reporters has grown in just the last few minutes.

"As I was explaining to them, Miss Markham," Jake says, "this is part of your tour of your family's Osmotic Power Systems facilities throughout the world. It was announced in a press release issued by the company last week."

I give him an uncomprehending look.

"I'm afraid Miss Markham can't discuss details of her meetings at Oxford, since they involve proprietary secrets that belong to the company."

Oh. He's good.

"Who's the bloke?" one of the reporters asks me.

Jake jumps in before I even have to form an answer. "As I already explained," he tells the man, "although maybe you weren't here ..." The reporter smirks because he obviously was here and just wanted to put me on the spot instead. "... that person in the car is an employee of OPS. He is also bound by the company's nondisclosure rules. I'm sorry, but he won't be able to speak to you."

Jake is very *good.*

"Is it true you were seen kissing him?" one of the female reporters asks me. "Or is that a company secret, too?"

That draws a laugh from her fellow reporters.

Jake loops his arm around my waist, pulls me toward him, and gives me a hasty kiss on the lips. "There. She's kissed me, too. If you want to see her kissing the driver, I'm sure we can arrange that. There's no story here—at least not one we can share with you yet. As I'm sure you know, Drs. Markham and Bellows are very serious about maintaining their privacy. Especially when it involves proprietary company information. In fact, Jefferson, didn't they sue your studio last year?"

The reporter in question grumbles.

Jake smiles in a polite and dismissive way. "Thank you all for your time. I hope you have a good day."

Then he strides toward the car and hands the bag he was holding to Wilkinson.

Wilkinson opens the door for me. Bryan tries to scoot in after.

"Not right now," Jake tells him. "Miss Markham needs to have her lunch. Maybe you can find a ride with one of your colleagues."

Wilkinson looks especially pleased as he hands me our sandwiches and then shuts the car door in Bryan's face. Jake slides into the front.

He inserts a button into his ear, and Daniel and I do the same.

"That won't keep them away forever," Jake tells us, "but it might buy you a few hours."

"Thank you," I tell him. "Nice job."

He gives me a little bow from the front seat. "It's what your parents pay me for."

Although I'm not so sure about that kiss ...

"You're a very convincing liar," Daniel agrees. Somehow the way he says it doesn't really come across as a compliment.

I put the ear button away and feed Red half a sandwich. He played his part, too. He deserves an extra treat.

That, plus all the biscuits Dr. Venn wants to give him.

I suddenly realize how absolutely empty my stomach is. I wolf down the rest of Red's sandwich and a whole other one of my own.

"We need to talk," Daniel murmurs to me.

I give him a very covert nod. Daniel is being as careful as I am. I think he shares my same suspicion that Jake might still be able to overhear us, with or without the ear buttons.

Or at least I thought I was being careful. But apparently not. And that's the question I've been dying to ask Daniel ever since the middle of the morning:

How did you know it was me?

16

"I began to suspect this morning," Daniel tells me when we're alone again and I can ask him.

Wilkinson dropped us off where he did before, and now we're walking back across the pretty, tree-lined courtyard.

"What did I do wrong?" I ask.

"Not wrong, just … Audie," Daniel says with a smile. "You called it theoretical physics, not philosophical the way we would. And you spoke of quantum physics, which no one here calls it."

"Oh."

"And then there were small clues ever since yesterday," he goes on. "But the main one was that in the past two days you've rarely looked me in the eye. That isn't Halli. Halli is very forthright. So I knew something was wrong, but I didn't know what it was. I thought something had happened to you, and she was keeping it from me. I never imagined what the real secret was."

"But then how …? I mean, you obviously felt sure enough to kiss me."

"No," he says. "I wasn't. But I knew I had to do something. You tried to make me leave Dr. Venn's office—I couldn't allow that. Not once you confirmed you were in trouble. So I took a risk. Knowing I might make an utter fool of myself if I was wrong."

I'm looking him in the eye now. "I liked it. Very bold move, Everett."

We're smiling at each other in a way that I'm used to, but I know we have to be careful. As much as I'd love to repeat that kiss right now, there are too many witnesses around us. Halli isn't as anonymous as I'd like her to be.

As if to reinforce the point, two young women peel away from a group of nearby students and come over to us.

"Halli?" one of them says.

"Yes?"

"We were wondering …" But that's as far as she gets before she loses her nerve.

The other girl gives her a friendly nudge and takes over. "You're a real inspiration—we wanted to tell you that."

"Oh. Okay, thanks." That's nice of them.

"Could we get a photo with you?" She pulls a small tablet from her pocket and hands it to Daniel. "I swear we'll keep it private."

"Okay, sure." I can be a good sport. The girls move to either side of me and both link their arms around my waist. Then they lean in close and rest their cheeks against mine.

I flinch a little at that. Strangers don't usually come up to me and feel so comfortable wrapping their arms me and invading my space.

Any more than the real me is used to someone proving a point to reporters by pulling me toward him and kissing me on the mouth.

But I suppose some people must view Halli Markham as public property. One of the side effects of her being famous.

"Thanks, luv!" the more outgoing one says to Daniel as he hands her back her tablet. She turns a little to the side and drops her voice to a whisper. "Is he your boyfriend, then?" she asks me.

"What? No … we're just friends."

"I'd like to be friends with that!" she says with a laugh before tugging on the other girl's arm and leading her back to their group.

Daniel points up ahead. "The schnauzer."

Sure enough, there's a little dog trotting along on his own, heading toward Dr. Venn's office in a very purposeful way.

"Let's wait a minute," I say, knowing Red might not appreciate the competition.

We find an unoccupied bench under one of the huge trees and sit down. A little gust of wind sends a few more yellow leaves drifting down around us.

"Are you ready for this?" Daniel asks me.

It's a reasonable question. I haven't really had enough time to process the morning. I could probably use a long soak in a tub.

"It's real, isn't it?" I ask him. I know it is, but for some reason I feel like I keep needing the confirmation.

"I'd like to put my arm around you right now," he says.

"I know."

"Or at least hold your hand."

"Me, too."

Instead I fold my arms across my chest to fight against the temptation.

The two girls who came over earlier are looking at us again, obviously talking about us to their friends. It's really not the way I'm used to living.

"Do you think it will ever be normal for us again?" I ask.

Daniel laughs. "It was never normal. Think of how we met."

"Oh. Right." I've always been a visitor from another universe. Being inside Halli's body for the second time though isn't really that much more incredible.

"There he goes," Daniel says. The schnauzer trots back out and heads just as purposefully toward wherever his next destination is. From the look of him, he probably has people all over this campus feeding him treats all day long. He's not a slim dog.

Daniel stands and offers me his hand. I take it, just for the space of time we can get away with while he lifts me to my feet.

"Tonight," he says. "We'll have a more proper hello."

I suppress a smile. "I kind of liked your improper one."

I see what he means: I really haven't been looking him in the eye for two days. Now I remember why. Because looking into his warm brown eyes right now makes me want to forget all about the hurry. The danger. All the choices I need to make minute by minute if I'm going to survive this time around. All I want is to be with him quiet somewhere, feel his warm comforting arms around me, and talk about our lives.

Okay, mostly kiss, but also talk a little in between.

"Shall we?" Daniel asks.

"We shall."

As soon as Red understands where we're going, he bounds on ahead. I feel strangely reluctant.

Daniel notices me slowing down. "What's wrong?"

"I'm just … worried," I confess. "About what he'll say. We still don't know how the other him died." Then

I say what's really holding me back. "What if I can't stop it?"

"Audie, look at me." Daniel smiles in that kind, confident way I've come to know and love. "Everything about you is a miracle. This will be no different."

I want to believe that. I'm lost if I don't. I know that. He's right.

But I can't help wondering, secretly, whether I'm smart enough to do all this—even with Daniel and Dr. Venn's help.

Dr. Venn's parallel self was a physicist working on the Manhattan Project. I assume he was smart, too.

But not smart enough to still be alive.

17

I can hear Red barking from far away. I take off at a run.

He's standing in the doorway of Dr. Venn's office, barking at a woman and a robot.

Dr. Venn's chair is in its extended position so he's standing upright again, supported by all the purple cuffs and cushions. That's what Red doesn't like. He doesn't seem to mind the woman so much. She's about my mom's age, and she has one of Dr. Venn's arms cradled between her hands while she's massaging his wrists and fingers.

"My nurse," Dr. Venn calls over the sounds of Red's alarm. "This will only take a few more minutes."

I grab Red by the collar and ask him to sit. Then I

crouch down next to him and pet him while the purple monster still looms above.

Then, just as Dr. Venn said, a few minutes later the nurse is done and he can compress his apparatus back into a chair.

The nurse brings her mouth right up against Dr. Venn's ear. "I'll see you tonight, Granddad." Unlike him, she has a British accent. She smiles at him, waves, then turns toward Daniel and me.

"A word of caution," she says. "I know it's easy to forget because his mind is sharp, but my grandfather is a hundred and three. Please don't wear him down. I've seen him bedridden for a week when he pushes too hard. He loves his work—sometimes too much. But you two will be mindful of that, won't you?"

She smiles the way a teacher might after telling everyone, *"If you cheat, I'll know it, so don't do it."*

Daniel and I both nod. The woman gives my shoulder a squeeze and leaves.

Meanwhile Dr. Venn has been trying to coax Red back toward him, but the dog won't go. "Here," Dr. Venn says soothingly. "I know. It's all right."

Finally Red does this sort of crab walk sideways for a few steps, obviously still afraid, until he sees the biscuit cupped in Dr. Venn's arthritic hand. Then everything is forgiven. Red reclaims his position at the base of Dr. Venn's chair and peacefully devours his treat.

Dr. Venn looks up at us. "I assume Madeline told you to take it easy on an old man?"

I hesitate, then nod.

"Good. Then you can help me right now." He gestures toward the earphones. I settle them over his ears, then resume my seat and pick up the microphone.

"We can come back tomorrow if you're too tired," I tell him, hoping he won't say yes. I don't think I can stand leaving right now and then wondering all night long.

"Nonsense," he says. "You'll know when I'm tired. I'll fall asleep. Until then, we keep going. And if you have to come back tomorrow and the next day and next week, you will. We have important work to do together, yes?"

"Yes." I think of what he said about working on the atomic bomb. How no one wanted to sleep. I get that. Right now I wish Dr. Venn were strong enough to talk to us through the night.

"So," he says to Daniel, "how far into the history did you tell her?"

I pass the mic over to him. "Scientists all around the world agreeing never to use their knowledge for war."

"Yes. A noble, humane idea," Dr. Venn says. "Simply wonderful. But do you see the flaw in it? From a physicist's point of view?"

I try to think of what he means. But nothing comes to mind.

"There were so many rules," he tells us. "We had to be very specific. Think about it: anything can be turned into a weapon. Even a paperclip or a shoe. It's the mentality behind the instrument that makes it dangerous—if someone wants to do harm, he can always find a way.

"So it took months of debating and redrafting before we had a plausible agreement. A list of rules about how much science we all could pursue, and where we would draw the line. Do you see it yet?" he asks me. "The flaw?"

"I'm sorry, sir. I don't."

"Space," he says. "What do we do about space? Airplanes carried the bombs to Japan. Imagine how much more damage someone could do if they launched a weapon from space. Rocket ships were only a hypothesis and the stuff of science fiction in the forties, but the dream was there. The theories to support it were there. And some of my colleagues didn't want to sign the Pact if it meant giving up their pursuit of knowledge."

"Einstein," I mutter. A flash of a memory. Of Halli and me in her greenhouse in Colorado, and me quizzing her about historical figures from my universe that she'd heard about, too.

She was pretty fuzzy on Einstein.

"He was a peaceful man," Dr. Venn says. "He hated war. But his answer was no. He had to know what he could know. So he and a fair many scientists ultimately refused to sign."

"What happened to them?" Daniel asks.

"Nothing. They went on. Life went on. Audie has been living in that world her whole life. And you," he says to Daniel, "have been living in this one. The one we made, my colleagues and I, that day we signed the agreement."

"Wait a minute," I interrupt. "Are you saying you deliberately created a parallel universe?"

"No. No more than you did when you tried to save Halli and now, as you want to save yourself. Everything changes once you make a different choice."

"Make a different choice," I repeat. "That's all it takes."

"That's all it's ever taken," Dr. Venn says. "No one seems to grasp that."

"But …" There are questions on the tip of my brain, but somehow I can't seem to shape them into words.

"Leave it," Dr. Venn says. "I've seen that look on too many students' faces over the years: too much theory, not enough story. So let me tell you a story.

"That other me—Edgar, we'll call him—goes to work one day, just like every day, except this day his colleagues are signing the Pact. For reasons of his own, he does not. That night he goes home, kisses his wife, has supper, reads a book, falls asleep.

"*I*, on the other hand, go to work that day, sign the

Pact, then go home, kiss my wife, have supper ... and so on. Would you hand me that pen, son?"

Dr. Venn gestures toward a pen on his desk and the pad of paper nearby. He detaches his arms from the purple cuffs, props the notepad on his lap, and then draws a long, shaky line across the paper.

"Edgar's life," he says, pointing to the line. Then he draws a second long line. It begins at the same starting point, but then angles steadily off in another direction. "My life."

He draws more shaky lines. "Your grandparents' lives, Audie. Your parents' lives. Yours." All heading in a certain direction. Then he draws three more lines starting from the same place, but angling off again: "Now Halli's grandparents. Her parents. Her." Dr. Venn looks up at me. "Do you see? Circumstance and choices. That's all it ever is. You're born into a partic-ular world, a particular country and city and neighbor-hood, and born to a specific set of parents. And then ... choices.

"And I'll let you in on a little secret," he adds. "It's not a line, it's a loop. But that's a different story. I need to know that you understand this one, first."

I study his drawing. Study the lines. There's the one for my life. That's me in Universe A, being raised by a nice mother, taking an interest in physics, having a crush on Will, deciding to see if parallel universes are real so I can have a hot project that will get me into Columbia.

And there's Halli's line. Universe B, abandoned by her parents, raised by an adventurous grandmother, a grandmother who dies and leaves Halli alone.

I pick up another pen from Dr. Venn's desk and start drawing new lines on his paper. Lines that branch off from the ones he drew for Halli and me.

Here is the line where I try to save Halli and end up stuck in Universe B instead. And here's the line where Halli starts living my life in Universe A and takes it in a completely different direction.

At some point about a week from now, that new line representing me would end. The story of Audie is over. The new line for Halli would keep going.

But wait! I move the pen back a few inches on my line and start drawing another new branch from there.

Something is wrong. Something doesn't make sense. I tap the pen against the paper while I think.

It's different. The past is different. That's exactly what it is.

"It's not just circumstance and choices," I tell Dr. Venn. "It can't be. Both times when I've woken up in Halli's body, the past was changed before I ever got here.

She hiked out on Sunday instead of Tuesday—I didn't cause that. And this time Jake and I ..." I catch Daniel's eye and stop myself.

When I told Dr. Venn and Daniel about everything that happened to me the last time I was Halli, I didn't tell them *everything*. In part because it didn't seem something that would help Dr. Venn with the science, but more because I didn't need for Daniel to know any of that.

And now that I'm thinking it through, there's another difference: not only how Jake reacts to me and how Red reacts to him, but also how Daniel is treating me.

Last time he acted like he couldn't make a move on me because he would somehow be cheating on me. With me. He couldn't get past the fact that I looked like Halli.

But this time? Not a problem. Once he knew it was me inside here, he had no problem kissing Halli's lips.

Not that I'm going to explain any of that to Daniel or Dr. Venn. So I just let my sentence trail off and hope Daniel will forget it.

"Okay," I tell Dr. Venn. "Let me say it all for myself and you tell me if I have it. When I decided to try to save Halli, I made a choice. A new universe split off."

"Yes," he says.

"But that universe had a different history than the first one, because in the new universe, Halli's tracking information showed she hiked out the Alps on Sunday instead of Tuesday. Right?"

"Go on."

"*I* didn't make that choice," I remind him. "I didn't know anything about it."

Dr. Venn nods. And I notice that he isn't just squinting anymore, his eyes are closed. They open a few seconds later, but there's no doubt about it: he's fading.

"Dr. Venn? You look tired. Should I stop?"

"No, but help me back in." His voice sounds weaker than it did just a few minutes ago. Daniel and I both hurry to help him slip his arms back into their cuffs.

Dr. Venn flexes his fingers on both hands. He gives us a reassuring smile, but says, "If I can't move these in the morning, Madeline will have my hide."

And ours, I think, but don't say it.

"Go on," Dr. Venn tells me. "You're very close. I'm not sleeping, I'm listening."

But his eyes are definitely closed.

"So now I'm back again," I say, speeding it up. "And this time the past is different again. Things I didn't choose, like Red growling at Jake—the two of them were friends last time."

Good save. Make it all about Jake and Red.

"And me staying with Mrs. Scott this time instead of at Halli's parents' apartment. I didn't *choose* any of those things."

"You did," Dr. Venn says faintly, "but you just don't know it." He takes a deep breath and forces his eyes open. I can see it's an effort. "I'm sorry, children. I can't anymore today. I have to sleep."

Daniel and I both stand up. "Do you need anything, sir?" Daniel asks.

"No, no …" Dr. Venn's head has already drooped toward his chest. I gently remove the headphones and unplug both them and the microphone. I'm not sure what else we should do.

"Do you think we should just … leave?" I ask.

"He's gotten along without us all this time," Daniel says. "I imagine his granddaughter will come for him. Or maybe he naps and then leaves on his own. He came alone this morning."

I feel weird about it, but we do just leave. It takes a little coaxing to get Red to come with us. He really seems to love sleeping at Dr. Venn's feet.

This time when we emerge from the office, no reporters. Jake's strategy seems to have worked.

I pull from my pocket the card Jake gave me this morning. The one he said I should use to "page" him.

"How am I supposed to work this?" I ask Daniel.

"What would you have done right now if you were still pretending to be Halli?"

I shrug. "Faked it."

Daniel smiles and takes the card. He presses his thumb to the center of it and holds it in front of my mouth. "Speak."

"Jake?" I turn my ear toward the card to listen for a response, but don't hear one.

Daniel is kind enough not to laugh. "No, it's one way. It's for sending a message." He speaks into the card himself and says, "Ready for the car."

The sky is already dusky, even though it's only about 3:30. The air is chillier, too. I should have brought Daniel's big coat with me.

The car is waiting for us by the time we reach the street. Wilkinson opens the back door and Red hops in.

"Miss, if you'd wait a moment," Wilkinson says. He lets Daniel go in next, then shuts the door.

Jake gets out of the front. "Slight problem," he says.

"Okay…"

"Your father is here, Miss Markham. We're to take you to him immediately."

18

I recognize the apartment building. Or "flats," as they're called here.

I recognize the doorman, even though he doesn't know me.

"Hello, Bates," Jake says. I stop myself from saying it, too. But I liked Bates last time. He was very nice to me and I liked his over-the-top doorman suit that made him look like a circus ringmaster.

"This is Halli Markham," Jake says, and Bates gives me a little bow. "Dr. Bellows is expecting us."

Jameson Bellows, Halli's father. On Red's and my ride up the elevator—Jake went up first so Red wouldn't have to take it all a step further and actually bite him—I'm already practicing what I'm going to call him. "Jameson" just seems too weird. But he looked at me strangely the last time I called him "Father." So I'll probably do the safe thing and just call him "you."

The elevator reaches the floor of the flat where Jake and Bryan and I stayed last time—the Rose Room. But Jake told me to keep on going all the way to the top.

He's waiting when we get out. "Ready?"

Oh, boy. "Yep." Red snarls at him in agreement.

Jake knocks once and then opens the door.

Every time I think I understand what being rich must be like, I find out I'm wrong. It's not enough that Halli's parents own their own private island and have that enormous four-story mansion in the middle of it, with employee quarters and a horse stable and a full gymnasium and all sorts of other buildings around it. Or that they own not just one jet, but two. And boats and cars and everything else the modern gazillionaire might need. And that their company has offices and factories and facilities all over the world.

To own just *one* place like the one I'm stepping into right now would make me feel like I had so much money I could afford to rip up a hundred dollar bill before and after every meal just for the fun of it.

Halli's father is standing in a front of an entire wall of floor-to-ceiling windows, drink in hand, gazing out at the lights of London. There must be an acre of space in here, all of it covered in hardwood flooring and thick, expensive-looking rugs. The lighting is soft and soothing. There are just a few pieces of furniture, all tasteful and perfect, just a little bit of art on the walls, not a speck of dust or dirt anywhere, and it all screams *I AM VERY RICH AND POWERFUL AND DON'T YOU DARE TOUCH ANY OF MY THINGS.*

"Red, no—!" But it's too late. Halli brought him up to make himself at home even when the couch is white and probably woven with strands of pure gold and is owned by her dog-hating parents.

"Sorry," I mumble, as I rush to pull him off. He jumps down onto the dark red rug instead, seems delighted by the plushness of it and decides he'd better roll, then settles on top of the nice extra carpet of yellow fur he's left behind. Thanks, buddy.

"I had a call from Johnson Chilton yesterday," Halli's father says. He finally turns around and looks at me and frowns at the dog. "He said you asked some very prying questions about the technical aspects of our hydro-catalytic process."

Great. I could have guessed Mr. Chilton would rat me out. He probably called Halli's father the minute I was out of his sight.

But it's true, I was curious. I understand enough of chemistry and some of the other science involved to know that Halli's parents have invented something amazing. They figured out a way to use just small amounts of water to power cars and airplanes and provide electricity to hospitals and schools and cities. So yeah, I was more than impressed. And of course I wanted to know how they do it. But Mr. Chilton wasn't very happy about telling me.

"I want to know how serious you are," Halli's father says.

"About what?" I'm trying not to be nervous because I know Halli wouldn't be, but I also can't help forgetting how mean Dr. Bellows was to me that weekend I stayed with him and his wife. He didn't like Halli and he didn't like me. I never seemed to say anything he approved of. He especially didn't like the way I interfered with the vote he wanted at the board meeting.

"Oxford," he says. "Your mother told me about your conversation last night."

Great. One lie, and it grows tentacles when I'm not looking.

"Very serious." What else can I say? Halli's father smells weakness. I'm going to have to put on my best performance here.

"Why?" he asks me.

I'm saved by a knock on the door. A man in a white smock and a chef 's hat wheels a cart into the room. Even though this is an apartment building, apparently it has room service.

"Over there." Halli's father gestures impatiently. The chef unloads a bunch of dome-covered plates onto the glass table in the corner, then quietly slips back out.

I have zero appetite, although I'm sure I'd be plenty hungry if I were in Daniel's cozy kitchen right now.

Still, I recognize an opportunity for stalling when I see it.

"I need to eat something," I say. Then I head for the table and start piling up a plate with one of every item I see.

Jake is doing the same, although I'm guessing he actually intends to eat all of that.

"You're doing fine," he whispers.

I scoff as quietly as I can. I take a bite of a soft doughy roll and hope it will settle my stomach.

Halli's father isn't eating. Instead he fixes himself another drink from a sleek looking mini-bar that slides out of the wall and then disappears back into it so there's nothing to interfere with the clean smooth surface of the wall. With that kind of technology, I'm surprised the floor doesn't open up where Red is so it can discreetly remove him and replace him with a whole new rug.

"I don't have all night," Halli's father says, and I'm thinking, *"Neither do I."* If not for this detour, I'd be home with Daniel and his family right now, enjoying a much better meal—even if all they had was toast instead of this fancy spread. And I'd be that much closer to finally being able to go somewhere alone with Daniel to discuss everything that's happened today. And then to spend some time in private not discussing anything at all.

So let's get this whole thing over with.

"What do you want to know?" I ask him. "Yes, I'm interested in going to Oxford."

"Why?" he asks again. "Sit." He points to the big white chair across from him.

Luckily, it's the only comfortable thing about this entire room. It's like sinking into a hug. The decorator must have picked it out on her own, to try to bring some humanity to the place. She was probably fired immediately because of it.

"I've been thinking about going to college for a while," I say. The stalling helped. At least now I have an answer. "I didn't want to tell you guys because I wasn't sure I could get in anywhere. I was trying to keep it secret, but …" I shrug like it doesn't really matter what he thinks about it. "Regina asked, and so I told her."

"Studying what?" Halli's father asks.

"Science of some kind."

I meet his gaze, knowing I won't flinch. This is a lie I can stand behind.

"What field?" he asks.

"Chemistry or hydroengineering." The same degrees Halli's parents have. "Or maybe physics," I add, just for me.

"To what end?" he asks me.

"So I can help run the company."

I used to think I hated lying. I didn't think I was any good at it. Now I think I love it.

Halli's father has the kind of laser, penetrating stare

that could make even a statue give in. Not me. I'm just waiting for the next thing he'll ask me. I hope it's something hard so I'll have to make up something even better.

Instead he has to ruin the game. "I always wondered if you had it in you. All right, then. The company will pay for it."

"What?" I try not to sound too disappointed. "Oh ... okay."

"But why Oxford?" he asks.

I've lost all interest in the conversation. "I don't know. Ginny knew a few people there." I might as well fall back on a lie I've already used.

"Like Venn?" Halli's father smirks and takes another sip of his drink. "I don't think so."

"What do you mean, you don't think so? Ginny told me about him."

"No, I mean you won't associate with that disgrace to the scientific community. Do you understand me? We've already had to field questions from reporters all day about you being seen coming out of his office. No daughter of mine is going to study with a nut job like that."

"Really?" I can feel the temperature rising in my chest. It's heading up my neck to my face. "What exactly makes you call him a nut job?"

"The fact that he was friends with your grandmother, for one thing. She collected people like that.

Swamis in India, yogis, mystics—of course she'd want to latch on to Venn."

I don't know whether to be more insulted for Ginny's sake right now or for Dr. Venn's. Maybe I'll just be angry about both.

"What do you even know about him?" I ask.

"A lot more than you do," Halli's father says, getting up to freshen his drink again. "Otherwise you wouldn't have wasted your time with him today. Ousted from the Physicists Consultancy Group he helped create after the Last War. Kicked off the faculty at Harvard. Couldn't find a position at any colleges in the States, so had to start knocking around over here. Finally one of his old Pact buddies took pity on him and found him a teaching position at Oxford—very low level. The man's outlived everyone who used to think he was a genius. Now everyone knows he's just a crank. He's probably been senile for the past twenty years at least."

"He's not senile," I say. I want to say more: *"He's brilliant. He's still a genius. How dare you make fun of him. You're living in a parallel universe that he and his colleagues made. Because of them you haven't had a war in this world since 1946. Do you know how lucky you are? Do you understand everything he's done? Instead you just sit there all smug and act like you know the truth. You don't know anything close to the truth."*

"We'd prefer you go to a school in the States," Halli's father continues, "but we can work with Oxford. We'll have to find you the right professors. Your mother and I will design your curriculum. If you're serious about wanting to be involved in the company, then you'll have to do it right. Your mother and I have a certain standard to uphold."

"Uh-huh," I say. "Right." I'm not even listening to him any more. I just want to get out of here. I stand up and head for the door. "Come on, Red."

"We'll put together a list," Halli's father says. "Jake can start taking you around to meet people tomorrow. We'll take care of admissions, but if you want to start in the spring …"

Red and I quietly exit the room. The dog sits next to me in the elevator and leans against my leg. He gets me. He knows that I'm both exhausted and infuriated by what just went on. He knows I need to pet his soft yellow head.

"Good night, Miss," Bates says as the dog and I stride past. I give him a wave over my shoulder. I'm done talking for a while.

The fresh, cold air blasts me in the face and feels like exactly what I need. I stand in front of the apartment building, just breathing in the London night. I'm not dressed nearly warmly enough, but I'll live. I just want to feel free for a few minutes.

Circumstance and choices. So much of what happens is outside of my control. But look at what Dr. Venn and those other scientists did back when it really mattered:

they made a decision to do things differently. They had no idea what would happen, but they knew they couldn't keep following the same path as before. That one led to bombs and death and destruction. So they made a different choice.

"Halli, you're freezing." Jake takes off his jacket and tosses it to me so he doesn't violate Red's safety zone. "I called for the car. It'll be here any second. But come on—you should wait inside."

"I've been to the North Pole," I remind him. "This is nothing." I put on the jacket and stand there with the wind whipping my hair around. My long thick hair that came with this costume. I don't think I've been appreciating it enough.

I don't think I've really been appreciating any of my advantages here enough.

I tuck my hair into the collar of the jacket and let it warm my neck. But that's just a small, easy change. I can do much more than that.

"I need some money," I tell Jake. "Where can I get some tonight?"

19

"There you are!" Sarah says as I step into their kitchen. "Daniel told us where you were—was it dreadful?"

"*Sarah*," her mother scolds her.

"Dreadful," I agree.

Francie gives me a somewhat maternal look over the top of her glasses, but she doesn't say anything.

"I hope your father doesn't expect to be invited to our party," Sarah says.

"Remind me," Francie says. "Did I raise my children with no manners whatsoever?"

Sarah waves her away. "We're all friends here, Mum. Halli Markham doesn't mind us speaking freely about her abominable parents, do you?"

"Not one bit," I say.

"Good." Sarah passes me a plate of cookies she's just been sampling. "Speaking of the party, you be the judge. Do you prefer the cinnamon or the chocolate?"

I eat two cookies with barely a pause in between. Then reach for and devour a third. Now that I'm back someplace cozy and safe, my hunger is here full force. "Both of them," I say. "All of them. These are delicious."

Sarah beams. "Thank you. One of my many minor talents to complement the majors. Please keep that in mind when you're interviewing cooks for your next expedition."

She's not exactly subtle: what is this, the third time she's mentioned it? Including the last time I was Halli, when she asked me if she could be my apprentice. What would the real Halli do? Would she ever actually consider taking Sarah along on one of her adventures?

"Who's coming to this party?" I ask. It's not something I've spent much time focusing on, but I know it's this coming Friday night. Daniel and Sarah's father is turning fifty. While their parallel versions back in my world—Gemma and her brother Colin—will be celebrating at their family's ball on Saturday, Sarah and Daniel's family is a lot more low-key.

And a lot less well-off, from what I can tell.

"Mostly boring friends of my parents," Sarah says. "Although a few of them are great fun. Will Mr. Mobrey be coming?"

"Probably," Francie says.

"Mind reader," Sarah tells me. "Terribly good at it. You might want to have a go at that."

Not on your life. *"I'm sensing ... you're an outcast from another universe?"* I'll be on the lookout for Mr. Mobrey.

"Have you had supper?" Francie asks me.

"Not really." I hate to ask her to heat something up for me, but I'm starving.

Sarah scoffs. "Do you see, Mum? He didn't even feed her. What kind of father—"

"That's enough," Francie warns. "What if someone said such rude things to you about your father and me? How would you feel?"

"Impossible," Sarah says. "My parents are without equal. There isn't a sane person in the world who wouldn't see that." She kisses her mother on the cheek.

Francie gives up. "I'll warm you some soup," she tells me.

"No, allow me," Sarah says. "Further proof of my skills as Halli Markham's expedition cook. Even under the gravest conditions, I'll still supply you with warm corn chowder and a hot buttered roll."

"That sounds wonderful," I say. "Thank you."

Sarah kneels down in front of Red. "And you, sir? Are you famished as well?"

I totally forgot about Red. I could have fed him all sorts of delicacies from Halli's father's room service. "That would be great, Sarah. Thank you for thinking of him."

"Of course!" she says, roughing up his fur and kissing him on the nose. "He's my little love." Red stares at her adoringly. I think he's in good hands for the moment.

"I'm just going to wash up," I say. "I'll be back in a few minutes. Is … Daniel around?"

"Studying in his room," Francie says.

Sarah gasps in mock concern. "He missed one day of school—he must be frantic."

"You could learn a few things about academic discipline from your brother," Francie says.

"I prefer to watch as a spectator. It's so exhilarating." Sarah smiles sweetly and begins gathering supplies for my dinner. I steal away for a few minutes of privacy.

Sam is in the living room reading a very thick book. Other equally hefty books lay stacked all around him. He takes off his glasses for a moment and pinches his eyes. "The ancient Celts," he says by way of explanation. "Fascinating people, but sometimes trying to read the original texts …. Anyway, how are you? How was Oxford?"

"Interesting," I say.

"Was Venn just as irascible as I remember?"

"Actually, he was really nice."

Sam shrugs. "I suppose even the crustiest old men soften over time. Or else it was just me he detested. He wasn't the first professor of mine to feel that way. Or the last." He smiles and goes back to his reading. I head up the stairs.

I knock softly on Daniel's door. "Daniel, it's m—"

He yanks the door open and pulls me inside. Then he kicks the door closed and wraps me in his arms. The two of us enjoy a long, much-awaited, much-needed, and very proper kiss. Then I just stand there for a little while extra, leaning into him, my head resting against his chest while my busy mind and tired body enjoy the calm of his embrace.

"You survived," he says.

"I did." I treat myself to one more strong hug from Daniel, then I give him a quick kiss and detach myself. It's time to catch him up on what's happened.

There aren't too many places to sit in here—the floor, the bed, the chair in front of his desk—and when Daniel takes the chair, I gratefully accept the bed. I remove Halli's boots and draw my feet up under me with my back propped against the wall. It's almost as comfortable as the puffy chair in Halli's parents' apartment.

I describe my meeting with Halli's father. Daniel doesn't seem surprised by the offer to pay for Oxford.

"You're their only offspring," he says. "Perhaps they really have been waiting for you to show any interest at all in what they do."

"Maybe ... but you should have seen him before— the last time I was here. They had that board meeting on their island where everyone was supposed to vote about buying out Ginny's old shares. Since they belong to Halli now, I tried to delay it until she could take over her life again and decide for herself what she wants to do. You can't believe how furious he was when I said I wanted to learn more about the company first. That wasn't a man who wanted his daughter involved in the family business."

"Unless that part of the past is changed, too," Daniel points out.

I slump down even further along the wall and let out a tired sigh. "I don't know what to think about any of this anymore. I keep waiting for everything to suddenly make sense."

"Well, while you're pondering that one," Daniel says, "I have another mystery for you. I've been doing some research." He picks up the tablet from his desk and is about to show me something when we hear footsteps coming up the stairs. Soon there's a knock on the door.

"Open up!" Sarah calls. "I come bearing provisions."

I jump up and open the door and Red rushes in. He launches himself onto Daniel's bed and stretches out his full length. He lets out a satisfied groan like someone lying down after a big Thanksgiving dinner. I assume Sarah fed him well.

Because she's certainly doing that for me. She carries in a tray and sets it down on Daniel's desk. Steam rises from a huge bowl of corn chowder. There's also a basket filled with rolls and my own personal plate of cookies.

"Wow, this looks fantastic," I tell her. "Thank you so much."

Daniel reaches for a cookie. Sarah bats his hand. "Those are for Halli Markham."

"I think I can spare one," I say. "But just one."

"Budge over," Sarah commands Red, then she stakes out a section of Daniel's bed for herself and for me. I bring the soup and a roll over to join her. After only the first spoonful I'm in heaven. "Sarah … wow."

"I'm only the rewarmer," she confesses. "You can thank my dad. But the biscuits are mine alone."

I know by "biscuits" she means cookies, and I'm sorry I didn't bring those over with me, too. But it's too much trouble to get up. For now I tear off a chunk of roll and dip it in the soup, then give a separate chunk to Red. He chomps it open-mouthed, then goes back to his post-dinner nap.

"Oops, careful," Sarah says. She catches a hank of my hair just as it's about to fall into the bowl. She drapes it back over my shoulder, then pauses for a moment with the strands still pinched between her fingers. "Do you remember me cutting your cousin's hair?"

"Of course," I say. Sarah cut my real hair—that lank, thin, pathetic hair—on one of our first days together in the Alps. She trimmed it up to my shoulders and got rid of the worst part of it. It actually looked and felt a lot stronger after that—almost like Halli's hair, only shorter.

Sarah sighs. "Is there really no hope of Audie coming here this week? How I'd love to see her again." She jerks her chin toward Daniel. "And that lot—he'd be ecstatic if he could have his girlfriend back, even for a day. Wouldn't you, Dan?"

Daniel smiles. "Yes, even for a day."

Sarah bounds up from the bed. "We should call her!"

"What?" I exchange a look with Daniel. "No, I don't think that would be a good idea."

"Why?" Sarah asks. "It's daytime in the States right now, isn't it? We wouldn't be waking her." She retrieves Daniel's tablet and stands with her fingers poised over the screen. "What's her comm number?"

"Um …" *Okay, liar, what are you going to do with this one?* "I'm afraid I have some bad news."

"What's wrong? What's happened?" Sarah asks. "Is Audie all right?"

Daniel gives me a quizzical look. But I have to keep a straight face. I have to keep playing my part.

"She's fine," I tell Sarah. "She just … look, there's no easy way to say this. Daniel, she's breaking up with you. She's in love with a different guy. She just hasn't gotten around to telling you yet."

"NO!" Sarah bellows. "Unacceptable!"

"Oh," Daniel says, doing his best to look heartbroken. "I see."

"I'm really sorry," I say. "Audie and I actually had a fight about it. I told her she was crazy to let a great guy like you go. But she's always had this thing for this other guy named Will, and he finally started paying attention to her when she got home from our trip, and … like I said, I'm sorry."

I read somewhere once that the best lies always have bits of truth woven in. It's true I have had a crush on Will for years. And it's true he did start paying attention to me finally—although the me was really Halli. But when it came down to it, I chose Daniel over Will. I actually feel bad about telling this lie right now, because I feel like I've betrayed Daniel. I have to remember that the real Audie made the right choice.

"Well!" Sarah says. "This is all terribly disappointing. I must say I'm not very pleased with your cousin right now. I thought she was a nicer girl than this."

"She is a nice girl," I say in my own defense. "It's just … sometimes people can't help how they feel."

Sarah scoffs at that. "At least she could have had the courtesy to tell my brother, rather than letting him pine away for the past week …"

"I haven't been pining," Daniel says.

"Oh, really? *If only we hadn't had to end our holiday so soon,*" Sarah imitates in her most melodramatic voice.

"I hope Audie and Halli can come to Dad's party. I hope I can see her again ... She's the finest girl I've ever met..."

Daniel glances at me and I can tell he's embarrassed. I try not to make it worse by letting him see how much I like the report.

"I'm really sorry," I tell him again. "But I hope ... you and *I* can still be friends."

"Of *course* you're our friend," Sarah answers. "It will take more than a fickle cousin to sever that bond. Won't it, Dan?"

"Without question," he agrees. "We're happy you're here, Halli. And I'm certain I speak for our parents in saying you're welcome to stay as long as you like."

"Thank you." I risk giving Daniel a private smile.

"Look how Audie has diverted you from your supper," Sarah says. "It's cold now, isn't it?"

I spoon in another mouthful. "It's not bad."

Sarah shakes her head. "And to think I once believed she was the perfect match for my poor, lonely brother."

"Sarah ..." Daniel warns.

"Don't deny it, you pathetic wretch. You'll bury yourself in your studies again and not look at another girl for years. I know you too well." She sighs dramatically. "I did what I could. It was not meant to be." She pats my leg and hops off the bed. "Halli Markham, he is yours to console now. I have more biscuits to bake. It is my personal pledge that no one shall leave our party with less than half a bellyful of them."

She pauses at the door. "By the way," she tells me, "I hope you won't mind if we invite your friend Jake to the party. It seems impolite not to."

"That would be very rude," I agree. This time it's Sarah and I who share a secret smile.

"Splendid!" she says. "I'll write him a note and you can deliver it to him tomorrow." Then finally she leaves us alone.

Daniel picks up his tablet and two cookies, and takes Sarah's spot on the bed before Red can reclaim it. He hands me one of the cookies, which I eat immediately. He takes my empty bowl from me and sets it on the floor.

Then he threads his fingers through mine and I lean my head against his shoulder as we listen to Sarah's steps descending the stairs. I could sit here like this for the next hour, sandwiched between Daniel and a big snoring dog. This might be the happiest I've felt all day.

Except for when Daniel first kissed me this morning. That might be hard to top on even the best day. Even if I live as long as Dr. Venn.

"You broke up with me?" Daniel asks.

"Yes, but now *I'm* falling in love with you. It gets very complicated. I hope you can keep up."

I kiss him because I can now, and because I know we have work to do and so I won't be kissing him again for a while. I unthread my fingers, sit up straight, and tell him I'm ready for whatever he wanted to show me.

"It's archival footage," he says. "It took me a while to find. But now I understand the connection with Professor Lacksmith."

Daniel pokes and swipes at the screen of his tablet.

Swirling lights gather above. The movie begins.

And there's our friend Dr. Venn.

20

I t's an old movie, from about twenty years ago, according to the date hovering below the image. It's nice to see Dr. Venn walking around on his own. He's using a cane, but he still has a pretty lively step for an 83-year-old.

"Dr. Venn?" someone is asking. "Can you explain your findings to our viewers?"

"No, I can't." He doesn't say it in a surly way like he's trying to get rid of the reporter, it's more just a statement of fact.

"Will you present your findings at the conference?"

"You mean *defend* my findings," Dr. Venn says. "I haven't decided yet."

"Professor—"

"*Doctor,*" he says icily.

"Dr. Venn, the world will want to know."

Dr. Venn stops walking and faces the camera. "I'm not a fool, young man, nor are you. The world will be afraid, as they always are. Now go off and bother someone else."

The footage ends. "And then there's this one," Daniel says, "a month later."

There's a crowd gathered in a large amphitheater. Maybe this is the conference the reporter was asking about. Dr. Venn stands at a podium on stage. He's waving his cane.

"Don't blind yourselves!" he shouts over the sounds of the crowd. "Test it if you don't believe me! Is there anyone here with the courage to try it for themselves and then tell me I'm wrong?"

A man in the second row stands up. He says something, but it's totally drowned out by the crowd. A woman holding a microphone hurries over to him.

"Dr. Venn, my name is Sydney Lacksmith." He's a tall, thin, stately-looking gentleman with a very proper English accent. "I would be honored to try your machine."

"Is that *your* Professor Lacksmith?" I ask Daniel.

"Yes."

"If it does what you claim," Professor Lacksmith says, "then this is an unprecedented breakthrough in physics and consciousness studies. In which case I will be the first to support you. If the experiment fails ..."

"If it fails," Dr. Venn tells him and rest of the assembled conference, "then you can call me a liar to my face and to the public. But I thank you for your scientific integrity. It seems everyone else here wants to skip the experimental phase and move straight to the name-calling."

The crowd grumbles and complains about that, but Dr. Venn has already left the podium. He makes his slow, deliberate way down the steps of the stage, then continues toward Professor Lacksmith to shake his hand.

"What's the experiment?" I ask Daniel.

"This is the first I've heard of it. Lacksmith has never mentioned it. I know he's exchanged information and ideas with Dr. Venn over the years, but he's never spoken of this conference. At least not in any of our classes."

"Did you find anything else?" I ask.

"Dozens of interviews over the years, but nothing significant so far as I can tell. Although I might not know what I'm looking for. These two caught my eye simply for the Lacksmith connection."

"What does your Professor Lacksmith do?" I ask. "Why is he a 'yorker'? And don't tell me it has something to do with cricket—I'm not buying it."

Daniel sighs. "Do you really want to know?"

"Yes! Of course." I think of what Sarah said: *If he considers you a true friend, he'll tell you.* I've been Daniel's girlfriend under two different names and in two different bodies so far. If that doesn't make me his true friend by now …

"All right," he says reluctantly. "But promise you won't laugh."

"I study fungus," he says.

"Fungus?"

"Specifically the neural networks of underground fungi in woodland environments, and their role in conveying information and nutrition among clonal colonies and differing species of trees." He pauses to give me time for that to sink in. "Fungus."

"Whoa," I tell him. "Back up. Give that to me in bite-size chunks, please."

Daniel smiles. "Now you know how I feel sometimes when you rattle off physics phrases that seem perfectly clear to you and sound like gibberish to me."

"Sorry. Now's your chance to do better."

"All right, then let me give you some context first," he says. "A few years ago I attended a lecture by

Professor Lacksmith. He described a phenomenon whereby trees under attack by a particular beetle in one part of a forest are able to send signals to their fellow trees at great distances away. Those alerted trees could then rapidly produce their own chemical defenses to ward off the beetles. So how do they do it?"

"I don't know," I say. "How do they?"

"Underground networks. The forest's nervous system. Tree roots connect to networks of fungi and transport information and nutrition from one plant to another."

"So that's what neurobotany is?" I say. "Studying the nervous systems of plants?"

"That's one way of describing it," Daniel says. "It's a fringe field. Not many scientists support it. Only humans and animals are thought to have nervous systems. Professor Lacksmith is one of a small collection of scientists who believe otherwise."

"And you believe it, too," I say.

"I do."

"So what's yorking?" I ask. "Is that part of this?"

"'Yorker' really is a cricket term," he says. "It's when the bowler—the pitcher, if it were baseball—delivers the cricket ball low to the ground. So someone decided that what we do is yorking—low and beneath the ground."

"How do you win at it?" I know Daniel won first place for it, but I don't see how.

"There's a yorking competition every year," he says. "The winner is the one who devises the fastest method for passing messages from one tree to another. It depends on the mixture of chemicals and whether you deliver it as a gas to the branches or as a liquid you inject or pour into the roots—"

"Wait a minute," I interrupt. Because now it's starting to sink in. Not what he's telling me—that part's pretty cool—but what the implications are as between him and me.

I fix him with a hard, steely glare. "Daniel Everett. Do you mean to tell me that all this time when I've been sharing with you every little detail of all my weird theories about quantum physics and parallel universes and all of that, you've been hiding your own weird plant experiments? Come on!"

Daniel looks uncomfortable. "Not hiding ... waiting."

"For what?"

"The right time."

"Which was?"

Daniel coughs. "Now seems right."

"No," I say. "To borrow a word from your sister, *unacceptable*. Daniel, why didn't you tell me? Didn't you think I'd be interested? Of course I'm interested! I would have loved to hear everything about every single one of your ..." But then the obvious answer pops into my brain. "Oh ... you didn't trust me."

"In my defense," he says, still looking embarrassed, "I understood what Dr. Venn meant this morning—about why he was so harsh with us when we contacted him yesterday."

"That he's learned to be cautious," I recall. Daniel nods. "Because not everyone wishes him well."

"I've had a few … unfortunate experiences of my own," Daniel says. "Without going into specifics, let's just say it has been made clear to me that most girls do not fancy a bloke whose life's ambition is to study fungus."

"Well, I'm not most girls. Which I think should be obvious by now. And besides, I've always wanted to date a guy like that."

Daniel smiles. He lifts my hand to his lips and kisses it.

"I've also always wanted to date a guy who does that." I pretend to swoon, but I don't have to pretend all that much. Daniel really understands the romantic gesture.

But there's something more important going on here, and it needs to be said.

"Seriously," I tell him, "don't you think we're beyond hiding things from each other? After everything we've seen and done, do you really think I would make fun of whatever weird thing you're interested in?"

"No, I actually don't think that," Daniel says. "I'm

sorry. Keeping it secret has become a habit. But I know it shows a certain lack of faith."

"It's more than that," I say. "It's just such a waste of time. I don't want to have to pretend with you—I'm doing it enough with everybody else. I want to know that when we're together we can be totally truthful. Because the truth is, we don't know how much time we'll have together."

I can see that Daniel doesn't like the sound of that.

But he also can't deny it.

"We'll find a way," he says.

"How? Maybe a way to let me live—that would be more than spectacular. That's my main goal right now. But it doesn't change the fact that this ..." I gesture to myself and the space around me. "... isn't right. I don't belong in this body or this universe. Survival is just the first part of the equation. What am I supposed to do about the rest of it? How am I supposed to put it all back together the way it was?"

There's a light tap on the door. Red perks up his ears. A quiet voice says something I can't quite hear.

I get up and open the door. Sarah is standing there with a plate of warm cookies.

She's staring at me with a wild look in her eyes.

Now I know why I couldn't hear her before. Her voice is barely a murmur. The hand holding the plate is trembling. Sarah looks like she's in shock.

"Who," she whispers, "are you?"

22

I quickly hustle her inside and shut the door.

"Sit down," I tell her, leading her to the bed. I take the plate of cookies before she drops it.

Sarah looks from me to Daniel. "You know?" she asks her brother.

Daniel is careful. "Know what?"

Sarah points at me.

I kneel down in front of her. I take her hands in mine. She flinches, which isn't a good sign, but at least she lets me hold on.

Sarah licks her lips as if she's just crawled for days across a barren desert. Her voice sounds that dry. "You're not Halli, are you?"

I hesitate, but then shake my head.

Sarah closes her eyes and lets out a sigh. "I *knew* it."

I grip her hands. "How? How did you know?"

Sarah looks at me right the eyes. Really looks at me, like she's trying to see the person behind. Then she lowers her gaze like she's a little embarrassed about what she's about to say.

"You're fonder of me than she is."

I prove it by giving her a hug. "Oh, Sarah. You're one of my favorite people ever. You know that, don't you?"

"If you're Audie, then yes, I do know." She smiles at me. "You are, aren't you?"

I nod.

"How long have you known?" Daniel asks her.

"Since last night."

"Why didn't you say anything?" I ask.

Sarah barks out a laugh. "Such as? *Pardon me, Halli Markham, but I believe you are a fraud. I suspect you are another girl entirely.*" She shifts her gaze to her brother. "Mum and Dad may be bonkers about the supernatural, but I doubt even they would believe this one. Especially if I'm the person who told them."

"When last night?" I ask. I feel like I've been playing hide and seek and had the best hiding place *ever*, and now someone easily found me. I want to know what I did wrong.

"Oh, Audie—shall I call you Audie?"

"NO," Daniel and I answer together.

"It'll be easier if you don't," I say. "That way you won't slip up."

"I suppose he calls you Audie, though?"

"Sometimes," I admit. "But he probably needs to be more careful, too."

I shoot Daniel a look that says *Don't argue*. I don't really think he'd make a mistake, but there's no reason for Sarah to feel like I'm singling her out.

"I'm not stupid," Sarah says.

"I know that," I answer automatically.

"No, really, I don't think you do. Budge over," she tells the dog, then she sits at the head of the bed with her back against the wall, legs crossed under her, and Red's head readjusted onto her lap. I sit down in the space leftover down at Daniel's end.

"It's true I am not a scholar like my brother," Sarah says. "But I do have eyes. I have ears. And I pay attention to people. You haven't been yourself since we came to find you yesterday afternoon. I didn't understand why, but I felt it. The way you carried your body. The way you looked at Daniel—or really, refused to look at him. That was so strange."

Busted. Again.

"But … and I mean no disrespect to the real," she mouths *Halli Markham* before going on, "but she always treated me differently than you did."

"How?"

"As if I were more foolish than I really am." Sarah smiles, but I can see the hint of hurt behind it.

"I don't think you're stupid," I say. "I never have. I think you're funny and clever and wonderful."

"Thank you," Sarah answers, unusually shy for once. "Mutual."

"How much do you want to know?" Daniel asks her.

"This is enough for now," she says. "I needed to know I'm not crazy. And please tell me, is she all right? The real …?"

"As far as I know," I say. "I saw her a few days ago and she was fine."

Sarah nods. "Good. I'm a huge admirer, as you know."

"I do know."

"But you're the one who should be with my brother. So I'm glad you're here. Is there anything I can do to help? I heard what you said about survival."

"I might need a lot of things," I tell her. "Thank you, Sarah. I might need a whole lot of your help."

"Finally!" she says, throwing her arms dramatically into the air. "I can be the apprentice of Halli Markham."

"That's exactly what I'm making you," I say. "Thank you for the suggestion."

I've been holding back on something. Despite what Daniel and I agreed to about not having any more secrets. I haven't known how to broach the topic. I've been worried about Daniel's reaction. But now with Sarah here, I think I'll have a better chance.

I stand up and dig into the pocket of my jeans. I pull out a large wad of cash. Then I set it on the bed near Daniel.

"What's this?" he asks.

I glance at Sarah, who seems to have gotten it right away. Her eyes are bright, and there's the beginning of a smile tugging at her lips. Good.

"I should have done this last time," I say.

"Last time?" Sarah asks.

"It's a long story," I say, borrowing Daniel's excuse. "I'll tell you later. Anyway, this is for you two."

I wasn't sure that I'd be able to withdraw money from Halli's account. If it involved a password or a PIN, I knew I'd be out of luck. But I also saw a memory of Halli's where she paid for groceries by having the cashier scan the microchip beneath her collarbone. And it turns out that's all it took to get cash from this universe's version of an ATM. The machine had a built-in scanner, and all I had to do was pull my shirt to the side and expose a little bare skin.

Daniel looks from the money back to me. "No."

"Yes," I say. "It's mine."

"It's Halli's," he says.

"*I'm* Halli. I decide what I do. And she would give it to you herself if she were here. You have no idea how much she has. This is *nothing*."

"I won't take it." He tries to hand it back. "Thank you, but no."

I clasp my hands behind my back so he can't return it. "Use it for college. Or your dad's party. Or a car. Or something else nice for your family. I don't care. But it's ridiculous to have so much and not share it."

Daniel stands up and gently pulls my hand from around my back. He presses the wad of money into my palm. "Thank you. It was a kind offer." Then he kisses me very sweetly on the cheek.

I transfer the money to Sarah. She wraps her hands around the bills and keeps them.

"No, Sarah," Daniel tells her.

"Yes, Sarah," she answers. "Halli Markham has given us a generous gift. I gladly accept for our family."

"And that's not the last of it," I tell her. "I'll bring more tomorrow and the next day—however long I'm here." Just like the ATMs I'm used to, there's a limit to how much I can withdraw every day—even though the limit here is pretty huge. Still, I suppose I could actually go into a bank and withdraw much more. I might look into that.

"We can't accept any of it," Daniel says. "Sarah, give it back."

"Don't you dare," I say. "Daniel, you don't understand: I'm *poor* where I come from. My mom and I barely scrape by every month. And paying for college … I understand about that. It's why I'm here right now.

I knew I needed a scholarship if I had any hope of going to Columbia—if they even admitted me—so I had to come up with something really *extra* extraordinary, like finding a parallel universe."

"Parallel universe?" Sarah says. "Is that what this is? Sweet mother of pearl ..."

"And obviously I'm grateful for that," Daniel tells me. "But if Halli tried to give you thousands of icies—"

"Which she couldn't," I point out, "because we spend dollars, not international currency. Her money wouldn't do me any good."

"But if she could," he says, "would you take it? Honestly? Because I don't believe you would."

It's a fair question. And I know I probably would have had a different answer to it a few weeks ago than I do right now.

"Yes, I would," I say. "And I'll tell you why. Because sometimes people want to be generous. It makes them feel good. And even though you think you're being noble and polite by refusing, it's actually a really unkind thing of you to do. Daniel, I *want* to help you. I want to help your family. I *love* you—"

"Well, now!" Sarah says. "Be still my heart! What do you say to that, big brother?"

"I say I love her, too, but I still won't take her money."

I'd love to just revel in all this love talk for a few moments, but I can't allow myself the distraction.

"Then look at it this way," I say. "I'm paying my apprentice from now on. I can set her pay however high I want. And she can decide what she wants to do with her earnings."

"If you're very sweet to me," Sarah tells her brother, "I shall share my fortune. Otherwise, it's all for Mum and Dad and me. You can continue thriving on bread and jam."

"We'll talk about it later," Daniel says.

Sarah bounds up from the bed, still clutching her cash. "Until then, I have a secret treasure to bury. Don't worry, Halli Markham. Your fortune is safe with me. No one will ever give it back."

23

Even after Sarah leaves, I can see that Daniel still wants to argue with me about the money. But it's time I shut that down, once and for all. I didn't want to say it in front of Sarah, but now I can.

"Daniel, I might die again."

"You won't," he says firmly.

"We don't know that. We still don't know what happened to the other Dr. Venn."

Daniel doesn't look happy about the reminder.

I reach over and take his hand. "No matter what happens, I don't want to waste another lifetime here. I'm Halli Markham and I'm a millionaire—a multi-millionaire, maybe even a billionaire. Whatever it is, a few hundred thousand dollars—icies, whatever—isn't going to make any difference to me. But it will to you and your family. So I'm doing it and I'm not going to argue with you about it anymore. I'll give it to Sarah for safekeeping if I have to. But I'd be just as happy to give it to you, and I hope you'll stop being stubborn. There. Done. Next topic."

Daniel frowns. But at least he lets it go, for now.

"I do have another topic to discuss," he says. "It's about tomorrow. I don't mind missing classes again—that isn't a problem, I can always make up the work—but Wednesdays are my tutoring sessions with Professor Lacksmith."

"Oh, Daniel, you have to go to that."

"I thought so, too, but I didn't want to abandon you with Dr. Venn."

"I'll be fine," I say. "I have my trusty dog. But if Professor Lacksmith can tell you anything that might help …"

"My thinking precisely," Daniel says. "I find it curious that he's never mentioned that conference before or his testing of some machine of Dr. Venn's. He's told us scores of other stories from his career, and he's spoken of Dr. Venn as a colleague, but never anything about what we saw on that film."

"Do you think he'll tell you if you ask?"

"I don't know. I have to try. At this point we need as much information as we can find."

I nod. But already my mind is drifting. Something Daniel just said is gnawing at its edges. *Wednesdays are my tutoring sessions ...*

Right now it's Tuesday night. I feel like I've lost all sense of time. So much has happened in just the last day and a half.

But I know what happened on the other Tuesday night. It's when everything started going wrong. Which means that by now back in my old world, I'd already made contact with Halli and she knew I was still alive.

But that didn't happen this time. So what does Halli think now?

I explain to Daniel what's on my mind. And why it matters.

"She made a lot of decisions last time based on the conversation she and Professor Whitfield and I had earlier that day. We told her the original Halli was dead —that there was no going back to that body. After that, it's like she went into full survival mode. Everything she did was because she knew she was on her own. She had to completely remake my life into something that worked for her. She wasn't just holding it in place until I could come back."

"So what do you think she'll do now?" Daniel asks.

"I really don't know. Last time she'd already been waiting a whole week without any word from me. She wasn't even sure I was alive. So now, if she still doesn't know, and pretty soon she'll have to start going to my school as me and take over my job ..."

The more I go through it, the more clearly I can see: Halli will still make her choices to survive. She still won't be able to pretend to be me much longer. She doesn't understand my school work, she doesn't understand my job, and she'll still lose patience with my mother trying to have any say over her life.

Halli is going to run again. I know it. Especially if she goes to the ball a few nights from now and meets Daniel's parallel version, Colin, again. He'll plant ideas in her mind and she'll see her way out.

"It's not just me we have to worry about," I tell Daniel. "I can't let Halli do the same things she did last time. I know it'll break my mother's heart. And she's messing up my future—if there really is any chance I have a future back in my old life."

I sink back onto Daniel's bed and use the snoring Red as a pillow. I stare up at the ceiling. "I only have a few days, I think. She started getting antsy on Monday, made her plans to drop out of school that afternoon, and quit my job on Wednesday. If she's still three days behind me like last time, it means I only have two days before all of that starts happening again."

I sit back up. "I'm not going to let her do it again, Daniel. I've worked too hard all my life to get where I am, and she doesn't get to throw it all away in just a few days. You and I both need to find out as much as we can tomorrow. I need to stop her. I want to save both of my lives: this one and the one I left behind."

"You know I'll do whatever I can."

"Good," I say. "Because we're running out of time."

24

—————

"How did you tell him?" Sarah asks. We're working at either sides of her gel-filled bean bag-looking chair to stretch it out flat into a bed. I lay in a chair just like this at Sarah's parents' history studio when I did my meditation session with Daniel. I know the gel molds around your body like you're slipping into a bubble bath without getting wet. It's hard to explain. But it's super comfortable, and knowing that that was Sarah's alternative when she offered to let me have her bed last night made it a whole lot easier to accept.

"I didn't tell him," I say. "He told me. He figured it out on his own."

"It must have been a shock," Sarah says. "To him, I mean."

"Oh, he's seen more than a few shocking things from me." The worst of which was probably the first time, when I disappeared right in front of him and left just a pile of empty clothes. Probably after that, everything else seemed more normal.

"You didn't seem all that surprised, though," I say. "Once I told you who I was."

Sarah shrugs. "I've grown up at my parents' studio. I've seen things most people would never believe— phenomena even Daniel doesn't know about. He's never been as keen as I am to spend time with my parents' researchers. I find it thrilling. I think he finds it … unnerving."

"Why?"

"He likes things that can be explained. He wants scientific facts. He doesn't approve of *mystery*."

I can see what she's saying. When Daniel first suspected that I wasn't Halli's cousin, the way she and I had been telling everyone, he laid out all his facts proving it was a lie. Then he calmly waited for my explanation. Whereupon I vanished. And then when I came back from that, Daniel wanted a detailed, rational explanation for who I was, how I'd gotten here, and every other nuance about my travels between our two universes.

Sarah is right: Daniel is more comfortable with facts than mystery.

"I notice you haven't asked me any questions yet," I say. "Like what's going on, how did it happen …"

"It's not that I'm incurious," Sarah answers, "but I suppose I'm the opposite of my brother: I don't want to ruin the mystery."

She undoes our stretching work on the chair by plumping up one end of it against the wall before plopping down into it. I sit on the floor next to her and lean against her bed. Red readjusts himself to curl up between us.

"Let me tell you a story," Sarah says. She pulls a blanket off the edge of her bed and covers all three of us with it. She hands me a pillow to sit on. This almost feels like a slumber party. Sarah is in her ice blue pajamas, I'm wearing my *Princess dreams of adventure* sleep shirt and Halli's sweatpants—all we need now to go with the story is a bowl of popcorn and some hot chocolate.

"When I was a little girl," Sarah begins, "six or seven years old, I had a teacher named Mrs. Lamb. I adored her. I thought she was the cleverest, prettiest woman in the entire world, second only to my mum, of course."

"Of course."

"Every morning when Mrs. Lamb arrived at school she smelled of lilacs and springtime. She always dressed impeccably in lovely floral skirts and pastel sweaters. She was the very essence of elegance. Her hair was perfect, her cheeks were rosy, her smile was like sunshine warming your face, her voice was like a song—can you picture such a woman?"

"I can." How could I not? Sarah really does have a way with words.

"Good. Then you'll understand. One weekend I was at the market with my mum, when we saw this disheveled, harassed-looking woman with a red-faced, squalling child. The woman wore sloppy, food-stained clothes, her hair was a rat's nest, she looked as if she hadn't slept in an age.

"And she paused in the midst of trying to discipline this hellion of a child to say, 'Oh, hello, Sarah and Mrs. Everett. How are you?'

"I honestly didn't recognize her. It wasn't until Mum called her Mrs. Lamb that I knew. And I was *horrified*. Little girl that I was, I'd just seen a monster personified. What had this creature done to my beloved teacher?

"I couldn't speak. I stood there mute while my mum and Mrs. Lamb exchanged a few pleasantries. Then Mum and I went on while Mrs. Lamb continued down the aisle with that horrid screeching beast-child in tow.

"I don't know if you can understand," Sarah says, "but that day nearly broke my heart. I was never happy going to school the entire remainder of the year. I had seen the truth, and the truth spoiled everything—even though the very next time I saw her, she was once again impeccably dressed and smelling of springtime. Ruined. Utterly ruined."

"I get it," I say. "Totally."

"Do you?" She clutches my hand. "I'm so glad. To this day, Mum accuses me of overreacting. She viewed me as an overly dramatic child, whereas I prefer to see myself as a romantic."

"No, I know what you're talking about," I say. "I stopped going to movies with my grandmother because every time I screamed at a scary part or cried over something sad, she'd lean over and say, 'Remember, it isn't real.' Completely ruined it. She didn't get that I *wanted* to be scared and I *wanted* to cry. I wanted to be caught up in the fantasy. Why would you watch a movie if you couldn't get involved?"

Sarah looks confused. "Sorry, but what do you mean, it wasn't real?"

"You know, maybe it was a cartoon or something with talking animals."

Sarah laughs. "Talking animals! Can they do that where you come from?"

Now it's my turn to be confused. "No, it's … you know, just a movie."

But then I understand. It's the same problem Halli had trying to enjoy my mom's and my favorite sitcom.

"You don't have movies like that here, do you?" I ask. "Stories about magic, or animation, or, I don't know, stupid comedies."

"No, although I would love a story about magic," Sarah says. "What my parents film in their studio is probably the closest anyone gets. And there are numerous critics who find their programming to be far from realistic."

Now I also understand something else. "The last time I was here, I went out to a café with you and a few friends of yours from your school."

"Did you? When? This is now the second time you've referred to being here before, and I have absolutely no memory of it. So I'm afraid you'll have to explain."

"Are you sure?" I say. "I don't want to ruin the mystery."

Sarah waves me on. "I'll stop you before you say too much. I'm highly attuned to the ruinous. But now I must hear the story."

I pause for a moment. Try to think of the best, most efficient way of filling her in. I've already told this whole story to Dr. Venn and Daniel today. I'm too tired to go through it all again.

"You heard me say something to Daniel about parallel universes," I start. Sarah nods. "Well, just take my word for it that this is one, I came from another, and there are at least two more that I know of."

"Truly? How exciting!"

"In this one and another one, I've been Halli both times—her body, me inside. Do you follow that so far?"

"Absolutely."

"So the last time I was Halli, I came to London and saw you and Daniel." I've already decided I'll never tell her how that life ended. So I have to be careful here. "And one day we went out to a café with some friends of yours—"

"Which ones?" Sarah asks. "Do you know?"

"I assume it's the same ones you invited yesterday."

"Oh! Is that how it works?"

"I think so. Anyway," I say, "we were having this conversation, and one of your friends said you should go into theater. And you said something about how you were tired of always playing Marie Curie discovering radium. Is that what your movies and theater are like? They're all historical reenactments?"

"Oh, yes. Loads of interesting material from every possible era. Plus all the recent stuff. No one will ever run out of subject matter and have to make anything up." Sarah frowns. "Pity. I would love to see one of your programs about a talking animal."

Sarah bites her lip and seems to be considering something. "All right, I do have a question to ask. But please don't answer if you think it will disappoint me."

"Okay."

"You mentioned your grandmother. Am I to assume she is not Virginia Markham?"

"No. They look the same, but they're completely different."

"And you, Audie, are one person, and Halli Markham is a different person who looks just like you."

"A little taller, more athletic-looking, but yes."

"So is there …" Sarah pauses. But I can guess what she wants to ask.

"Are you sure you want to know?" I ask.

Sarah bites her lip again and nods.

"Yes," I tell her. "There is another version of you in my universe."

Sarah's eyes go wide. "Do I … am I …?" She shakes her head. "No, don't tell me. Not if you think I won't like the answer."

That's a tough call. But I think I know how to finesse it.

"Her name is Gemma, and she's awful," I say. "She's absolutely nothing like you—at *all*. In fact, she's the complete opposite of you. You're wonderful. She's horrible. You'd hate her if you met her for even five minutes—"

"Oh, stop," Sarah says, slapping her hands over her ears. "No more. *Ruin.*"

Now I feel guilty. "Okay, maybe she's not *that* bad," I admit, and Sarah uncovers her ears again. "It's not like she's a criminal or anything. It's just that she's so … unpleasant. She's snotty and conceited and basically not a nice person. Like I said: not like you at all." I almost leave it at that, but decide I should tell her the whole truth. It's only fair. "Plus she got to date this guy

I was secretly in love with for years, so that didn't exactly make me like her."

"Oh," Sarah says, raising an eyebrow. "Now I see."

"No, it's not just because I was jealous," I hurry to say. "She really is awful. Take my word for it."

But Sarah doesn't look convinced. "And who is this other bloke? The one my evil twin has usurped from you. Is he here in this parallel universe, too? Should I warn my brother he might face a rival?"

"He's not a rival," I assure her. "But yes, he is here."

"Who is he?" Sarah asks excitedly. "Do I know him?"

"I'm not going to say." I agree with Sarah's description of herself as a romantic. I think she'd rather find out for herself that she likes Jake, without me telling her she's dating the Will version of him in my world. *If* they're still dating after what happened at the ball. I won't be telling Sarah about that, either.

Sarah gives me a suspicious look. But then she shrugs. "You may keep your secret. I trust your judgment. Oh, speaking of which …" Sarah climbs out of the chair and stands on her tiptoes to reach something hidden on a shelf above it. She pulls out the wad of cash. "I accepted this on principle because my brother was being so stubborn about it, but I want you to know that I have no designs on it if you'd rather I gave it back."

"No," I tell her. "Not at all. But it is for all of you, so I hope you'll figure out a way to share it. I plan to give you a lot more, so be thinking. I really want to do something nice for your family."

"You're very generous. Thank you." Sarah hides the money again, then sits back down under the blanket with Red and me.

Then she looks at me with that kind of open, vulnerable expression I'm used to from her. "But tell me," she says, "please don't say you were joking about me being your apprentice. I really hope you will accept me for the position."

"Sarah … I'm not Halli."

"I know who you are," she says, "and I am at your service. Now, last week, always. Please allow me to help you. It would truly be my honor."

I nod, a little choked up, and Sarah points at my sleep shirt. "I do dream of adventure," she says. "And there is no question you are having one, Audie-Halli, or however I should address you in private. I hope you'll include me from now forward. I might be of great help to you."

"You might," I agree.

"Splendid," she says. "Then I'm sure you'll agree I should come with you tomorrow, whatever you're doing."

"I'm going back to Oxford, but I don't think—"

"Please," she says. "I'm quite serious about this. I want to be involved."

I'm not sure whether having her along would be an

asset or a hindrance. But I also hate to tell her no. So I try a different angle.

"Remember, your parents wouldn't let you take off from school today to go with me."

"Only because they don't know the truth about who you are. But once we tell them—"

And I surprise myself by how immediately and firmly I answer, "**No**."

25

I never thought I'd willingly admit this, but it really does all come down to math.

Or at least an equation, in my case. Decision X plus a series of decision Ys equaled death.

Circumstance and choices.

So far I've kept to my plan and not done anything the same.

Daniel knows who I am now, but not because I told him.

Sarah knows, but she didn't know last time.

But her parents? They knew. And as helpful as they meant to be, nothing went right after that.

"You can't tell your parents. Please, Sarah. It's very, very important."

"But … they'd understand," she says. "They know people who might be able to help you."

"*No*. Please." Even the memory of all that pain I felt when Olga and her daughter "helped me" is enough to make me wince. "Look, Sarah, I think your parents are wonderful. I love spending time with them. I like them as much as my own mother—my real mother," I clarify, since Sarah doesn't approve of Halli's mother any more than I do. "But I have to be really careful about not letting anyone know. It was an accident that you and Daniel found out. But it really has to stop with you two."

"May I ask why?"

"It's dangerous. That's all I can tell you. Some things happened last time—bad things. You just have to trust me on this."

"Of course I trust you."

"So I'm sorry you won't be able to come with me tomorrow, but I do have another job for you."

"Yes, please," she says. "Whatever it is."

It's the kind of thing I'd do myself if I had time and knew how to work the technology. And even though I could ask Daniel, he's going to be busy enough with Professor Lacksmith.

Sarah is my logical choice.

"There's a professor at Oxford I'll be visiting tomorrow," I tell her. "His name is Edgar Venn. He's very old —a hundred and three—"

"Gracious."

"He was actually one of your father's professors at some point, so please don't let him know what you're doing. Anyway, Daniel found some film of Dr. Venn from about twenty years ago, but I'd like to go back even further. He said there are dozens of other interviews, but he didn't know what he was looking for. I don't, either, but I do know I want to see everything I can about Dr. Venn. So you think you could do that research for me?"

"Absolutely. I would love to."

"Good. Thank you. You can show me tomorrow night."

"Audie-Halli …" Sarah makes a face. "I don't know what to call you anymore."

"'Halli' will be fine."

"But you're not," she insists. "You're an amalgam. A blend."

A new creature.

"I'm Audie Three." I feel a little self-conscious saying it out loud, but I know Sarah won't make fun of me. "You can't tell that to anyone else, though. It's just for you and me and Daniel to know. So keep calling me Halli."

"Will you … stay this way?" Sarah asks. "Or will the real Halli ever come back? And then will you return to how you were?"

Those are the right questions, even though Sarah has no idea about any of the science behind them.

I do have an idea of the science, but I still don't know the answers.

"I'm sure it will all work out somehow."

You're sure, huh? Liar.

What I won't tell Sarah is that those questions of hers are really Step 2 of my whole situation.

Step 1 is just trying to stay alive for longer than this week.

26

"Our friends are here," Sam says when I come downstairs for breakfast. He's reading another thick book, or maybe it's the same one from last night, and sipping a cup of tea. I can smell coffee in a pot on the counter. Sarah said they bought some for me at the market the other night since they know that's what we drink in the States.

Good. I could use some. Even though I was so exhausted last night by the time Sarah and I finally stopped talking, it still took me forever to fall asleep. I had way too much on my mind.

Sam points out the window. I part the curtains to see rain drizzling down on a group of people out huddled at the end of the walkway in front of the Everett-Wheeler house.

Reporters.

I mutter something I probably shouldn't say, but I can't help it. I'd just like a calm day for once.

"It's pretty miserable, what they're doing," Sam says.

"I know! Why can't they just leave me alone?"

Sam laughs. "No, I meant having to stand out there in weather like this and wait for their quarry to emerge. I certainly put in my time just like they are. I don't envy them."

I knew Sam was a history reporter before he became a producer and then started his own history studio with Francie, but I never pictured him hounding people the way Bryan Stewart and the other reporters have been doing. I don't quite know what to say.

"Did you take them some tea?" Francie asks as she joins us in the kitchen. She's dressed in thick slacks and a cherry red wool sweater. I'm wearing one of Daniel's sweaters. It's the color of oatmeal and it's too big for me and I love it.

"Tea and muffins," Sam tells his wife. "They inhaled them like no one has fed them for weeks. Another liability of the job," he tells me. "You're always, always famished."

"And cold. And wet," Francie adds. "Or hot and sweltering. And always in a rush. Except when you're standing around like right now and waiting for hours and hours."

"Are you saying I should feel sorry for them?" I ask.

"It's awfully hard when they feel like mosquitos buzzing around my face."

"Mosquitos with bills to pay and husbands and wives and children to support," Sam says. "But no, you shouldn't feel sorry for them. They generally like what they do. I did. Although I prefer what I'm doing now much more. For one thing, I'm inside right now."

"So, Halli," Francie says, "what's on your agenda for today?" She pours herself a cup of coffee and brings me one, too.

"Thanks," I tell her. I should have gotten it myself. I hate for people to think I expect them to serve me. Halli never acts that way. "I'm going back to Oxford as soon as the car gets here."

"Seeing Venn again?" Sam asks me.

I nod. "He gets really tired. We couldn't go for very long yesterday."

"What's he like?" Francie asks. "Still mentally sharp?"

"Very," I say.

"How old is he now?" she asks.

"A hundred and three."

Sam whistles.

"Nice man?" Francie asks. "Decent?"

"Very."

Sam scoffs at that.

"He was to me," I tell him. "I really enjoyed talking to him. He's got a lot of amazing stories."

"Does he now?" Francie says. She taps her finger against her cup. "Do you think he would ever do a program for us?"

Sam tugs at his earlobe. "Sorry, I thought I just heard you ask if you could go into that cage over there and pet that lovely tiger. 'Oh, but his fur looks so *soft.*'"

Francie laughs, but won't give up. "The man won't last forever. Shouldn't we preserve what he might have to say? Otherwise you'll turn up some irresistible tome some day," she gestures toward the book Sam is reading, "and think, 'Venn knew all about this. I should have asked him when I had the chance.'"

Sam shuts his book. "It's true the man does know a few things about a few things, but I really don't see—"

"I don't think he'd do it anyway," I interject. "He's pretty private." I think of those two snippets of archival footage I watched with Daniel last night. Dr. Venn might have been nice to us, but obviously he can be a bear to reporters and anyone else who wants to challenge his work.

"No," Sam says with an air of finality. "That tiger bites. Forgive my keen sense of self-preservation."

"We'll talk about it later," Francie whispers to me in a voice loud enough that she obviously means for Sam to hear.

"Right, then," Sam says, rising to his feet and tucking his research book under his arm. "I have easier tasks at the moment. Do you want to work on those Olga edits with me this morning?" he asks Francie.

A cold shot of electricity races up my spine. Yesterday was Tuesday. I met Olga at their studio Tuesday afternoon. Her session still went on without me.

I can still feel her soft, small hands gripping tightly to mine. See her sitting across from me with her eyes closed as the images of what happened to Halli and me flitted across her mind. *"You have given me a puzzle. How exciting. Thank you."* Then the answer coming to her, words that were sweet to my ears: *"Alive! She's alive! Go to her!"*

So I did.

A mistake I can't repeat.

But how am I supposed to stop Halli from doing everything she did if I can't talk to her? The truth is, I haven't really allowed myself to think too much about it. There's a nice, protective barrier in front of it in my mind, and I know on the other side is a whole mess of problems I'm not ready to confront. It's easier right now to just worry about myself. But I know at some point I'm going to have to think through the Halli puzzle, too. And do something about her.

Just not right now. Right now I have reporters to deal with.

"What can I do to make them leave me alone?" I ask Sam and Francie.

Sam shrugs. "Give them what they want. Most of those people out there have been sent by their heartless producers out into the rain on a cold, dismal morning to bring back some sort of footage on Halli Markham. They'd probably all love to go back to their warm, dry studios. Or at least go on to something else besides standing there freezing their bums off."

"But what if I don't want to talk to them?"

"I'm afraid that won't satisfy their producers," Francie says.

"What if I've already agreed to give an exclusive to someone else?"

"Have you?" Sam asks.

I describe the deal I made with Bryan.

"Might do," Francie says. She gets up and pulls a box off the counter. "Let's go ply them with some of Sarah's biscuits and speak to them like the civilized people we all are." She turns to Sam. "Would that have worked with you?"

"Biscuits, yes. A reasoned, civilized argument—no. Because then I'd have to explain to my boss why I've come back with crumbs on my shirt, but nothing else to show for my last three hours on the job."

"Is that how long they've been out there?" I ask. The idea is kind of horrifying.

"Not quite," Francie says, "but long enough to nab Sarah and Daniel on their way to school."

Now I really feel bad. "Do you know what they said?"

"I heard the word 'vultures' from Sarah," Sam says, "and I believe Daniel was of the 'no comment' variety. There was some insinuation that he's your new beau. But he's with your cousin, isn't he?"

"They … broke up." Lie or don't lie? "Daniel and I do … kind of like each other."

Francie's eyebrows lift. "Well! You are full of surprises. I think I understand why they're so persistent. Although I do tend to agree with the 'no comment' approach. Citizens are entitled to their privacy, no matter how tantalizing their stories might be."

I have the feeling Dr. Venn would see it the same way. I can't imagine him sitting down with anyone in the media and telling them any of the secrets he's told me.

Sam glances out the window. "Your car is here."

Francie offers me the box of cookies, but I don't think Sarah would want me to waste them on the vultures. I pull Daniel's big coat from its hook by the door and grab an umbrella out of a tall basket. I summon Red, who's been sleeping on the couch in the living room. That dog does make himself at home.

"Talk to him," Francie says. "Dr. Venn, I mean. It wouldn't hurt to ask."

"Here, tiger, tiger …" Sam coos.

"Especially if he's willing to talk about the rift," Francie adds.

"The rift?"

"With his fellow physicists," she says.

Halli's father had mentioned something about that, too. How Dr. Venn had been ousted from a physicists' group.

"Do you know anything about it?" I ask.

"Apparently someone died," Sam says. "But no one has been willing to go on the record as to why."

If he's talking about the other Edgar Venn, I'm about to go ask the same question.

I t comes in handy to have a dog who doesn't like strangers.

He can't stop the reporters from shouting at me, but he does keep them a respectable distance away. Wilkinson stands in the rain holding the door for me, while Jake gets out to smile pleasantly at the reporters and tell them, "Miss Markham will spend the day on confidential company business. That will be our only statement today. Thank you."

Red hops in, I hop in, then the car is blissfully quiet. Wilkinson starts it up and goes back to sipping his tea and reading. Jake taps on the divider between the front and back seats.

I look up to find a list displayed there. Names and times and subjects.

I don't even have to ask.

Jake wedges in his ear button and I reluctantly do the same.

"Will you be visiting any of these people?" he asks me.

"No."

"Do you want me to?" he offers.

"No."

There are ten names of professors and the subjects they teach. Someone—Halli's mother or father or some employee of theirs—has obviously set up appointments with each of them. The schedule is filled from 10:00 to

4:30 in half-hour slots. They were good enough to give me an hour for lunch.

"What will you say when they find out you didn't talk to any of them?"

"That's my problem," I tell him. Then I take out the ear button, close my eyes, and lean back to ride in silence. Red gives his customary pre-nap moan and lays his head across my lap. Between him and being bundled up in Daniel's clothes, this is as cozy as I can get.

I try to concentrate on the questions I want to ask Dr. Venn today: obviously about what happened to the other Dr. Venn. That's number one. But also about the topic we just barely touched on before Dr. Venn faded yesterday afternoon: how it is that both times when I've been Halli, her past was changed before I even got here?

If everything really is circumstance and choices, then who made the choice to change those pasts? Dr. Venn mumbled something about it being me, even if I don't know it.

Well, he's right—I don't know it. He's going to have to explain that one to me.

I shift in the seat to get more comfortable, and feel the edge of Sarah's envelope poking into my back. It's gotten a little crinkled in my back pocket, but once I smooth it out it's almost as good as new.

She left it on top of her pillow where I could find it

this morning. She was nice enough to sneak out very quietly and let me sleep an extra hour while she got ready for school.

I tap the divider and hold Sarah's invitation against it. Then I lower my window, Jake lowers his, and I pass it to him outside the car. I insert the ear button for what I hope will be a short conversation.

"What's this?" Jake asks. He opens the handmade card I watched Sarah create last night. Some people have natural artistic talent, and she's one of them. All she needed were a few colored pens to turn a plain piece of paper into a mini work of art.

"There's a birthday party Friday night for Sarah and Daniel's father," I say. "Sarah hopes you'll come."

Jake gives me a look that I don't know how to interpret—amused? Flattered? He stuffs the note in his coat pocket. "So does that mean we're staying through Friday?"

"*I* am. You can do whatever you want."

"Then I guess I'm going to a party Friday night."

I shrug. I'm about to remove the ear button when Jake says, "Wait. There's one more thing. I got a comm from Bryan last night."

Great. That guy. "Saying what?"

"He wants to know when you'll be ready for your sit-down. He suggested later today. He's getting impatient."

"I don't care if he's impatient," I say. "I'm busy. Tell him I'll talk to him this weekend. Maybe. If I'm free."

"Halli, I don't want to try to tell you what to do, but it might make your life easier if you just got the guy off your back. Give him his hour. Get it over with. Otherwise he's going to keep bothering you."

How can Halli stand all this? People constantly *at* you. Expecting you to talk to them, take your picture with them, answer whatever questions they have just because they want to pry. Halli isn't their property, and neither am I.

"I changed my mind," I say. "I'm not going to give him an interview. As of right now, I'm off limits. To everybody."

"Okay ..." Jake says. He lets that sit for a few moments while he seems to think it over. "So you're saying ..."

"No interviews, no pictures, no exclusives—nothing."

"Your parents might have a problem with that. They agreed to let Bryan—"

"Jake, I. Don't. CARE." I stare at him through the transparent divider and hope I'm conveying exactly how serious I am about being completely over all of this. If this is my last week of this life, I'm sure not going to waste it doing what other people want.

And if I'm fortunate enough to keep living for a

while, then I might as well start enjoying this life right now.

What would the real Halli do? Exactly what I am right now. I've seen her in action, and I know. I might not have liked it when she was bulldozing her way through all the choices I made for myself about how to be Audie, but in a way, it was actually inspiring. She did what she wanted. She didn't like how things were, so she started making all new choices to fit her own tastes and preferences.

"In fact," I say, "from now on I'm not interested in any more meetings with my father or comm calls from my mother. You can handle all of that for me."

I saved his job, so now it's time he repays me. And even if he doesn't want to do it, do I really care? What do any of these people have to do with me? With *me*, the real Audie 3?

The question isn't what would Halli do, it's what will *I* do? What do *I* want? Who's standing up for *me*?

I know now that I can get money any time I want. Maybe Halli's parents can take the car and Wilkinson away from me, but Daniel and Sarah can teach me how to get around. I can stay with their family or go back to Mrs. Scott—I'm sure she'll help me.

I don't know why it hasn't occurred to me until this very second, but the truth is I'm *fine*. I don't have to play the Halli game. I can start making up all of my own rules.

"Do me a favor," I tell Jake. "Please don't let them know until the end of today. It will make things easier if I have a ride home."

"What makes you think I'll tell them anything?" he asks.

"Because you work for them."

"What if I worked for you?"

I narrow my eyes at him. He smiles.

I don't get this guy.

"So what are you saying?" I ask. "That you'll give up your position with my father—stop being his apprentice, and whatever else you do for my parents—and you want to come work for me instead?"

"That's what I'm saying," he confirms.

"Doing what?"

"Whatever you need me to do."

I give my head a good solid shake. I feel I should be following this better, but I'm not.

"Jake, what makes you think I can pay you whatever they're paying you?"

"You're rich."

"What makes you think I have any kind of work for you to do?"

"Everybody has work they want done," he says. "I'll bet you could think of ten things right now off the top of your head."

Well, at least two: keep the reporters and Halli's parents off my back.

But the problem is, I'm not really sure I trust him. Jake of the easy smile and the slick conversation and the two-faced way of dealing with Halli's parents. How do I know he isn't some kind of double agent? How do I know he isn't going to feed them information about me the same way he feeds me information about them?

But what is there to know about me, anyway? My tracking information already reveals too much. So they know where I am at all times—so what? So they'll find out I didn't talk to any of the Oxford faculty they recommended—yeah? And?

"I have to think about it," I tell him. "This is obviously a surprise."

"Is it?" he asks. "Hm." He doesn't seem convinced.

"For one thing," I say, "do we really want to have this conversation in front of someone else?" I gesture with my eyes toward Wilkinson.

"He would be happy to work for you, too. Wouldn't you, Wilkinson?"

I can't hear his answer, but I see him nod.

What's going on? How have I suddenly gained two perspective employees?

"I'll think about it," I say again.

I can see the towers and spires of Oxford in the distance. Once again my pulse starts to speed up in response.

"Whether or not I hire you," I say, "I'd really appreciate it if you kept everyone away from me today. Reporters, my parents …"

"Of course, Miss Markham," Jake says with a smile.

It would be easy to take that smile as sincere—easy to take Jake up on his offer right here and now—but something is still bugging me about the whole thing. About him.

Why doesn't Red like him? No, it's more than that: why does Red seem to actively hate him? Is it just some weird anomaly of this universe's version of the dog and Jake, or is there something more behind it? And is it supposed to mean something to me?

Wilkinson pulls up to the curb where he left Daniel and me yesterday. The rain has picked up, and Wilkinson is nice enough to hold an umbrella over us as Red and I get out. He hands me that one—a big, wide, obviously higher-quality umbrella than the one I borrowed from Daniel's house—and takes the lesser one for himself.

Jake lowers his window just enough for me to hear him. "Do you want us to pick you up for lunch?"

"Actually, can you just go get sandwiches again?" I ask. "I'll come and get it when I'm ready."

Instead Jake hands me another one of those cards I'm supposed to use to page him. "I'll be happy to bring it to you."

"So these are the kinds of things you'd do for me?" I joke. "You'd give up your dream of becoming a chemist like my father just so you can bring me a sandwich whenever I want it?"

"Halli," Jake says, "I'd be happy to do much more for you, if you'd let me."

We share a look for a moment and it's clear to me what he means. I'm going to have to shut that down right away. I've already walked that road once and it ended very badly.

"No, thanks," I say, maybe a little more sternly than I have to. But the wall needs to come up, and fast.

Besides, let Sarah have a chance with him. He has to know right now that he has none with me.

"You'll be all right, Miss?" Wilkinson asks. "I might be able to find somewhere closer to park."

"I'll be fine," I tell him. "Thanks for the upgrade with the umbrella. Come on, Red."

I take off at a dash. Anyone watching me right now might think I'm running because of the rain.

I'm running because I'm finally going to get some answers.

28

"Red, my boy! Good morning!" Dr. Venn detaches his arms from the cuffs of his chair and holds them wide for the dog. Red wriggles his way forward, his whole body in a wag.

"GRANDDAD, KEEP THEM ON THE CHAIR," Madeline tells him. "YOU'RE STILL TOO COLD."

Dr. Venn ignores her for the moment and digs out a few treats for Red. The dog obediently sits. Dr. Venn is less obedient, trying to lean forward and pet Red's head at the same time his granddaughter is still tucking a blanket around his legs and lower torso.

"I've turned up the heat on the gel," she tells me, "but it won't do him any good if he's not in contact with it. GRANDDAD, ARMS BACK IN, PLEASE." She carefully repositions his arms inside the cuffs. She might be bossy, but she's gentle. "We tried to make him stay home this morning—it's obviously too wet and cold. But he insisted on meeting you."

I'm grateful, but I also feel a little guilty. "What can I do to help him?"

"First," Madeline says, "you can respect my grandfather's age and health. He doesn't account for it himself, I'm afraid."

"Of course I will."

"Second, you can ensure he's always warm. I've turned up the heat in here, but the blanket is essential as well. Please, if you notice any signs that he's cold, stop and let him elongate the chair. Standing for a while can restore the circulation. He can't do it for too long because it tires him, but a few sessions of it a day really help."

"I promise," I tell her. "I'll do whatever I can."

Madeline smiles and reaches out to squeeze my hand. "I'm sorry. I know I'm sounding awfully harsh with you. But it's only because we love him and want to protect him, my family and I. But I'm well aware that my grandfather has A WILL OF HIS OWN AND IT IS VERY STRONG." She gives her grandfather a mock sneer which he returns before they both soften back to smiles. "You're obviously not to blame," she tells me. "He's always been defiant. It's why he is who he is."

She gives me a few more instructions for where the controls are for the heat in the room and in the chair.

Then she kisses Dr. Venn on the cheek and tells him she'll see him this afternoon.

As soon as we're alone, Dr. Venn says, "My headphones, please."

I slip them over his head, then take the chair across from him and pick up the microphone.

"The yorker isn't with you today," Dr. Venn says.

"No. He wanted …"

I'm not sure if I should tell him Daniel will be talking to Professor Lacksmith today. Just in case Daniel finds out anything bad. "He had to go to school."

"But you're here, and I'm here," Dr. Venn says. I nod. "It's because we both understand, don't we? That this right now is the most important thing in our lives."

"Yes, sir, it is."

"Good," he says. "Then we won't waste time. Yesterday you asked me about your past—how it could change before you came here. Let me tell you about one of my experiments."

29

"Imagine I set up an experiment where I show you a series of holographic images," Dr. Venn says. "One after another, just a few seconds apart. A picture of a bicycle, a dog, a hat—that sort of thing."

"Okay."

"I program my machine to show you one hundred images in a row. Then once it's done, I ask you to quickly list as many of the images as you can remember. That's the test. That's the only test you take."

"Okay." I don't see what this has to do with my question about the past, but I'll let him tell it his way.

"Then after the test, I have you sit and watch twenty-five of those same images again, chosen at random by the machine. And do you know what happens?"

"I have no idea."

"You remember those images you saw twice *better*. Significantly better."

He pauses, smiling, as if what he just told me is impressive.

"Right," I say. "That makes sense. If you see the same image twice, you'll remember it better."

"But there's only one test," Dr. Venn reminds me. "Do you understand? I only test people after the first viewing. But they score higher on all the images they'll see for a second time *after that*."

He pauses again to give my mind a chance to catch up.

"Wait a minute," I say. I close my eyes to try to picture it. "So you're saying people remember better the things that they won't even see until after the test is over?"

"Exactly," Dr. Venn says. "It's why I always told my students they should pay attention in my classes when we go over the correct answers to an exam. They didn't know it, but they were part of my experiment, too. The ones who paid attention to what the right answers were *after* the test made fewer mistakes to begin with than the other students.

"Now, I know what your objection will be," he says before I even have time to form it. "You'll say, 'Well, obviously the students who come to test reviews are the better students anyway, since they care more about their grades.' But I eliminated that element by making it mandatory at least once every term to attend a post-test review and take notes next to every question they missed. And across the board, every student did better on whichever test I chose for the experiment that term. I picked different tests every time. And the same thing happened again and again."

"That's amazing."

Dr. Venn grins. "Isn't it? But you're wondering why I've told you this story."

Actually, I've been so absorbed by it, I forgot what we were originally talking about.

"It's called *retro-causation*," Dr. Venn tells me. "And you've done it both times you've appeared here as Halli."

He removes one of his arms from the cuff on his chair. "Just for a moment," he tells me before I feel the need to say anything, although I'm not sure I would. I don't exactly feel comfortable ordering around an elderly scholar who is obviously more brilliant than I'll ever be.

Dr. Venn picks up a pen and draws three dots on a sheet of paper. "I'll let you label them," he says. "Past, present, future."

I write one word under each dot.

"Why did you put them in that order?" he asks me.

"Because … I don't know. That's how you said it. And it's normal."

"It's normal because we think of them that way. But you could just have easily written Future, Past, and Present under the dots in that order. Or written all three words on top of each other under just one dot. It doesn't matter. They're all three here all the time, occupying the same space. But that's very hard for us to understand, isn't it? Even if someone could prove it to us mathematically."

"I have trouble with math anyway," I confess.

"You won't need it," Dr. Venn says. "I need you to picture something instead. You told me you've studied quantum physics. How would you describe a *possibility wave?*"

"It's a feature of the uncertainty principle," I say. "It has to do with not being able to predict what a subatomic particle will do. We can measure either its spin or its velocity, but we can't measure both at the same time. So there will always be one aspect of its future that's unpredictable. Until it settles down and we can measure it, everything it does is just a possibility."

"What happens when you do observe the outcome?"

"Then all of the possibility waves collapse," I say, "and only one of them becomes a certainty."

"And that applies to more than just subatomic particles, correct?" Dr. Venn asks. "Other, larger things can have unpredictable behavior, too."

"Right. Because larger things are made up of subatomic particles."

"Good," Dr. Venn says. "There's a coin in my desk drawer. Get it."

I find a few silver icies in the tray of his drawer and hold one up.

"Toss it into the air," Dr. Venn tells me.

I flick it upward off my thumb.

"Now—quickly," he says, "what are its possibilities?"

"Heads or tails," I say.

"More than that," Dr. Venn reminds me. "The coin might disappear into another dimension, or it might defy gravity and float upward and never land. Those outcomes aren't likely, but they are possibilities, aren't they? Isn't that what we do with quantum physics? We try to account for all the possibilities, no matter how strange they might be?"

"Yes," I say, "but there are some things that are more *probable* than not. And the probable outcome is either heads or tails."

"So now it's landed," Dr. Venn says. "Which is it?"

"Heads."

"What is the *probability* now that it will still land tail side up?"

"None."

"And the probability that it will land head up?"

"One hundred percent. It already has. I can see it."

"Good. You can keep Mr. Gandhi as your reward."

"So *that's* who it is!" I say. "I saw one of these when Halli and I were in the Alps, and I thought I recognized the face, but I just couldn't remember."

"Those were issued in honor of Mr. Gandhi's one hundredth birthday."

I'm about to just accept that information and move on, but I can see Dr. Venn staring at me with particular interest. As if he's waiting for me to get it.

"One hundred?" The memory of one of my history lessons tickles my brain. "But I thought …"

"That he was assassinated when he was in his seventies? You would be correct. In your world."

"But here?"

"He lived to a hundred and two. Youngster." Dr. Venn smiles. "He played a key role in the world as you see it now. We wanted peace, and he was the man to design it. We owe a great deal to his vision."

"So did someone still try to kill him, but they failed?"

"No," Dr. Venn says, "it never got that far. We were already different just a year after the war. And it's fair to assume the would-be assassin was different, too. For the same reason we're talking about: *retro-causality*."

"Okay, you're going to have to explain this all to me," I say. "I feel like I have little pieces of it here and there, but I don't see how they go together."

"Let me add another piece," Dr. Venn says. "Do you know what the *Zeno effect* is?"

"I think so. It's when there are two identical particles, both under observation, but with one of them, the scientist only observes it twice: at the beginning of its life cycle and at its end. With the second particle, the scientist checks on it all the time from start to finish."

"And what happens when you compare the two particles at the end of their cycle?"

"They're both very different," I say. "Because every time you observe something or measure it, you change it. It's called the observer effect."

"Very good," Dr. Venn says. "I want you to hold all of those principles in your head for a moment. Now hand me that pen and paper again." He takes his arms out of the cuffs, then flattens the paper on his lap with the pen poised above one of the dots. "So. The last time you saw Halli alive, in the flesh—not when you looked ahead and saw the avalanche, but when you were with her in the Alps—that was on Sunday, you said. Correct?"

"Correct."

He pokes a hole through the Past dot.

"Next, you woke up in her body on Thursday, safe in her bed in her Colorado house. Also correct?"

"Yes."

He pokes a hole through the Present dot. "So. Tell me, Audie, if those were your only two observation points—

this known past and this known present—what are the possibilities of what could have happened in between?"

"But … I know what happened in between. I saw it. I saw the avalanche."

"No, you saw one *possibility* that led to a different present—the one where Halli was dead. You woke up in the present where she lived—or more specifically, where you lived inside her body. Forget what you think you know. I want you to tell me what one of the possibilities was for how her story went from this point in the past to that point in the new present."

"Well … I guess the one that her tracking information showed. That she hiked out with Daniel and Sarah on Sunday."

"And Daniel confirms that, yes?"

I nod.

"So those are at least two facts that make that history the more probable one," Dr. Venn says. "And make the history where Halli dies less probable. Like you observing the coin lying face up, and so it's unlikely it landed tails up instead."

"Wait a minute—hold on. Those are not the same thing."

"Why not?" Dr. Venn asks.

"Because … I mean … one is just a coin. The other is a whole life. It's a lot more complicated."

"Is it?" Dr. Venn asks. "Then let's take another

example: your second time through as Miss Halli. You said there are things that have been changed. How could that have happened?"

I stare at the paper on his lap. Past, Present … and all that blank space in between.

"Just suppose something for a moment," Dr. Venn says to me. "Humor me. Let's say the conscious you arrives at some point in her timeline, and thinks, *'Hm, that didn't go so well. What could I do better next time?'* And let's say the conscious you thinks, *'Where in the previous timeline did things start to go wrong? What if I went back to that and started doing things differently?'*"

I'm listening very intently. Because what he's saying sounds like it could possibly be true.

"And so," Dr. Venn continues, "you decide to make some changes. Circumstance and choice. And so here you are, a new Present, but what Past would best support it? *'Oh, I know—I won't have done this. I'll skip doing that.'* And now you've claimed a different possibility for what might have happened between Past and Present. And the moment you start living forward again, you've set those changes in place. They have now become your probable history."

"But … wait a minute." I set the microphone on my lap so I can lean forward and give my head some support. It wants to be cradled a little right now. Anchored between my palms. It's feeling a little airy and unweighted at the moment. It needs to know we are real.

I sit back up and try again. "I don't control the dog. He hates Jake this time. Why?"

"Because maybe in this past you reacted to Jake in a way that made the dog feel protective. Is that possible?"

The word *possible* has taken on a new meaning for me. "Yes, I suppose it's possible. And I guess it's possible that I knew Halli's parents would make Mrs. Scott leave the island before we could make plans for me to stay with her, so this time I made sure I talked to her in time."

"It's my students studying the test after they take it," Dr. Venn reminds me. "You saw the better answers, and so you fixed it."

"Wow." What seemed bizarre just a few minutes ago is starting to make more sense.

"It's because time flows in loops," Dr. Venn says, "not in a straight line. Possibility waves flow from the past to the present and back to the past, carrying information in both directions. It does the same from the present to the future, with waves coming back showing all your possibilities.

"But there will always be one that resonates with the wave you're sending forward," Dr. Venn continues. "Future you says, *'These are the answers to the test you're about to take. You'll see them at the test review you'll go to two days from now.' 'Oh, okay, thank you.'* Or present you says, *'I want to be a doctor.'* Future you answers, *'All right, here's the life where you're a doctor. Do you want to know how you got here? You did this and this and this.'* 'Oh, okay, so I'll make those choices right now and going forward, and become that version of me in the future. Thank you for the information.'"

"Are you serious?" I ask. "That's really what happens?" It's a beautiful story, but it sounds too unreal to be true.

"That's what my research shows. And my own personal experience. The possibilities coalesce into one probable course. I send a wave into the future and it searches for the resonant wave coming back. Then I start getting hunches, nudges—all from the future me. *'Go talk to that person. Stay away from this one. Read this book. Go for a walk now because you're going to see something that will change your life.'* I can choose to follow those suggestions or not—the choice is always mine—but the track has been laid for me if I want to make it easier on myself."

"So … hold on." He's giving me so much information right now, I feel like my brain is on overdrive. "So when I came back as Halli this time, I sent out a possibility wave about how I wanted things to change. And one of the waves coming back from this present connected with that and we made a new history together. Is that what you're saying?"

"That's close," Dr. Venn says. "We could spend all

day on it—and maybe we will later—but first I want to know something else: have you noticed any other changes?"

"You mean … besides the things about Red and Jake and Mrs. Scott? No, I think those were the only big ones."

"Any changes … in yourself?" Dr. Venn asks.

"Like what?"

"I don't want to plant any suggestions in your head," he says. "Just examine it yourself."

Do I feel any different? Maybe...

"Okay, I don't know if this means anything," I tell him, "but there have been a few times … no, forget it. It's probably nothing."

"It's probably not," Dr. Venn says. "So tell me."

"I've noticed … okay, there are a few times, especially when I've been dealing with Halli's parents, when I feel like I really am her. Not just pretending. I feel angry and … offended, I guess, in ways I don't think I should, you know? They're not *my* parents. Why do I get so upset?"

Dr. Venn nods. "Anything else?"

"Maybe a little … bolder this time?" Despite what I just said, I feel shy saying it. It's weird to have to describe yourself to someone else.

"Bolder how?" he asks.

"Stronger than I used to feel. More confident. More sure of what I have to do and how I should go about doing it. And also … I guess I'd have to say more defiant."

"Defiant," Dr. Venn says, smiling. "*Yes*. That's a wonderful word for it. And do you want to know why you feel that way?"

"You mean it's not just my imagination?"

"Oh no, not at all," he says. "It's very real. I've experienced it, too."

"You have? Then what is it?"

"It's the strands of Halli in you. You aren't strictly Audie anymore. You carry Halli with you now, too. Along with strands of the girl you were right before this. And strands of the life Halli is making now, living as you. And of course strands of the original you. They're all woven into you, like threads twisted into rope. So of course you feel bold. Of course you feel strong. And yes, *defiant*."

He raises a gnarled, arthritic fist. "You're not the same seventeen-year-old girl you were a month ago—you've traveled universes. Lived multiple lives. Of course you're a different person. And why? *Circumstance and choices*. Possibility waves flowing backward and forward and sideways. You've chosen the best parts of all of you to construct the girl sitting before me right now. How do I know? *Because I did it, too*." He barks out a laugh. "So! What do you think of that?"

What do I think? What can I say? I just sit here staring at this old man who is grinning like a kid, his body encased in purple casts, his eyes bright behind thick glasses. He must be exhausted from all this talking, from all this teaching, but you wouldn't know it to look at him. The man is exuberant. The man is *alive*.

"Dr. Venn," I say, "you have officially blown my mind."

"Audie, my dear, we have only just begun."

"Can you tell me more about the strands?" I ask. "That sounds so amazing, but I'm just not sure I get it. And what do you mean you've done it yourself? When? What are you talking about?"

Dr. Venn chuckles and pats his hand in the air the way I saw him do with Red when the dog was barking hysterically at the chair. "All in time. We have so much to talk about, you and I. But I'm afraid my days of rambling through the night are long behind me. If I rest now, we can have at least a few more hours this afternoon."

"Oh, of course!" I try not to let him see I'm disappointed. Every minute with this man feels like a gift. I shouldn't be greedy. "Are you warm enough, sir? Can I get you anything—maybe some hot soup or something?"

"Yes, soup sounds nice," he says. "I brought a sack lunch, but something hot would be very welcome."

I stand up and pull on Daniel's coat. "I'll go get you something right away."

"Audie?"

"Yes, sir?"

Dr. Venn smiles at me. "You are a very enthusiastic and intelligent pupil. I want you to know I greatly enjoy our time together."

"I do too, sir." I have to cough to clear the sudden obstruction in my throat. But he has no idea how much that means to me. "Let me go get you something nice to eat. We'll be right back. Come on, Red."

"The dog can stay."

Since Red hasn't made a move, but is still peacefully snoring at the foot of Dr. Venn's chair, I think the professor is right.

It's raining again, so I grab Wilkinson's fancy umbrella before I head out.

I dig into the pocket of Daniel's coat and pull out Jake's card. I press the center of it the way I watched Daniel do. "Jake, I'd like a sandwich, and can you also bring a container of soup for Dr. Venn? And maybe some bread or crackers? Thank you."

I put the card back, then button every button on Daniel's coat and turn up the collar. I leave my hair tucked inside it. Between the coat and the birdcage-shaped umbrella that slopes wide enough to shelter my shoulders, I'm pretty well hidden from the world.

A perfect cocoon for thinking. At a time when I've never had more to think about.

Retro-causation.

Time loops.

Possibility waves.

Strands.

I'm going to need to walk for this.

I take off at a brisk pace with no particular destination in mind. I just have to move. My body and mind feel antsy, edgy. I need to burn off some this excess energy.

I join the stream of students and faculty striding along the wet path. No one recognizes me, no one bothers me. It's perfect.

So what if what Dr. Venn said is true?

That I really had a hand in rewriting the past to match the present I needed to have?

And that there's a future me sending out waves to this present, waiting for some resonant wave coming from me so we can write the future together? Is that really how this works?

If so, then what do I do now?

I guess start with defining what it is I want.

My first choice would be returning to my own universe and my own life and picking up where I left off. Bring with me everything I've learned in the past month of being me and combinations of me, but definitely go back to being Audie.

The problem is, I don't know if that's realistic. I hate to even think that, but I need to deal with truth. And the truth is, if Professor Whitfield was right about his hypothesis, then Halli doesn't have a body to go back to. That one was destroyed. This one I'm in right now was never hers, and so it won't recognize her. It would be like a body rejecting a donor organ. It's just not as simple as thinking Halli and I might switch bodies and go on our merry way.

And no matter how callous Halli was about the decisions she made with my life, I'm not going to make her die for that. Of course I still have to save her. There's no question about that.

I have to believe she'd feel the same way if she were in my situation. She's not cruel, she just wants to survive. But I don't think she'd sacrifice me if she had a choice to save us both.

And that's the point: I can and will save us both.

So how do I do that?

I glance around to see if anyone is listening. Of course they're not—I'm nobody. People are too busy rushing to get out of the rain, or talking to their friends, or thinking their own thoughts.

But still, I feel kind of silly saying it out loud. Like a

kid making a wish before blowing out the candles on her birthday cake.

But here goes:

"I want to save Halli and me," I whisper. "Both of us. Step one."

I look around again. Still safe.

"Step two. I want to go back to my own life. And let Halli have her own. That is what I want."

I try to picture some future version of me feeling that wave come toward her. Nodding. Sending a matching wave back.

I'm so engrossed in the vision, I almost don't stop in time.

I've reached the edge of the outer courtyard. Ahead is the street where Wilkinson dropped me off this morning. And parked behind Wilkinson's car is a matching black car.

Jake is standing outside it talking to a familiar figure dressed all in black. Long black expensive-looking raincoat, black slacks, expensive-looking shoes that he probably hates to get wet. It makes me glad to be wearing Halli's hiking boots.

I consider hiding. Ducking behind a wall or a car and sneaking back the way I came.

But I'm not her. I'm not a girl who hides. I'm part Halli, part Halli 2, and all Audie 3. This girl stands her ground.

The driver of the second car holds an umbrella over

Halli's father's head. Jake has to hold his own. I watch as he hands Halli's father a familiar piece of paper.

Thanks to all her elaborate decorations, I can tell from this distance that it's Sarah's invitation to the party. Halli's father reads it, hands it back to Jake, says something. Jake nods and says something back. From the looks on both their faces, they're having a serious conversation. I don't like it.

Halli's father pats Jake on the shoulder, then his driver opens the door for him. He gets in and soon the car pulls away.

And now I do hide. Jake has just reached into the first car to retrieve two sacks when I twist around and hurry out of sight.

This body is built for running, so I don't have any trouble at all taking a roundabout way back to Dr. Venn's office and still arriving there well ahead of Jake. I even have time to slow my breathing back down to normal.

"Hi!"

"Hi." Jake looks around. "No Red?"

"Nope, he's inside." I smile in what I hope is a casual way. "Is that lunch? Great. Thank you."

I take the bags from him and set them on the bench next to me.

"So," I say. "What have you been doing all morning?"

"Not much," Jake says. "Mostly just wandering

around. There are a lot really interesting buildings here."

"There are," I agree.

The silence stretches out for a few long seconds before Jake asks, "How has your morning been?"

"Great. Thanks. Well," I say, standing up, "I should get this soup to Dr. Venn. Thanks again."

"Sure. What time should I pick you up?"

"Oh, around four should be fine. I'll page you."

I stand there for a moment or two more, waiting for Jake to say something about having just talked to Halli's father.

Nope, nothing.

"Okay, see you later," I say, then head toward Dr. Venn's door.

"Halli?"

I turn around. "Yeah?"

"I got another comm from Bryan. I told him you didn't want to do the exclusive after all. He wasn't very happy."

"Yeah, I'll bet. Anything else?"

Jake shakes his head. "I'll see you later this afternoon."

"Yep, see you."

Liar.

What are you up to, Jake?

31

"Ahhh," Dr. Venn says as I unpack his lunch and set it up on his desk. "Thank you, Audie."

The soup container is too hot and heavy for him to hold, and I almost offer to do it for him, but he's already adjusting the height and angle of his chair so he can come right up to the edge of his desk and safely spoon in the soup himself. His hand shakes a little, but he manages it.

"How long have you…" I gesture toward his chair, then realize a second too late that maybe that's not a polite question to ask.

But Dr. Venn doesn't seem to mind. "It was gradual. Age weighs a body down. But I designed this machine myself so I can still stand when I want to."

"You designed this? How cool."

"Normally everyone looks to only the mechanical physicists to design their machines. But I know how to make things, too. I've always known." He says it with a kind of rebellious pride.

Defiant.

He pats the arms of his chair. "You'd be surprised by how much more tolerable it makes being in my condition if I can stretch myself to standing whenever I want. I watch old people all the time crumpled in their chairs or hunched over their walkers. Fills me with pity."

"Then why don't more of them have a chair like yours?" I ask.

"One of a kind," he says. Not with pride this time, but regret. "I designed this only a few years ago. When Dr. Edgar Venn was already out of favor."

It seems as good a time as any.

"Sir, can you tell me now what happened?" I ask. "To the other Dr. Venn."

This one looks at me with cloudy eyes from behind his glasses. "Let me rest first, child. It's a complicated story. And not a very happy one, as you might imagine."

"Sure," I say, even though I wish he wouldn't send me away yet. But there's no point in exhausting the man. "I'll take Red with me. He could probably use some fresh air." I haven't touched my sandwich yet, but now I tear off a corner of it to wave in front of Red's nose. He'll always wake up for food.

"Madeline will be here soon," Dr. Venn says. "Then my schnauzer friend, Lewis. Let's talk again after that."

"Okay. Come on, Red." I gather my coat, umbrella, and lunch, then Red and I head back out into the cold.

I don't know why, but I feel really sad all of the sudden. Maybe it's the gray weather, maybe it's the fact that I can't have answers to all my questions right away—

Or maybe it's the fact that Dr. Venn has already let me know I won't like the answer I'm getting from him next.

But I have to know how the other Dr. Venn died. Even though I'm hoping I'm already out of danger. Here it is Wednesday, and I'm standing here healthy and strong in Oxford instead of sick and drugged up in a hospital in London. That has to count for something.

Maybe the strong, healthy, alive me sent a possibility wave back from the future to show me how to be this.

It's such a cool and crazy thought, and I love it.

Red is already out in the wet, muddy grass handling his business. I bundle myself up in the coat and pop open the umbrella and stroll out to join him. He seems jazzed by the weather, and has this kind of bouncing, rocking gait. Already my mood is lifting. I reach down for a stick and throw it. Red is in the process of bringing it back when he drops it and growls.

"What are you doing with Venn?" a voice asks me.

I whirl around. Play time is over.

Bryan Stewart stands a few feet away from us with his binocular camera up in front of his face. I have to assume everything I say from now on will be filmed.

So I don't say anything.

I remember seeing that in Halli's memory: her grandmother giving her some great advice after Halli felt compelled to answer a reporter's uncomfortable questions. *"Not everyone needs to know what you think,"* Ginny told her. *"Your thoughts are your own. You never have to tell anyone a single thing about yourself, or what you think or feel, if you don't want to—even if they ask."*

It goes against my good girl, polite upbringing, but that upbringing belongs to Audie 1. From what I've seen so far, I'm guessing I didn't bring much of the polite girl strand with me.

"We had a deal," Bryan says.

I pick up another stick and throw it to Red. "Turn off the camera," I say with my back to Bryan. "That's the new deal."

"My producer isn't very happy with me right now," Bryan says.

"And I wasn't very happy to come out of my friends' house this morning and find a horde of reporters there."

"Wasn't me," Bryan says.

"You might say it soured me on all of you. Come on, Red." The dog brings the stick with him and lopes along to my side. Bryan hasn't moved yet. And he still has the camera aimed at my face. Red growls as we get closer. "Good boy," I tell him and reach down to give him a pat.

"Why Venn?" Bryan asks again. "Are you aware of his history?"

"I don't know. Shut that off and you can tell me."

"Has he told you what happened to Dr. Sands?"

Dr. Sands? That's a new name. "Yes," I lie.

"So you know he died in that very office where you've spent the past day and a half?"

"Bryan, what do you want? And shut that thing off or I'm going back inside and these are the last words you'll ever hear from me. You can count on it."

Bryan sighs, but at least he lets the camera drop to his side. It might still be recording sound, though, so I have to be careful.

"I want what you promised me," he says. "An exclusive. We'll even keep it to the one hour. And I would deeply appreciate it, Miss Markham, if I could interview you tonight so my producer will let me leave this wet, freezing, miserable place so I can go back home where the high was seventy today and I hear there was actual sunshine."

At least that sounds close to an honest answer. And I have to say that's an honestly gloomy look on his face.

I think about it for a few seconds. "It's about Ginny and me only," I say. "No questions about Dr. Venn— none of any kind. Do you understand?" The least I can do is protect him. I have no idea who this Dr. Sands is that Bryan is talking about, but I'm pretty sure I don't want to be surprised while Bryan is filming me. I'm grateful he brought up it now so I can lay down some ground rules.

Although I wouldn't mind finding out what Bryan knows. It could save me some trouble.

"So what do *you* think happened to Dr. Sands?" I ask.

"Went in healthy, came out dead. So you tell me."

32

"Almost done," Madeline says cheerfully. She's kneading the pad of one of Dr. Venn's thumb. The professor has his eyes closed and his expression alternates between pain and relief.

"Thank you for bringing him a hot lunch," she says. Dr. Venn doesn't have his earphones on, so he can't hear us. "Some days he forgets to eat at all. I appreciate you looking out for him, Halli."

"Can I ask you something?" I'm not sure if it's the wrong thing, but lately I'm never sure. I decide to just go for it. "Someone just said something about a Dr. Sands."

Madeline isn't so cheerful anymore. "Dreadful business. Please don't ask my grandfather about that."

"Okay, but ... can you tell me anything? This person said he came in here healthy and left dead."

Madeline scoffs. "Is that what they say now? I suppose it's best to know. It's easier to fight a lie when it's out in the open. No, Professor Sands wasn't a healthy man. He had a heart attack. There was an inquiry by the medical branch and by the legal authorities. My grandfather was unequivocally cleared. And the whole incident left him a fairly broken man. It's *his* health that was destroyed. Along with a distinguished, noble career."

"But why was his career destroyed if it was just a heart attack?"

"Because of the suspicions before he was cleared. Some members of the faculty and the scientific community couldn't accept the result. They made my grandfather's life very difficult. It was an awful time for our family."

"So ... were the two of them just talking, and then suddenly Dr. Sands had a heart attack? Or what?"

"ALL DONE, GRANDDAD," Madeline shouts as she pats his hand. Dr. Venn smiles and tells her thank you. Madeline turns so that only I can see her face. "Please don't stir this up, Halli. It's a very sad, bitter memory for my grandfather. It was a long time ago, and I'm sorry anyone felt it necessary to bring it to your attention."

She turns and waves to Dr. Venn. "SEE YOU

TONIGHT. STAY WARM. WAIT FOR ME SO I CAN
WALK YOU BACK. IT'S RAINING."

Dr. Venn nods. Madeline gives my arm a squeeze
and then she leaves us.

Red takes Madeline's vacated spot beside Dr. Venn's
chair and settles in for a nap.

The door opens again and Madeline sticks her head
in. "Hand me a few biscuits, will you? Lewis is here. I
expect you don't want to invite him in?"

"No. Thanks." I fish out a few dog treats from the
container on Dr. Venn's desk and hand them to his
granddaughter. She smiles at Dr. Venn, then closes the
door.

Dr. Venn reaches for his earphones. I help him fit
them over his head. Then he says, "You asked her about
Sands."

I pick up the microphone. "How did you know?"

"I could hear some of what she said."

I should have realized that with her raised voice and
how close she was standing next to him, he might pick
out a few words.

"I'm sorry," I say. "Someone asked me about him just
now, and so I thought … but I shouldn't have brought
it up."

"Why not?" Dr. Venn says. "I would have told you
anyway. It's part of the story." He gestures for me to sit
down. I take a moment to remove my wet coat, then try

to get comfortable. Even though I'm too anxious now to be very relaxed.

"Where did I leave you on my history?"

"After World War II," I say. "The split. The Pact."

"I wasn't like you, Audie. When my new universe branched off, I didn't know anything was different. It's not as if I woke up in a different body. No, it was still the same me, kissing my wife goodbye every morning, going to work every day, coming home to help raise our son. Life went on.

"And it was a very exciting life. We were making large changes in the world. Peace was finally on every-one's minds at the same time, and when the whole world wants peace, suddenly other things become more important."

"Like what?" I ask.

"Medical advances. Health. Prosperity. Knowledge, exploration, travel—pursuits your friend Halli and her grandmother were perfectly suited for. With the world more open and accessible now, people wanted to know what there was to see. It's why adventurers became so popular. Halli and Virginia weren't the only ones, of course—there were many before they came along—but now explorers were the heroes people wanted to hear about, instead of soldiers or anyone involved in any kind of violence. Aggression of every kind went out of fashion very, very quickly, I'm happy to say."

"I can't even imagine that," I tell him. "Sometimes it seems like every other person in my world has a gun. And you wouldn't believe some of the movies and TV shows and games we have—some of them are crazy violent."

"I know," Dr. Venn says. "I've seen my share. I can tell you that that kind of 'entertainment' never would have flourished here. I'm proud of that. We didn't know that would happen when we signed the Pact, but it was a welcome result."

"You've seen some of them?" I ask. "How?"

"I've spent considerable time in your universe," Dr. Venn says. "But I'll get to that.

"Decades went by. I pursued my work. Instead of designing bombs, I was free to explore some of the ideas I'd first had as a young man—questions about the mind, and what it's capable of, and how human consciousness might affect what we witness in the natural world."

"I'm interested in that, too," I say.

"Of course you are. What physicist wouldn't be? It's the most fundamental and fascinating question we can ask: What makes the universe tick? Is it possible that we, these small, seemingly insignificant beings living their short lives on a small planet in a vast cosmos, can have any affect at all?"

"But I thought you said you couldn't study space."

"No," Dr. Venn says, "we couldn't *explore* space. There's a difference. We could think about it all we wanted. Ponder it night and day. We just couldn't build anything that would let us see what was really up there. We had to limit ourselves to math and theory."

"That must have been kind of sad," I say. "I know how excited people were when we finally sent men to the moon. And now we have rovers examining the surface of Mars. Your world has missed out on all that."

"We have," Dr. Venn agrees, "but we chose humanity over the stars. Was it a poor bargain? I didn't think so at the time I signed the Pact, and I still don't think so. But, then, I've had the benefit of both worlds for the past forty-one years. I'm sure many of my colleagues would have loved the opportunity to say the same—if only they were brave enough, and had opened their minds to the possibilities back when I gave them the chance."

I do a quick calculation. "So you were … sixty-two? What exactly happened?"

"I made a machine," Dr. Venn says. "A machine that changed my life."

33

"What kind of machine?" I ask.

"A very simple one, in principle," Dr. Venn answers. "Simple parts: cloth, metal, rope. I improved it over time, but that first prototype was something I constructed from supplies I brought from home.

"If you would." He detaches his arms from the cuffs and gestures for me to set up his notepad and pen in front of him on the desk. Then with a shaky hand he draws a long, narrow oval with a short line extending from the top.

"It's a swing, of sorts," he says. "But you stand in it. I have padding here and here at the legs," he says, drawing two horizontal lines across the oval, "more at the waist, and then more to brace the chest and arms."

He looks up from the paper. "It's what gave me the idea for my chair here. I discovered that the more crooked and weak my spine became, I could still find relief by climbing into the swing. I could feel the blood circulating through my legs again. My back stopped aching as long as I could stretch it out. I started spending several hours every day defying old age and gravity. Then about five years ago, when walking finally became too difficult, I had a friend build this chair to my design."

"So … the swing changed your life," I say. This whole thing isn't nearly as dramatic as I thought it would be. But I guess if your body is in pain and you figure out a way to feel better, then that qualifies as changing your life.

"It isn't just a swing," Dr. Venn says. "It's a space-time machine."

Now we're talking.

"History, Audie. We scientists don't pay enough attention to it. How do you feel about history?"

"It's … okay." If he means my history classes, then I'm not going to lie and say I've loved them. There might be a few interesting stories here and there, but mostly it feels like we're just supposed to memorize a bunch of facts and dates so we can pass the next test.

"You might have noticed that our culture here celebrates history," Dr. Venn says.

"Oh, I've noticed." When I was in the hospital, the

nurse flipped through channels for me, and everything was a history show: history of science, history of adventure, even "current" history like, *"Who's that mystery guy Halli Markham was seen with last week? Daniel Everett, ladies and gentlemen!"*

And then there's the kind of history studio Daniel's parents run, delving into archaeology in their own unique way.

"Some scientists believe that everything we do now in modern times is an advance," Dr. Venn says. "That methods from the past were primitive. Even laughable."

"I think they feel the same way where I come from."

"But sometimes the old methods still work," Dr. Venn says. "Maybe even better than anything we might devise now." He points to the unit on his desk that both of us are hooked into—him with his earphones, me with the mic. "I tried the tiny amplifiers that fit inside the ear, but they never gave me the kind of reception I can get from this old machine.

"So when I read a reference in an ancient translation about a tribal leader who built something to allow him to travel through time and space, of course I paid attention. Science is about discovery, not pride. Our job is to learn and to teach. For the sake of the human race."

I don't think I've ever thought of it in such noble terms. But I can see his point.

"So were there drawings of it that you could follow?" I ask.

"No, just a few very vague details. But I had time, I had an interest, and so I applied myself to the problem."

I can understand that perfectly. He's talking to a girl who sat in her room for hours every day for six months in a row trying to figure out how to contact a parallel universe.

"I built over a dozen different prototypes," Dr. Venn says. "I failed time and again. But it's just how you described, Audie: suddenly, there he was. The other Edgar Venn."

"Really?"

A buzz moves along my skin. Funny how a few words can generate electricity.

"My method of travel was different from yours," Dr. Venn says. "My body stayed here, but my mind duplicated it in full in the other universe. Do you understand bilocation?"

"Halli told me about it. She said the ancient yogis knew how to do it. They could sit in a room in deep meditation, and appear in a completely different town at the same time. Their students could hug them, talk to them—they couldn't tell the difference."

"Exactly so," Dr. Venn says.

"So, what … you just showed up one day out of the blue? How did he react?"

Dr. Venn chuckles. "Let's just say it wasn't very dignified. I told him it would be our secret."

"So where was he at the time? What was he doing?"

"We were lucky," Dr. Venn says. "He was alone in his office, daydreaming."

That sounds familiar, too. The first time Halli and I made contact, it's because both of us were meditating at the time. I always thought that that's what did it: creating this kind of pathway or connection between us at the vibrational level. Now this story from Dr. Venn makes me think I've got it right.

"It took a few minutes for both of us to get over the shock," Dr. Venn continues. "I knew I might be able to travel to other places and times, but I had no idea I might meet another version of myself. Edgar and I sat for a while just looking at each other. First afraid, then laughing."

I smile. Because I get that, too. Once you get over the freakiness of what's going on, you can't help but be excited that you've met your other self.

"So what did you do?" I ask. "What happened? Tell me everything."

"We did what any trained scientist will do," Dr. Venn answers. "We began studying our situation. And we did so for the next twenty-three years. And continued expanding our research into other universes, and other selves."

"Excuse me, what?"

"Forty-three of us, Audie. That we found so far. Different versions of us in different universes and different eras. And not all of us scientists, either. Or, for that matter, men."

"Okay, hold on." Once again I have to set down the mic for a moment to regather my brain. It's like eating a huge meal. You can't just shove it all in at once without getting sick.

"Okay," I say after a short break. "Go."

"Do you remember what I said about how you could have written Past, Present, and Future all on top of each other in one spot?"

I nod.

"This might be hard to conceptualize," Dr. Venn says, "but try to imagine that all of time is happening right now, all in this same moment. So a Viking and a medieval peasant and a young woman in Italy in the 1800s and I, Edgar Venn, and the other Edgar Venn— all of us living our lives in our own places and centuries, all right now at the same time."

"I'm sorry, I'm having a really hard time picturing that."

"See if this helps," Dr. Venn says. "Here in this moment it's after two o'clock in England. At this same moment it's several hours later in China. And at this same moment it's many hours earlier in California. Do you have trouble with that?"

"No … but it's because I'm used to it, I guess. I know it's true, so I don't have to question it anymore."

"Why do you know it's true?"

"Because I had this really cool teacher in third grade," I say. "Mrs. George. She did a whole demonstration one day with a model of the earth and the sun. So we could see that as the earth rotated, everyone on the planet got to have sunshine at different parts of the day. That always stuck with me."

Dr. Venn nods. "This is how I see it: when I was a boy, I loved to go to the carnival that came through our town every year. We were poor, and I always wanted to win a prize to take home to my mother. So I became expert at the bag toss—the one where you knock down bottles with a sand-filled bag. Do you know the game?"

"Yes."

"I noticed that the man running the game would only let a few customers try and fail before he took the bag himself and showed that it could be done. It was very important, I realized later, for the psychology of the customers that they knew what they were trying was possible. Otherwise they just felt cheated. And this way, once they saw the worker do it, they felt even more motivated than before and even bought extra tries."

"Okay … but what—"

"What does that have to do with the simultaneity of time?"

"Right."

"Because I'm telling you that I have done it," Dr. Venn says. "I have seen it. I am the carnival worker who shows you what's possible. And I can tell you that without a doubt I have shared a meal with my Viking counterpart in his sod-roofed house in the year one thousand twenty-four. I was there. I ask you to believe me."

"Dr. Venn, it's just so … weird."

He gestures toward me. "Look where you are, Audie. Look *who* you are. Tell me that is any less unbelievable."

"So you traveled there—you bilocated—while you were in the swing."

"Yes."

I shake my head. "I believe you, but…"

"You need to verify," Dr. Venn says.

"I need … yeah. I need to see something to believe it. I'm sorry."

"Don't apologize," Dr. Venn says. "Blind belief is useless to the scientist. I want you to *know*, Audie. But I also need you to know that it's possible, and it's real."

"But I also need to know something else," I say. "Why did the other Edgar Venn die? Was it connected to all this?"

"Sadly, yes. By the time we realized what the problem was, it was too late—the damage had already been done. And the damage became more progressive, until finally Edgar died. In exactly the way you were experiencing that last time you were here."

"So what was it?" I ask. "What killed him?"

"Free will," Dr. Venn says. "He tried to violate free will. The human mind simply won't allow it."

34

"Think about it, Audie," Dr. Venn says. "You were able to insert your mind into your former body. But Halli's mind had already taken up occupation there. And each time you were suddenly 'pulled' out of your body, as you described it to me, you felt excruciating pain. That was your interpretation of it, correct?"

"Yes." It was obvious that was the problem. The first time, Halli was so excited to find me inside my old body, she practically screamed with delight. That shocked me out of the experience. Then the second time, I was in a quiet, dark room with Daniel, having a long conversation with Halli and Professor Whitfield, when suddenly Sarah and Jake and Bryan burst into the room. Once again I was violently pulled out of the experience and felt like my brain was splitting in two.

"You weren't pulled out of it," Dr. Venn tells me. "You were attacked."

"Attacked? By what?"

"By Halli's mind. Without her knowing it. You see, toward the end of his life, Edgar had begun experimenting with a different way of contacting our other selves. He'd had a particularly frightening experience bilocating to a South American village where one of us lived in a very isolated, close-knit tribe. When Edgar suddenly appeared on the scene one morning, our other self went half-mad. He attacked Edgar quite savagely. And while Edgar wasn't actually hurt—it was just his bilocated form, and it can't be harmed—the real damage was to our tribesman self. The man was terrified. Edgar realized he could never do that to him again.

"But he still wanted to investigate what the man's life was like. That's what Edgar and I were doing: he built his own swing—by now it was more of a machine—and the two of us went off on our separate travels to find our others, then we shared everything we learned. Once we realized we existed in so many different lives in different places and times, we had to know everything—as much as we could. Can you understand that?"

"Of course. I'd probably do that, too. I mean, are you saying that Halli and I probably aren't the only versions of us that exist?"

"Most certainly," Dr. Venn says. "You've already been three different girls yourself. Of course there are more of you."

I don't set down the mic this time, but I do close my eyes for a moment just to give myself a little time to absorb it all. Then I open my eyes and nod to let him know I'm ready for more.

"So the next time Edgar went back, instead of bilocating, he tried a different method—the one you discovered on your own. He simply inserted his mind —his consciousness if you prefer—into the tribesman's brain. With the intention of quietly, secretly investigating what the man's life was like. How he thought. How he lived. With disastrous consequences."

"What happened?"

"The same thing that happened with you," Dr. Venn says. "As soon as Edgar brought himself back out, it was as if someone had taken a sledgehammer to his head, he told me. He collapsed. Because he was in his private room at the time, he lay suspended in his machine for half a day and most of the night before he was well enough to contact me. Then I bilocated to where he was and helped him back to his office where he could lie down. We didn't dare go for medical help. I took care of him as best I could.

"We tried to analyze what had gone wrong," Dr. Venn continues. "Just as you did—was there some noise? Some distraction? Something that interfered with the effects of the machine? But then it happened again, with another visit to a different us, and then we knew for sure.

"You can't invade the territory of someone else's mind, Audie. The brain won't allow it. It treats the invader as a virus. And it attacks ruthlessly and viciously. Mortally.

"Edgar Venn, my original self, a man who had become my brother, my best friend, my colleague, and my fellow explorer for twenty-three years, died within two weeks."

Dr. Venn has tears in his eyes. He also looks pale and exhausted. I realize I've let him go on too long. But there was no way I was going to stop him.

"Sir, can I get you some water?"

His voice is hoarse. "Some tea would be welcome. Thank you." He points to a thermos on the shelf behind his desk. "Madeline brings me some in the afternoons. I forgot to have it."

I'm happy for a task to do. I don't know what to say to him. Everything he's told me today—retro-causation, time loops, and now all of this—is so large, so mind-shaking, I almost don't want him to say anything else until I have time to process it all. As in home in the Everett-Wheeler's tub taking a long, contemplative bath.

But at the same time, I want to keep talking for as long as Dr. Venn can take it. More, more, more, please.

"Here you go." I pour out some hot tea into the cup sitting next to the thermos. Dr. Venn's hands shake as he tries to bring it to his lips. I do my best to help him.

"That's fine," he tells me after a few sips. "Thank you." He lowers the cup and motions for me to return to my chair. "I'm afraid I'll need to nap soon, so let me tell you just a few more things for now.

"What we discovered, Edgar and I in our travels, is that there are three ways of observing. And you've discovered a fourth.

"The first way," he says, "is to inject ourselves into a time and place through bilocation. The second—your method, which I admire since Edgar and I could never accomplish it—was to send yourself somewhere in your full physical form."

"But not all of it," I correct him. "Some things never came over. Like my CD player and my headphones. And even though my clothes came with me, I could never wear Halli's clothes coming back—they stayed behind. I could never figure it out."

"Ghost clothes," Dr. Venn. "I'll tell you about them some other time."

He's looking a little droopy. He's right, I can't waste time.

But I do need to correct him on one last thing. "Also, even though my whole body came over, I saw an outline of the wave form of me on the monitors at Professor Whitfield's lab. Halli's wave form was in the room, too, even though she'd never physically been there."

"Do you know why?" Dr. Venn asks.

"It was just a guess," I say, "but the professor and I thought it might mean Halli and I were entangled somehow, the way some particles are."

Dr. Venn nods. "Interesting."

"But go on," I say. "What are the other two ways?"

"The third you know," Dr. Venn answers. "It's what you and Edgar did, inserting yourselves into the body and mind of another person. I understand the temptation—especially in your case, Audie, since the body used to be yours—but I think we can both agree that that method should never be attempted again."

"No," I agree. "Never."

Dr. Venn gives a tired sigh. "So that brings us to the the fourth way: you send your mind to the moment, but you leave your body behind."

"You mean like the kind of thing Professor Whitfield had me do?" I ask. "Remote sensing?"

"Yes, but with an added feature," Dr. Venn says. "What Edgar and I learned was that even when we were watching from outside ourselves, we could still communicate. It wasn't a conversation so much as it was giving ourselves suggestions. Does that sound familiar?"

"You mean ... what you were saying before about

time loops?" I ask. "About your future self passing along information to your present self?"

"Exactly," Dr. Venn says. "That method is safe. Edgar and I spent a great deal of time—maybe too much time, now that I look back on it—visiting our younger selves. Trying to nudge us in more positive directions. *Don't say that to your wife, go apologize,' 'Don't let that person get to you—he doesn't matter in the long run.'* Small adjustments like that. But once you realize you have the power to go back, it's very hard to resist trying to achieve some kind of perfection in the way you've been living your life. If we'd known we had limited time, I think we would have spent it exploring outward more, instead of always going back. Who knows how many more versions of ourselves we might have found?"

"So ... wait a minute," I say. "Do you mean you don't do it anymore? You don't travel?"

"No. Not for years."

"But why?" I can't imagine giving up such a huge discovery and just walking away from it.

Dr. Venn smiles sadly. "Too many memories. Too many thrilling discoveries. And no one to share them with. The truth is, Audie, I've been very alone for the past eighteen years. Even with my family all around me. I've missed the intellectual friendship. It feels very hollow to carry on all by myself. Can you understand that?"

"I think so, sir. But ... don't you have other friends? Professor Lacksmith, or ... somebody?"

"No one who has seen what I've seen," Dr. Venn answers. "No one who has experienced what you and I have, Audie. We've traveled farther than anyone we've known. Even if we try to describe it to other people, we're the only ones who really *know*. So you must understand why I was so grateful to meet you yesterday."

"Yes, sir, I do."

"Good, good..." He closes his eyes for a moment. I wait and hope he'll open them again.

When he finally does, he gazes at me very directly. "I want you to continue my work," he says. "Continue my travels. Discover everything you can. I'll show you my machine. I'll show you how to use it. If you're willing and you're not afraid."

It's not an easy thing, staring into this old man's eyes and seeing all the pain and hope and exhaustion there.

And wondering how much of that I'll feel, too.

But for the first time since I showed up in this life, I'm not worried about dying anymore. That's not the issue at all.

The issue is what's possible.

And Dr. Venn knows more about that than anyone I've ever met. How could I possibly say no?

"I am afraid, Dr. Venn. I won't lie. This whole thing

is…" I let out a breath. "Yeah. But I'm also very willing —I won't lie about that, either. Except…"

"Except?"

I'm not sure if I should ask, or if this is the right time, but since we're being honest—

"Sir, how did Dr. Sands die? Was it in the machine?"

Dr. Venn hesitates. Then answers, "Unfortunately, yes."

35

"It wasn't a heart attack," Dr. Venn says. "That was a convenient lie. Not so convenient that there wasn't an inquiry, but in the end, heart attack was the easier reason for everyone to believe."

"What was the real reason?" I ask.

Dr. Venn sighs. "You have to understand how to operate the machine." His words are coming more slowly now. He's definitely starting to fade. "There's a skill to learning to focus and defocus while you're in it. Dr. Sands … did not have that skill. I tried to instruct him, but he was in too much of a hurry."

"So what happened?" I ask.

"The short answer, Audie, is that he went somewhere and forgot how to come back."

I have to sit quietly for a moment to let that sink in. Even though I'm running out of time.

"But you can show me," I say. "How to go and come back. You're sure about that?"

"I'm sure about *you*," he says. "You don't seem reckless or foolish. Algerson Sands was both."

Dr. Venn's eyes are doing that slow, ever-slower blink.

"Dr. Venn? Sir?"

"Yes, Audie. I'm listening."

But his eyes stay closed.

"Will I be able to find Halli using your machine? Do you think that's possible?"

"Yes … you'll find her…" Then a soft snore takes over.

I'm not ready to leave. I have eight thousand more questions. Every answer today feels like it bred a whole galaxy of new mysteries. I need hours and hours of Dr. Venn's time.

But I'm simply not going to get it.

I unplug the mic and then gently remove the earphones from Dr. Venn's head. I make sure he's adequately covered with his blanket.

I kneel down beside Red and scratch him behind both ears. I kiss the top of his head. I'm feeling lost and sentimental and frustrated and afraid and lonely all at the same time.

I wish Daniel were here.

The clock above Dr. Venn's desk shows it's almost 3:30. I can either fill the extra half hour on my own or page Jake to come get me early.

I decide the best use of my time right now is to borrow some of the paper from Dr. Venn's desk and make myself a list. Of everything I think I understand, and all the things I still don't.

The door to Dr. Venn's office opens an hour later. I've filled five sheets of paper, and I'm not even done yet.

"Oh, I didn't realize you'd still be here," Madeline says.

"I lost track," I say, rising to my feet. "I didn't realize how late it is. Is there someone out there waiting for me?"

"A young man, dark hair, quite handsome?" she answers with a smile.

"I have to go." I don't care about keeping Jake waiting, but I need to get back to London to talk to Daniel. I have so much to tell him, and I hope he has a lot to tell me. I put on his coat and then fold up my notes and shove them deep into one of the pockets.

"How is he?" Madeline asks, gesturing toward her grandfather.

"He's amazing," I answer before realizing that's not what she was talking about. "I mean, he's fine. He's been sleeping for the last hour or so. But up until then he was really alert."

"Good." Madeline gently shakes Dr. Venn awake. "GRANDDAD, IT'S RAINING OUT. I'M GOING TO BUNDLE YOU UP A LITTLE MORE AND THEN TAKE YOU HOME."

I help her cover him in a wool coat and then a rain-coat, both laid over his front like a haircutter's smock. Madeline fits a brimmed hat over his head. "READY?" She presses the console on Dr. Venn's chair and it begins to move toward the door.

I open the door for them, and as he passes me, Dr. Venn removes his hand from the cuff and reaches out to grip my arm. He pulls me closer so he can whisper.

"You're a brave girl." Then he smiles at me, a wide smile that makes his tired eyes crinkle behind their thick glasses. He looks like a grandfather now, not like a rebel or a pioneer or like that wary, crabby man who first spoke to me on the comm. And not like the angry scientist yelling at his colleagues at that conference. You wouldn't know looking at that kindly, gentle face that behind it rests a mind that holds more wonders of the universe than anyone could imagine.

I'm tempted to kiss him on the cheek the way I would have my own grandpa. But I resist. It would be too weird.

"I'll see you tomorrow," I tell him.

He nods, and then Madeline holds her umbrella over him while the two of them venture out into the cold rain.

Jake is sitting on the closest bench. Red yawns and stretches his legs out long in front of him. Then he resumes his post at my side as soon as Jake stands up.

"Good news and bad news," Jake says.

"Nope, I'm only accepting good news this evening," I say as I start off across the courtyard. I'm tired and I'm wired and I don't really feel like talking.

"Okay, then the good news first," Jake answers. "Your father was able to reschedule all those appointments for tomorrow."

I stop and look at him. "Not funny."

"Sorry," Jake says, "but at least that's better than the next news: he wants to see you. We're going there next."

"That's a no," I say. "Anything else?"

"Okay...." Jake has to hurry to keep up with us. Red and I have purpose in our step. "How about this, then? Bryan says he's meeting you at my inn at seven o'clock tonight for an interview you agreed to?"

"Yes, because even though I specifically asked you to keep him away from me, he showed up at lunch today. So I'm giving him his interview to get rid of him once and for all."

Jake seems stung by the criticism, but too bad. Everything I just said is true. Plus I'm still waiting for him to confess that he saw Halli's father already today and for whatever reason showed him Sarah's invitation. Until I hear some explanation for that, I'm not exactly feeling all warm and fuzzy toward Jake.

"Anything else?" I ask.

"No, Miss Markham." All the playfulness has left his voice. "What should I tell your father?"

"I'll tell him myself. You can call him on the comm as soon as we're in the car."

You're a brave girl.

I didn't used to be, Dr. Venn, but I'm getting there.

36

We're rolling toward London when Jake is able to make contact. Halli's father's head appears on the screen between the front and back seats.

I get right to the point.

"I understand there was some confusion about how I was spending my time today."

"Confusion?" Halli's father says.

"Yes. I should have been clearer before: I have meetings with Dr. Venn all the rest of this week. Maybe even into next week. I won't be able to meet with any of your people until after that."

That last part is a lie—I have no intention of meeting with any of them—but I don't feel like having a fight unless I need to. If Dr. Venn's machine can really bring me into contact with Halli, then maybe there's a chance to change this whole situation. I won't know until I try.

"I told you to stay away from Venn," Halli's father says.

"That's not your decision," I tell him.

It's amazing how much easier it is to be brave when you're tired. Right now I don't care if the man yells and screams at me. I have much bigger issues to deal with than disappointing Halli's father.

"What are you talking to that lunatic about?" he demands.

"Physics. And Ginny. We've been talking a lot about Ginny. I assume it's all right if I miss my grandmother?"

Halli's father grumbles, but he actually seems to accept that answer. Maybe I need to stick to the Ginny excuse with everybody. No one can claim that I'm lying.

"So you're still interested in Oxford?" he asks.

"Nothing has changed."

Everything has changed.

Halli's father pauses to take a sip of his drink. He swirls an ice cube around in his mouth and then spits it back into his glass. "And you'll meet with the faculty your mother and I selected?"

"When I'm done with Dr. Venn, yes." It feels like a harmless concession. Especially since I won't be honoring it.

The lights on the screen swirl around, then the divider between the seats is clear again.

Halli's father just hung up on me. Pleasant man.

"I need to rest now," I tell Jake. "Please see that I'm not disturbed."

"Yes, Miss Markham."

It's weird to have him being so formal again, but I don't try to fix it. Maybe it's better to re-establish some distance.

I remove the ear button, then settle into a comfortable position and close my eyes. Red nestles further onto my lap, and I rest my hand on top of his head.

Now. Finally. I can process.

I slip my free hand into the pocket of Daniel's coat and grip the folded pieces of paper. Five sheets of questions and theories and even some answers.

What a day.

But for right now, one particular answer is still echoing in my head.

"Yes ... you'll find her..."

Halli.

And if I find her, then that means I've found my old universe again.

And this time I'll have a time machine.

How did Dr. Venn put it? That once he and Edgar realized they had the power to go back in time to their younger selves, it was hard to resist trying to give them advice. Nudge them in certain directions. Achieve some kind of perfection for how they'd been living their lives.

So … what if?

What if I can go all the way back to myself earlier this year, when I first came up with the idea of looking for parallel universes?

What if I try to convince myself that's a really bad idea?

What if I give myself some other idea for a project to do to impress Professor Hawkins and the admissions people at Columbia University?

What if I can make none of this ever happen?

My eyes pop back open. And I know without a doubt that I'll do nothing of the kind.

Yes, things have gotten out of control. Yes, I miss my old life and most of all my mother, and yes, I wish I could just wake up in my own bed in my own body in my own universe tomorrow morning and find that everything has just worked out perfectly and I never have to worry again.

But there are too many other things I don't wish.

I don't wish I'd never saved Halli.

I don't wish I'd never found her in the first place.

And I don't wish I'd skipped all the adventures I've had in the past month. Even when they've been hard, the truth is, they've been INCREDIBLE. I've seen things and done things and met people I never would have if I were still my same old Audie sitting in my room reading physics books all the time, never really going out and living in the world.

Halli has shown me a better way. *I've* shown me a better way. So no, I'm not under any circumstances going to visit my earlier self and whisper in my own ear, *"Don't do it!"* Never going to happen.

But is there some point in time that I *could* go back to that would make some kind of difference? Help me avoid some of the bad stuff without erasing any of the good?

I feel a cold flash of electricity up my spine. Along with the certainty of an idea that has just popped into my head fully formed. I lean forward and cradle that head right now, because the thought is so huge, so right and true, it feels totally overwhelming.

Because all at once, *I get it*.

I've already had this conversation with myself.

I've already looked at my whole history. I've already analyzed everything that's happened and where things went right and where they went wrong.

I've already made a choice.

Because what did I need most this time? To get to London. To talk to Daniel. To find out what he and his parents learned from some Oxford professor about why my head was splitting in two.

And when was I in London last time? When did I see Daniel?

Two days ago. In the lobby of Halli's parents'

London headquarters. Exactly when and where I returned this time.

I've already thought this through.

I'm exactly where I need to be. I'm exactly *who* I need to be. If Dr. Venn is right, and I've gathered certain strands of Halli and me together to form this particular version of us both, then I must have known what I was doing. Just as I must have known what I was doing in picking that specific time and place Monday afternoon to start over here.

Which means some future version of me has already had a conversation with myself and helped me make specific, logical decisions.

I move my hand to cover my mouth to keep from laughing out loud. This idea is so crazy, and it's so possible, I wish I could just blurt out the whole theory to Jake and Wilkinson right now just so I can share it with someone.

I'll have to make do.

"Red," I whisper. "I figured it out. I understand it perfectly."

Red lifts an eyebrow, but otherwise doesn't stir. He's right: we have to stay calm.

But that's hard right now because the implications are so huge. It isn't just that maybe I've sent some message to myself back from the future to help push me in the right direction—which means there *is* a future version of me who survives all this and knows how I did it. That alone is a thrilling and comforting thought.

It means something else, too. Something that matters to me almost as much. It's tangible proof of something I don't think I've ever had in my almost eighteen years of life: that maybe I can actually start trusting myself.

I'm so used to doubting that I know the way. Doubting that my instincts are right. Doubting that I'm capable of handling whatever's thrown at me, because who am I? Just Audie Masters. No one special, just me. I'm used to feeling awkward and uncertain and self-conscious and afraid. I'm used to feeling like everyone knows better than I do how to move through life and make the right choices and figure it all out.

But if there really is a future Audie Masters who's taking the time and trouble to send back possibility waves to me, or maybe even to visit me in the same way the two Dr. Venns used to visit their younger selves, then maybe I can finally start believing that my instincts, my intuition, my ideas are right. That I might actually know what I'm doing. That I can trust myself to find the way.

If that's not worth having a party here in the back seat, then I don't know what is.

I'm so giddy with the whole thing, I almost miss the landmark. I tap on the divider and motion for Jake to put in his ear button.

"I need to stop at that bank again. Please tell Wilkinson to go back."

"Yes, Miss Markham."

Because that's one of my instincts right now: to help Daniel and Sarah and their parents in whatever way I can. It's the least I can do for everything they're doing for me.

The car stops and Wilkinson opens my door and I bound out into the rain. I don't even bother with an umbrella. Red jumps out with me, and the two of us dash up to the money machine to withdraw another stack of icies. We return to the car with now both of my pockets bulging with paper.

I can barely sit still for the rest of the ride to Daniel's. I have so much to tell him.

But I'm even more interested in what he has to tell me.

37

"Excellent," Sarah says as soon as I walk into the kitchen. "An expert taster. Please judge these."

As if that's any great chore. I happily sample her sugar cookie with chips of homemade praline and a chocolate and praline version, too.

I close my eyes to savor every morsel. "Sarah … heaven."

She smiles and gives me a little bow. "Thank you, Miss Markham. Two dozen of both should nicely round out the collection."

She glances over her shoulder at her parents, who are both sitting at the kitchen table enjoying their cookies with tea while they go over a set of reports. Although "enjoying" might not be the right word, based on their expressions. They seem pretty engrossed in their conversation. Sarah motions with a tilt of her head for me to follow her out into the hallway.

"Nothing yet. I'm sorry," she whispers. "Mum's had me helping with the party food ever since I came home for school. But I promise I'll do your assignment the moment I'm released from service. It shouldn't be much longer."

"That's fine," I say, although the truth is I'm disappointed. But I also know that everyone has their own lives to live. It's not like they can drop everything to work on my problem day and night. "How's it all coming? The party, I mean."

"Splendid, if it isn't until next week. Slightly frantic if it really is the night after tomorrow."

"Can I help?" I ask.

"No, but thank you. Mum has her own particular way of fancy-cutting the sandwiches. I'm afraid it's a secret she's willing to share only with her beloved daughter. I imagine you're terribly jealous. Please say so."

"Very," I answer with a laugh. Sarah always seems to be able to get one out of me, no matter how tired or worried or preoccupied I am. "But I was thinking I could help in another way." I flash her the tip of tonight's wad of money.

"Good gracious," Sarah whispers.

"So could I pay for your father's party? I'd really love to."

"That's Mum's decision," Sarah says, "but I shouldn't think she'd agree. She's very principled. And you are our guest."

"A guest she's very generous to keep housing and feeding, even though I could clearly afford a hotel. Should I try talking to her?"

Sarah shrugs. "You could. It might convince her we could afford to serve something slightly upmarket to the sandwiches."

"Okay, I'll try. Is Daniel home?"

"Upstairs. I'll be up as soon as I can. I'm cooking dinner, too, while my parents go over accounts. Rather grim, I'm afraid. It's their monthly ritual. In any case," she says brightly, "tonight's fare is my famous potato and leek soup. Hope you're ravenous."

"Starving. Thanks, Sarah. I'm so impressed by you."

"Why, Miss Markham! How good of you to say so." She gives me a little bow. "And you, sir," she says, kneeling down in front of Red. "I would be pleased to serve you a redolent mixture of the house's finest dog food."

He may not understand the words, but understands the tone. Red gives her an enthusiastic wag of his tail. Sarah fluffs up his neck fur, then escorts him into the kitchen for dinner.

I'm tempted to follow. To plop a wad of icies in

front of Francie and Sam and tell them they never need to worry about money again.

But I don't want them to just reject it right away out of politeness or some sense of pride. I'll have to talk to Daniel and Sarah later about the best strategy for getting their parents to say yes.

I climb the stairs.

Daniel answers at the first knock and gathers me in for a warm hug and an even warmer kiss. We have a lot to talk about, he and I, but I don't see any reason to rush this part. I take my proper portion of kissing, then lean against him for as long as I want and let him hold me nice and tightly. It's a restorative feeling. Even better than Sarah's cookies.

Finally I peel myself away. "I don't have a lot of time right now, unfortunately." I explain about the interview. "So let's just give each other the highlights for right now."

I pull out my five sheets of paper to show him, then take off his wet coat and drape it over the chair. I take off my wet boots, too. Then the two of us sit on his bed, shoulder to shoulder, leaning against the wall.

"Okay, the short version," I say. I use my notes to help organize my report. It would be so easy to run off on a tangent and not get to everything.

Daniel listens with intense interest. He asks only a few questions.

"Now you," I say. "Go."

Daniel takes a breath. "Right. Well, the timeline isn't quite what we believed. We assumed from that footage of the conference that Professor Lacksmith was the only one who accepted the challenge. But there was another. He approached Dr. Venn after the conference and became the first to test the machine, ahead of Lacksmith."

I take a guess. "Dr. Sands?"

Daniel nods. "You can imagine that after that disaster, Professor Lacksmith wasn't so keen to try it himself anymore."

"Oh, boy..." I close my eyes and slump a little more against the wall. That doesn't seem like very good news. I was really hoping someone else tried Dr. Venn's machine and lived to tell about it.

There's a knock on the door, then Sarah comes in carrying a tray with three bowls of soup. Red angles past her to jump up on the bed.

Sarah hands Daniel and me our dinners, then sets the tray on his desk. "Do you mind if I listen? I've finally been released from my duties downstairs."

I guess she's not so worried anymore about me ruining the mystery. "Of course you can stay," I say.

She sits in Daniel's chair and all three of us take a minute or two just to eat.

"Mmm, delicious," I tell her. "As usual."

She smiles. "Thank you. I really would have made an excellent expedition cook, don't you agree?"

"I do." I'm tempted to tell her she might still have a chance if I find Halli tomorrow and somehow sort this all out, but since I don't actually know if I can pull off either of those, I decide to keep that private hope to myself.

"So where does that leave us?" I ask Daniel.

"Quite a bit further than yesterday," he answers. "Professor Lacksmith might not have braved the machine himself, but he's been studying Dr. Venn's results for years. He wasn't too eager to tell me—apparently it's been their secret—but once I explained my personal interest..."

"You didn't tell him who I am, did you?"

"Not precisely," Daniel answers. "I told him I'd met another person with similar experiences. I shared a very broad outline of how you and I met. Needless to say, he wanted to know far more. So we worked out an exchange of information. We spent hours at it."

I glance at the clock. Quarter to seven. I'd rather be late than hungry, so I finish the rest of my soup.

"Okay, I told him one hour. I wish I didn't have to do it, but if it gets rid of him once and for all..."

"Sorry, who?" Sarah asks.

"Bryan Stewart. That reporter."

"He's here?"

"At that inn where Jake is staying," I say. "I told him he could have his interview with me tonight."

"Can I watch?" she asks.

"Actually, I wouldn't mind it if you'd come and watch Red for me. Jake will be there, too."

"Both?" Sarah says with a smile. "Well, then."

"Perhaps I should go instead," Daniel says.

"Don't you dare," Sarah answers. "I am Halli Markham's apprentice, am I not?"

"Oh, that reminds me," I say, digging the wad of bills out of my pocket and handing it to Sarah.

Daniel frowns.

"Get over it," I tell him. Then I kiss his cheek before hopping off the bed. "We'll talk about all of this when I get back. You can look at my notes and see if those help."

"Sarah, if you'll excuse us for a moment," Daniel says.

"As you wish," she answers. She loads our empty bowls back onto her tray and leaves us alone.

Daniel wraps his arms around me. "Are you certain about this?"

"Certain I'll be happy when it's over. I need fewer people following me around. This one's going to keep bothering me until I get rid of him."

"But you'll be impersonating her on camera while being questioned by someone who presumably has done his homework."

I tap my head. "I have enough material in here to fill an hour. And I already told him I reserve the right not to answer any question I don't like."

"Reporters can be devious."

"Not as devious as I am," I say. "I've been lying for two lifetimes."

3 8

The night is chilly, but at least the rain has stopped.

I'm still wearing Daniel's oatmeal-colored sweater and his same damp coat, but it's only damp on the outside. Inside it's cozy and warm. Red bounds ahead of Sarah and me, sniffing everything that's been freshened by the rain.

Sarah threads her arm through mine. "I like you for my brother."

"Okay," I say with a laugh. "Thank you."

She rests her head against my shoulder for a moment. "Do you think you'll stay?"

"Stay? I … honestly don't know." And it is honest, since I've barely given myself the chance to think beyond these next few days.

"I know it might be difficult," Sarah says, letting go of me so she can bury her hands in the pockets of her coat. "I can't imagine having to pretend to be someone else for so many hours a day, but you'd always with safe with us. We could even tell my parents—they wouldn't mind, you know. They'd actually be very excited."

"I know, Sarah. And I feel bad keeping it from them —they've always been so nice to me. It's just for now, you know? Until I see how everything works out."

"But then … I mean, if you do sort it out…" She turns to me and I can see just enough of her face in the light of the street lamps to see the hopefulness there.

"I don't know," I tell her again. "I'm just being honest. I really don't know what my future holds."

"Yes." She nods. "Of course you don't. I'm sorry for pressing. I used to be the same with my dolls. I'd *squeeze* them so hard because I loved them so much. Then I wouldn't understand why their limbs fell off so easily."

"Okay, I'm drawing the line at that."

"Please do," Sarah says. "It's dangerous."

Jake is waiting for us outside the inn. Red lets his feelings about that be known.

"Hello, Jake," Sarah says with a smile. She turns to me. "I'll take Red around to the side for now, shall I?"

"No, we'll all go inside," I say. "It's too cold out here. You and Red can wait in the entryway again."

I'm about to head toward the door when Jake pulls me back. "I need to talk to you first."

"Okay." I step back a little so he has to release me.

"I wanted to apologize. You were right about what you said earlier. I should have done my job better and made sure Bryan didn't bother you. I'm sorry about that."

I shrug. "It's done. Let's get this over with."

"I wanted to tell you something else," Jake continues. "Sort of in my own defense. I did keep your father from interrupting you with Dr. Venn."

I keep my expression perfectly neutral. "Oh? When?"

"This afternoon," Jake says. "Over lunch. He'd heard from one of those professors you were supposed to have an appointment with that you hadn't shown up. He wanted to confront you about that himself."

"So what happened?"

"I talked him out of it," Jake says. "I told him it would be better if we came to see you at the end of the day."

"What did he say?"

"He didn't like it, but he agreed. Then you … handled it another way." Jake smiles. "Very well, I'd say."

I'm waiting. But he still doesn't explain why he felt it necessary to show Halli's father the invitation from Sarah, or why Halli's father was so chummy with the way he patted Jake on the shoulder. Something about the whole thing still doesn't seem right. But Jake is done with his confession.

"It's cold," I tell him. "Let's go in."

I lead the way. Jake follows, then Sarah waits until we're into the lobby before going in with Red.

"I'd appreciate if you'd have someone bring Sarah some hot tea," I tell Jake.

"Of course. Right away."

While he goes to speak to the woman at the front desk, I survey the scene in the sitting area to my left.

Bryan is using a larger binocular camera tonight, mounted on a tripod. He's set up lights behind two flowery chairs angled to face each other. There are other people standing around, maybe guests waiting for some excitement. Bryan sees me and heads over.

My pulse picks up. Suddenly I'm not so sure I can pull this off.

"Ready?" Bryan asks.

"Sure."

He pulls out a small container of powder and a fluffy brush, and gives my face a little dusting. "For the reflection," he tells me. "I have some other things in my kit if you want to add some color before we start."

"I happen to like this face. Just as it is," I remember Halli telling my friend Lydia as Lydia tried to put makeup on her before the ball. I feel the same way about Halli's face. I accept the powder, but that's it.

Jake has returned from his errand. He draws me aside again. "It's not too late. If you want to cancel this whole thing."

And this must be the Halli in me: just someone telling me I don't have to do something or I shouldn't do something is enough to make me feel stubborn about going through with it. *Defiant.*

I sit down in one of the chairs.

"Did you bring the dog?" Bryan asks.

"Yes."

"I'd like him in the picture, if you think he'd do it."

I can tell from his face that Jake doesn't like the sound of that. Which again makes me want to do it.

"Sure. I'll have Sarah bring him in."

"Sarah's here?" Bryan asks. Look at that eager smile. Sarah leaves a lasting impression.

"Jake, can you send someone to go get them?"

"Hello there, stranger," Sarah says when she comes in and sees Bryan. "Did you miss me?"

Bryan looks flustered. It's possible he even just blushed. Good. Sarah might be exactly who I need to throw Bryan a little off his game. I think I might need every advantage.

Bryan clears his throat. "If you could bring him over here, Sarah. Thank you."

"Certainly," she answers cheerfully.

"Come here, boy," I say, and Red trots over on his own. Bryan is still too busy staring at Sarah to notice. "I only have an hour," I prompt him.

"Yes," he says. "Right." He clears his throat again. I glance at Sarah and give her an approving smile. Jake has retreated into a safe corner of the room, well outside Red's danger zone.

Bryan takes a seat.

And we're off.

"We're here with world-renowned explorer Halli Markham and her faithful dog, Red, for an intimate conversation about what life has been like since her beloved grandmother and fellow adventurer Virginia Markham passed on a year ago..."

The questions are pretty standard: how have I been, what have I been doing, how have I spent the past year? I know enough of Halli's life to answer all of them without hesitation.

Then Bryan delves a little deeper, asking me how I feel about going on without Ginny.

"It's hard," I say, "obviously. She was my only parent for sixteen years. I felt like an orphan."

Halli's parents aren't going to like that one bit. Fine with me.

"But you've since reconciled with your parents, haven't you?" Bryan asks. "Technological titans Jameson Bellows and Regina Markham?"

"They're fine, if that's what you're asking," I say. "I mean ... I don't have any issues with them."

"Do you love them?"

I give a little laugh. "That's ... kind of personal."

"This is an intimate evening," Bryan says with a polite smile. Behind his eyes there's a certain glint. He's poking at me, and he knows it.

"I admire them," I say. "I think they've done outstanding work in the scientific and technological field. I have nothing but respect for their work."

"And for them as people?"

"We all have feelings about our parents, don't we, Bryan?" That's as much as he's going to get out of me.

Not everyone needs to know what you think.

"Let's move on, Bryan."

He glances at his notes and asks me another series of harmless questions: what are some of my favorite memories of Ginny, what do I miss most about her, what do I think her legacy is in the adventuring world?

"I think Ginny stood for courage," I say. "For trusting yourself. For being smart and careful, but also being willing to go out and test yourself in the unknown."

Bryan nods. "Well said."

I have to admit I think so, too.

But then he hits me with the zinger.

"So how do you think your grandmother would feel about you completely abandoning your life as an adventurer to become the dutiful daughter of two people she despised?"

I stare at Bryan for a moment. He stares calmly back.

Then I laugh.

Bryan smiles uncertainly.

I fold one leg up under me on the chair and visibly, purposely relax. "Okay, Bryan, you really want to talk?"

His face lights up. He looks eager. Hungry. It must be the kind of moment a reporter waits for, when he finally breaks through the calm, poised exterior of an interview subject, and she breaks down and tells him the truth.

My truth.

"My grandmother was brilliant, okay? Brilliant. And she taught me more about living than any other human ever could. She also taught me about *business*. And do you know what I know about business?"

Bryan shakes his head.

"I know how to pick a winner. Now, my parents, Regina Markham and Jameson Bellows, are winners. Big, fat—no offense to them—winners. Of course I'm interested in what they do and what they know and how they run their company. Because I'm not stupid. Ginny was smart, they're smart, and I'm the offspring of all of them. You following me so far?"

"Yes." Bryan manages only half a smile. I can tell he's not so sure anymore that he likes where this is going.

"But that's not the only thing I'm interested in. Yes, I love a big adventure—obviously. That's how I've spent my whole life so far. But is it really that much of a surprise that now that my wonderful grandmother is dead, I might strike out for new lands? Search for new opportunities? Of course not, Bryan. To think that would be ridiculous."

I glance over at Sarah, who is capital L, capital T, Loving This. Jake … doesn't seem so sure.

"So, what kinds of opportunities am I looking at now, Bryan?"

"Yes," he says, as if he's in any way in charge of this interview anymore, "what?"

"Well, for one thing, I might want to study at Oxford. Study science of some sort."

"Is that why you've been visiting Edgar Venn? Notorious for—"

I cut him off. "I'm interested in a lot of different people's work there. It might take me months to get through all the discussions I want to have. I'm curious about *everything*, Bryan, and as I think my track record has shown, I go out and meet the world head on. I don't just sit around and wonder."

"I think that's a fair point," he says, "but what about—"

"The second big opportunity I'll be pursuing," I say, "is to invest in a history studio. One of your competitors, Bryan. A studio whose work I believe in and whose owners have my absolute confidence."

I hear a muffled cry of glee. I know who made it.

"I'm announcing here that I plan to invest in History 14, the studio owned by Francie Everett and

Sam Wheeler, and help them continue their excellent, insightful, ground-breaking programming.

"And that," I say, standing up, "is your hour. Thank you, Bryan. It's been a pleasure." I thrust out my hand and Bryan shakes it. He looks a little stunned. Good. "Come on, Red, let's go."

I stride for the door, not pausing for anyone or anything. I have no idea what the fallout from all of this will be, but right now, I'm just enjoying the feeling.

I was brave. I like it. I like it even better than lying.

I'm out in the cold night air before either Sarah or Jake can catch up with me. Jake stands at a distance. "Halli—Miss Markham—can I talk to you?"

"In a minute." First I need to accept a bone-crushing hug from Sarah.

"Thank you, thank you, thank you," she whispers in my ear. "You're so precious to me I'm going to squeeze your arms right off."

"What will your parents say?"

"It better bloody well be *yes!*" she answers.

She hugs me one more time, then I ask her to hold on to Red for a moment while I go talk to Jake.

"Halli … you've put me in a really bad position."

I chuckle. "Okay."

"This interview won't air until tomorrow," he says. "They'll need to edit and finalize it first."

"Yes, and?"

Jake sighs. "See, if I worked for you right now, it wouldn't be a problem. I'd follow whatever your instructions are. But because I still work for your parents…"

I'm not going to finish his sentence for him. He's going to have to tell me himself.

"I have to call them," Jake says. "I have to report. And I don't think they're going to like it."

"What won't they like? I complimented them all over the place in that interview."

"The investment part," Jake says. "They won't agree to that."

"It's *my* money. Remember? You said it yourself this morning: I'm rich."

"But you're still under guardianship," Jake says. "With Monsieur Bern. And he would have to approve anything large."

Monsieur Bern. That square-faced, small-lipped apparition who hovered above the conference table at Halli's parents' board meeting. The man who was going to vote to sell all my shares—Halli's shares—in the company to her parents.

No.

"I'll deal with all that," I say, although right at this moment, I'm not sure how.

What I do know is that I'm not going to lose this feeling of being in charge of what happens to me. I've gone too long without it. I want to hang on to it forever, if I can.

"So," Jake says, "what should I say to your parents?"

"Tell them the truth," I answer. "Tell them what I said. They'll know by tomorrow anyway."

I gather the collar of Daniel's coat closer around my neck. "Is that all, Jake? Because I'm cold."

"Yes, Miss Markham," he answers, sounding tired all of the sudden. "That's all."

"Then I'll see you in the morning."

"Halli?" he says as I walk away.

"Yes?"

"Are you sure you know what you're doing?"

I smile, and take a moment to reach down and pet my dog. "It's all just an adventure, Jake. It's what I do."

39

"May I please now tell you that I love you and will pledge my life to you from this moment, and would like to bake you into a cream pie so that I can eat you up, or spread you like butter across toast, because I LOVE YOU SO MUCH I can barely form the words and might possibly expire right at this very moment, I am so ecstatically moved. Thank you," Sarah says breathlessly. "The end."

And I am laughing so hard at that, it feels like the weight of two universes has finally dropped from my body.

"Oh my gosh, Sarah, I have no idea what's going to happen from that."

"I don't care," she says. "It was delicious. I only wish

Daniel could have been there. His protestations of love might have even exceeded my own."

I feel like running. So I do. And Red and Sarah run right along. The three of us crowd in through the door of the house, panting and energized.

Francie looks up from what she's reading in the living room. "Well! That was spirited."

"Oh, Mum—can I tell her?"

I shrug. "Might as well."

"Au—" Sarah quickly catches herself and coughs. "Halli just did the most brilliant thing during her interview. Where's Dad? Dad!" She calls. "Daniel! Come down here!"

Soon Sarah's audience is assembled.

"So that Bryan bloke asks Miss Markham here something about why she's abandoned her life of adventure and become the dutiful daughter or some such of two people her grandmother despised."

"He didn't," Francie says. Of course she wouldn't approve of his lack of manners.

"So Halli gives him all sorts of what for," Sarah goes on, "but then here was the most glorious part: she announced to all the world that she intends to invest in a history studio. A studio known for its excellence. *Our* history studio."

Francie looks at her husband. Then back at her daughter. Then at me.

"Halli, is this true?"

"I'm sorry," I tell her. "I probably should have discussed it with you first ... but yes, it's true. I'd love to be an investor if you'll accept me."

"Dear Halli," Francie answers. She rises from the couch and places her cold, soft hands on my cheeks. Then she hugs me the way no one on earth ever has except my mother. And that fact alone is what brings tears to my eyes.

When Francie pulls back, she's crying, too. She wipes away her tears and asks with a laugh, "Why are you crying, then?"

"I was afraid you'd say no." It's not exactly a lie, it's just not the real reason.

"If she'd said no," Sam says, "I would have carried her right out of the room." He gives me a hug, too, much more formal, and then finishes it off with a pat on my back. "Is it rude to ask how much?"

"A lot," I say. "I'm prepared to invest a lot."

Francie waves her husband away. "All to be discussed at a later time. Just accept your early birthday present and say thank you."

"Thank you," Sam says with a smile. "Thank you, indeed, Halli."

The only one who hasn't said a word yet is Daniel. But all it takes is one look in his eyes to know he approves of what I've done. No more frowning at me for bringing home wads of money. Somehow *invest-ment* passes his test for helping out his family.

"Biscuits," Sarah says. "I happen to have a few."

"And some tea, I should think," Francie adds.

"Halli, can I speak with you for a moment?" Daniel asks.

Sarah lures Red into the kitchen while Daniel and I step out to the front of his house.

"How long?" he asks. "How long have been planning this?"

"Not long. Probably half a second before I said it. But I knew once I thought of it that it was right. It's a hundred percent right. I think Halli would agree, too."

Daniel does the only romantic thing possible and kisses me here under the light from his parents' front door. It feels so good to be part of his family right now. That constant ache I felt last time over missing my mother and missing my old life is nearly gone.

"There might be a complication." I explain about Monsieur Bern. "But I'll be eighteen in February. Then I'll never need anyone's permission."

"Audie." Daniel says my name quietly since we're out here in the open. "I think it's wonderful what you want to do for my parents—for all of us—but..."

"But?"

"Nothing about this is simple, is it? February is only a few months away, but yours isn't a normal life right now."

Some of the joy I've just been feeling starts to drain

away. "It feels like you're about to give me some bad news."

"Not bad," Daniel says, "just … vital. I need to tell you what Professor Lacksmith and I discussed today. It sheds some light on your whole situation. It wouldn't be fair to let you make promises that you might not ultimately want to fulfill."

"Daniel, why wouldn't I want to do exactly what I said? I really do want to invest in your parents' studio."

"I know. But let's go upstairs. I have a lot I need to tell you."

40

We settle into our familiar positions, Daniel and Red and I, the three of us crowded onto the top of Daniel's bed. Sarah is in her bedroom right now searching for footage of Dr. Venn. I've taken off Halli's boots for the last time today, and changed into more comfortable clothes. If Daniel has a lot to tell me, I want to feel as relaxed as possible first, since I have the feeling I won't be this relaxed once we really get into it.

Daniel has his tablet on his lap. He's created a holographic chalkboard the way I've seen him do before, and it hovers above us in 3D, ready for him to draw on it.

"I need to talk with you about trees," he begins.

"Trees? Okay."

"Specifically about clonal colonies."

"Oh, yeah. I wondered what that meant." I remember those words speeding past me when Daniel first described what it is he's studying.

"Imagine a typical forest." He draws a horizontal line on his tablet, which shows up on the chalkboard in front of us. Then he sketches in four simple trees above the line, and a bunch of wavy roots leading from the base of each of them down below the horizontal line. "There might be a variety of trees growing there—pine, aspen, oak, others. I already told you about the underground networks—the roots and fungi that transport information and nutrition."

"Right."

"Well, there's another phenomenon at work with clonal colonies."

"But I still don't know what clonal—"

"Just watch first." Daniel sketches in more trees. "Imagine that all of these are one species—aspens, for example." He then draws in a second horizontal line, this time below all the squiggly lines representing roots. He points at the 3D image in front of me. "This lower line is the Mother Root. It comes from one single organism—the original aspen, in this case—and over thousands of years, it pushes further and further through the soil and sends up individual shoots that become new trees. But they're all clones—not merely offspring, but genetically identical to the original tree."

"Hold on," I say. "Wait. Halli and I are not clones. We might be entangled in some quantum physics way, but that doesn't make us clones."

"No, I agree," Daniel says. "As does Professor Lacksmith. But the model still applies. In a regular forest, even trees of the same species have to rely on the underground network of roots and fungi to communicate. It's because they're all separate individuals that have grown from their own separate seeds.

"But a clonal colony is different," Daniel says. "They haven't grown from seed, they've all grown upward from the same Mother Root. And that means they can bypass the standard underground network used within the forest. Instead, all of the trees within the colony have direct access to each other at all times. If a beetle attacks one of them a hundred miles away, every other tree in the colony instantly knows and can defend itself."

"Okay, I think I understand that," I say, "but I don't see how it applies to Halli and me."

"You explained entangled particles to me once," Daniel says. "You told me that even when they're separated across great distances, they can communicate instantly—faster than the speed of light."

"Yes."

Daniel points to his hologram. "So can these. I know your theory was that you were able to find Halli the first time because the two of you were vibrating at the same level and found some sort of resonance, but what if that isn't what it was?"

"Well then, what was it?" I ask.

"What if it was that you were both *made* at the same level?"

"What do you mean? Like by some ... cosmic Mother Root for humans?" It sounds even weirder than most of my theories.

"Over the past two decades, Professor Lacksmith has charted forty-four parallel versions of Dr. Venn. Only one of them so far has been his identical: the other Edgar Venn. All the others vary in age, gender, race, body type, appearance—so why is that?"

I press my palms hard against my temples. There's so much information in my brain right now, I need some support to keep it all in. "I don't know," I answer. "I don't understand any of this anymore."

But then suddenly I do.

"Strands."

Daniel smiles. "Dr. Venn's term for it, yes. Professor Lacksmith prefers to think of it as *grafting*."

"What's that?"

Daniel erases his current drawing and starts on another. "Let's say you want to grow a particular kind of citrus tree. Say, a ruby orange tree. You love the fruit, but those trees won't grow in your climate."

Daniel sketches in a tree trunk and makes a mark on its side.

"So you find a citrus tree that *will* grow in your climate—a lemon tree, for example—and you make a cut in its bark. Then you insert a thin piece of branch from a ruby orange tree. You bind the two together, and after a few weeks the tissues from the two of them begin growing together. Eventually you have a lemon tree that bears ruby oranges. Do you understand?"

"Yes."

"Good. So now we come to Professor Lacksmith's theory about Dr. Venn."

Daniel draws a root downward from the grafted tree and then sketches in a second horizontal line beneath it again.

"Even though above the ground this tree looks different, it's still part of the same clonal colony and can communicate with all its sisters and brothers very easily. That's how Dr. Venn could find so many of his other selves. They were in other times, other centuries, even other universes, but they were still all connected at this singular base level. He just had to be patient and seek them out."

"Wait," I say. "So you're telling me there are all these people, men and women, people who don't look anything like each other and live all over the place, and they're still all versions of Dr. Venn?"

"Not Dr. Venn as the person," Daniel says, "but versions of this." He points to the lower line. "Offshoots of the Mother Root. And all of them have undergone a form of grafting. It's a question of *when*—at what stage in their growth—they were grafted."

I pause a moment to think about that. "Okay, so when Dr. Venn was talking about how he visited the Viking version of himself in the year one thousand something, he was really visiting some person who grew out of the same Mother Root. Right?"

"Yes," Daniel says, "that was the origin. But then the grafting—"

"Took place right away," I say, pointing to the area below the soil. "Down here. Before that person was ever born."

"Yes, that's the theory."

"But with Halli and me," I go on, suddenly excited that maybe I have a grasp on this, "I've done some sort of grafting *above* the surface, creating versions where it's her body, but me inside. And Dr. Venn did the same thing when he and the other physicists signed the Manhattan Pact and split off into a new universe. He created a second Edgar Venn from the first one."

"I think so," Daniel says. "That's what the theory implies."

"But what does that *mean*?" I ask, because that's really the important question here. I'm used to having theories about how all of this happened—Professor Whitfield and Albert and I had tons of them back in their lab—but theories don't get me anywhere if I can't find a way to use them for my benefit.

"Go back to idea of the original root," Daniel says, pointing to that lower line. "Professor Lacksmith prefers to think in terms of plants, obviously, but he said Dr. Venn has always spoken of the origin in terms of a greater consciousness linking all the various lives together. He calls it the Great Mind."

I try to process that. "Okay, so let's say one big, massive mind creates all these people. And because they're all linked together in the forest of time and space—" *Forest of time and space.* I love the sound of that. "— they can visit each other or communicate together no matter where they live, or during what time period. Dr. Venn can go visit another member of his colony even if he or she lives in a different universe or a different century."

"Yes," Daniel agrees. "I think that's what they're saying."

I let out a breath. There's a lot to try to take in here. But I know if I can really absorb this, I might finally be able to answer a lot of my own questions.

I borrow Daniel's tablet. "So let's say this is the Greater Mind that goes with me." I trace my finger over the tablet surface and draw a few trees growing out of the lower line. Then I point to them in succession. "Tree Audie. Tree Halli." Then I draw in new branches on the Audie tree. "So when I saved Halli, I ended up grafting a Halli branch onto my Audie tree.

That created a version where it was Halli's body with me inside.

"Then that branch died." I draw in a withered end to the branch. "So I looped back into the past a little ways, and grafted a new branch onto this one. I'm still me inside Halli's body, but this time I've created a stronger plant. With stronger qualities to help me survive."

I look up from what I'm drawing. "Does that sound even close to right?"

Now it's Daniel's turn to press his fingers into his temple. "I've already spent hours discussing this with Professor Lacksmith. I don't know if any of it makes sense anymore. It's all like a hurricane in my mind at the moment."

"Let's stop, then," I say, handing him back his tablet. "I need to get up and move or something. My brain is on overload, too. We both need a break."

I climb past Red and stand up. Stretch my arms up high. Crack my neck from side to side. Bend at the waist to lengthen my legs. Hang there for a while to let the blood rush to my head.

"The problem is," I tell Daniel once I come back up, "I feel like I've done this kind of thing before."

"Done what?" he asks.

"Run after some theory. Professor Whitfield had all of his. I had some of my own. Then for the past few days it's been all Dr. Venn. And now this new stuff from Professor Lacksmith. I don't know if any of it is right. I keep thinking, *'Yeah, that's it!'* but then some-thing new comes along, and I think, *'No, that has to be it.'*" I shake my head. "It's frustrating because I never know if I'm wasting my time and chasing some idea that's completely wrong."

"I understand," Daniel says. "But it's science, isn't it? We circle around and around a problem until we finally approach what seems the most likely solution."

"So are we still circling here?" I ask. "Or is this the solution?"

There's a knock on the door. Sarah sticks her head in. "Busy?"

"Busy being confused," I say. "Come on in. Have you found anything?"

"Oh, *have* I." She holds her tablet out in front of her. There's a holographic image frozen in midair.

"You believe you're confused now?" she asks. "Wait until you see this."

41

"Watch," Sarah says. She restarts the film.

It's the same footage Daniel already showed me. There he is, Dr. Venn in his early 80s, walking with a cane and being questioned by a reporter.

"We already saw this," Daniel tells her.

"One moment, please," she says. She stops the film and brings up a new one. Dr. Venn once again is shown walking somewhere, this time in front of his house, maybe. There's a voiceover about him, but no one stops him for an interview.

The film ends.

Sarah turns to us, a smug smile on her face. "Well?"

"Well what?" I ask.

"Did you see it?"

"No," I say.

"Let's try again," Sarah says. She plays both pieces of footage once more.

I shake my head. "I don't get it."

Sarah groans. "Daniel? Anything?"

"No," he says, "sorry."

"Can we have a hint?" I ask.

"Look at his gait," Sarah says. Then she plays the footage for the third time.

"Just tell us," Daniel says afterward. "I don't see anything."

"Then prepare yourself," Sarah says. "Now that I know it's possible, it is clear to me that those two are *not* the same man."

"What? Show us again," I tell her.

This time she slows down each one and points at the moving image. "Watch the left leg. See how the foot turns out there? And watch his hand position on the cane. All right, have that in mind?"

She then restarts the second film. "There." She points to the left foot. "It's forward. Watch every step—see how it even turns inward right there? And look at his right hand. His grip on the cane is completely different. And watch how he holds his head. It's different than in the first one."

"Yeah, but this one is later, right?" I ask. "By how many years?"

"Two," Sarah says.

"He's old," I say. "Bodies change."

"Two years is not that much older," Sarah answers. "I'm telling you, this second man is *different*."

It isn't impossible. That man in the later footage could be the other Edgar Venn, briefly captured on film during one of his bilocation visits.

Although the truth is, I can't see any of the differences Sarah is pointing out. Both men look exactly the same to me.

"How are you getting all this, anyway?" I ask her.

"Because I pay attention," Sarah says. "I have an eye for it. Don't I, Dan?"

"She does," he admits. "She always notices the most peculiar things about people."

"Peculiar," she scoffs. "Body movement and hair style and clothing are fairly regular, thank you. The fact is, people just don't look. They don't *see*."

"I could look all day," Daniel answers, "and still not see what you've claimed about Albertson Foles."

"His eyes are moist and the left one has a twitch," she tells me, "but only during his evening broadcasts—never the morning ones. Obviously he's an afternoon drinker."

"Or that time you knew Mrs. Laird next door left her husband," Daniel says.

"Anyone could have seen that Mr. Laird had let himself go," Sarah says. "Stopped doing the wash. Wore the same shirt and trousers five days in a row one week. Hair so greasy you could have wrung it into a pail. No man who's loved abandons his appearance like that."

"Can I ask you guys something?" I interrupt, even though I'm very interested in what other feats of observation Sarah has demonstrated. But what she just said about Albertson Foles, whoever he is, reminds me that I've been meaning to ask this for a while. "What's with all the first names here that end in *son*?" One or two might not have seemed so strange, but there have been too many of them: Halli's father Jameson Bellows, the driver Wilkinson, that personal trainer on the island, Ferguson, the man at the London headquarters, Johnson Chilton— and probably more that I'm just not thinking of right now.

"It was the fashion, wasn't it?" Sarah says.

"What fashion?" I ask.

"Primarily in the 50s and 60s," Daniel answers. "When families began changing over to the mother's surname for the children instead of the father's."

"Some of the fathers felt subordinated," Sarah says. "Completely ignoring the fact that for centuries women were never given their proper due—"

Daniel heads her off. "Which is a topic for another time. But to answer your question," he tells me, "it became the fashion for some time that parents gave their sons the fathers' first names and added 'son' to the end."

"What about the girls?" I ask.

"It never worked," Sarah says. "The names would be hopelessly long. And not very poetic. *Samsdaughter* for me. No, thank you."

"Anyway," I say, trying to get us back on track, "I'm not saying these two Dr. Venns aren't different, but two pieces of film really aren't enough."

"A fair criticism," Sarah says. "Which is why I have several more to show you."

One after another she switches back and forth between older and more recent footage. And the more she points out the differences, I can almost start to see what she's talking about.

"It's the same as I noticed about you," Sarah tells me. "The way you hold your body and carry it. It wasn't like Halli. Maybe it's subtle—too subtle for you, Daniel—"

"I knew it was her," he says defensively.

"Bravo, you," his sister answers, "perhaps you've finally opened your eyes, but everyone has their own habits of dress and speech and movement. They're as telling as wearing a sign about your neck announcing, *'Hello, I'm in love now! I've lost my job! My wife has run off with our accountant!'*"

"Daniel," I say, "what if that really is the other Dr. Venn? We don't really know what he did when he bilocated here. Maybe he stayed for a while. Explored around Oxford. And some reporter just happened to film him."

"That sounds intriguing," Sarah says with a yawn, "but I believe I will leave the two of you to sort it out. I have school in the morning, unfortunately, and then many more hours of cooking for our dear father's party. Thank goodness we're only called upon to celebrate him once every fifty years."

As she closes the door behind her, I glance at Daniel's clock. It's late, and I'm pretty tired, too. Although that may be more mental than physical. But I still wouldn't mind putting this head to bed and waking up fresh in the morning. Maybe I'll understand more after a good night's sleep.

"I think we should call it a night," I say.

Daniel suppresses a yawn of his own.

I squeeze his hand and give him a quick kiss. "Thank you for talking to Professor Lacksmith today. And thank you for explaining all of that to me. I don't know what it all means yet, but I know it's probably important."

I'm just about to wake up Red so I don't have to climb over him, but Daniel still hasn't let go of my hand. "Audie?"

"Hm?"

"If that really was the other Dr. Venn, out for a walk when someone filmed him…"

Daniel hesitates. That only makes me more curious.

He isn't like me, blurting out every idea that comes to him the second it crosses his brain. He always seems to take more time to think things through. By the time he's ready to tell me something, he's usually already processed it for a while. Look how long it took him to tell me he studies fungus.

"This could work," he says. "No matter what."

"What could work?"

"You and me. Together," he says. "Even if you find a way to go back."

42

"It's too early for this," I mutter to Daniel.

But there's no stopping the face that swirls into focus on the screen between the front and back seats of the car.

"Good morning, Regina," I say.

"It's midnight here," she corrects me. "I've had to stay up just to talk to you."

"Then let's keep it short so you can go to bed."

"Are you out of your mind, young lady?" she demands. "What were thinking, announcing to a reporter that you intend to invest in that crackpot history studio?"

I consider telling her the son of the crackpot studio's owners is in the car with me, but she won't care anyway.

"It's my money," I remind her.

"It's your inheritance," she reminds me, "which you don't control until you're eighteen."

"Then I'll wait until I'm eighteen."

She doesn't have an immediate answer for that.

"We've managed to kill the piece," she says instead.

"What do you mean?"

"Did you think we'd let them air that? Thank goodness Jake was there. It might have gone live before we knew anything about it."

"Yes," I agree, "it's a very good thing Jake was there."

I'll deal with him later.

"Is that all, Regina? Because I have other things to do."

"You're determined to continue being seen with that clown, Edgar Venn?"

"As I told my father," I answer, "Dr. Venn and my grandmother were very good friends. It's a great comfort to talk to him about her. You know, about your *mother*."

Regina Markham dismisses that with a shrug. "I told your father you'd be impossible to control."

I can't believe she just admitted that. But I like it. I like being the kind of person Halli's parents can't control. It fills me with immense pride.

"You look really tired, Regina. You should probably go to bed."

If I knew how to hang up on her, I would. But I just have to wait for her to do it to me.

"Why is he there?" she asks.

I glance at Daniel. I hoped he was sitting far enough away from me that he wouldn't be in range. But I have no idea how these holo screens work.

"He's my boyfriend. Daniel Everett, let me introduce you to my mother, Regina Markham. She's a brilliant scientist and entrepreneur. You've probably heard of her."

I can tell the compliment throws her off guard. But she quickly recomposes herself. "I know who he is. I saw the reports two days ago."

I wonder if she means the reports of Daniel and me coming out of Dr. Venn's office on Tuesday, or the reports that someone saw us kissing. Either way, I don't really care what she thinks about it.

"I imagine you're feeling very pleased with yourself right now, aren't you, Mr. Everett?"

"Pardon me, ma'am?" he says.

"Seducing my daughter to secure your family's future."

"Okay, that's it," I tell her. "We're done here. Sleep tight, Regina."

I knock on the divider, and when Jake turns around I give him the signal to cut off the comm. A second or two later, the screen goes blank.

I slump back against the seat. I can't say what I

really want to right now, which is that every time I deal with her parents, I have more and more sympathy for Halli. But since I'm still not sure whether Jake can hear me back here, even without the ear buttons, I have to keep my thoughts to myself.

Daniel puts his arm around me. I'll take that. And Red is sleeping on the other side of me, his warm head on my lap. I'll take that, too.

It was kind of a rough night. Sarah had no trouble falling sleep, if her soft snores were any indication, but I lay awake for hours, rolling everything around in my mind.

Especially that whole thing about grafting. I really get what Professor Lacksmith was saying. It makes sense when I think about the two lives I've lived as Halli. It's the other stuff—the underground grafting— that's harder for me to grasp. Even when I substitute Dr. Venn's term of Greater Mind for the Mother Root.

I just don't know. I'm hoping I'll understand more of it today.

Dr. Venn is already in place behind his desk when we walk in. He's wearing a wool cap and a thick coat over flannel pajamas. There's a blanket tucked over his lap. Instead of his regular shoes, he's wearing a worn pair of slippers. He greets us with a deep, wet cough.

"Children," he says, his voice very hoarse. "I'm afraid we only have a few minutes. Madeline will be back any moment. Young man, come here."

Daniel and I exchange a glance, then Daniel joins Dr. Venn behind his desk.

"Here are the monitors," Dr. Venn says. He pauses to cough in a very deep, phlegmy way. He's obviously very sick. But also obviously in a hurry to convey this information.

"Heart rate," he says, pointing to a red knob, "skin temperature, brain waves—"

The door to his office opens, and Madeline comes in, carrying a small duffel. "No. You two have to leave. Come on, now, out."

"No," Dr. Venn manages before he succumbs to another coughing fit.

"Do you see?" Madeline asks us. "I begged you not to exhaust him, and then yesterday, with the rain and the cold—he was supposed to stay in bed this morning, but he sneaked out. The man has a fever. You're endangering his life."

"No," Dr. Venn argues.

"I'm sorry," I tell Madeline. "I'M SORRY," I repeat to Dr. Venn. And I mean it—he looks and sounds horrible.

"Don't be," Dr. Venn manages in a strangled sounding voice before he gasps and coughs again.

"COME ON, GRANDDAD, WE'RE GOING," Madeline says. "I CALLED THE HOSPITAL. WE'RE GOING STRAIGHT THERE."

He shakes his head like a bratty little kid. He points

his finger at his granddaughter and says, "NO." He coughs again while he points to me. "I must talk to this girl. Please, Maddy. Two minutes. Alone."

She is clearly furious with both of us—Dr. Venn and me. But it's also clear that she loves her grandfather, and doesn't want to tell him no.

"Two minutes," she says. She pulls a thin tube out of her duffel, along with a small oxygen tank. She loops the tube around Dr. Venn's head and inserts the two nasal outlets into his nose. Then she unfolds a second blanket and tucks it tightly around him. "Two minutes," she repeats, and to me, adds, "This is very serious. Don't you dare kill him."

Then Madeline stalks out of the office. Our two minutes have begun.

"Through there," Dr. Venn tells us. His voice sounds weak and hoarse. Madeline is right: I've pushed him too hard. Or let him push himself too hard, at least. If he dies because of me…

"WHAT'S THROUGH THERE?" Daniel asks.

"Machine. Can't wait for me. Might be in hospital … a long time. Or never come out. Might be…" He lapses into another horrible coughing fit before he can finish with, "Pneumonia."

Daniel opens the door Dr. Venn indicated. I don't want to leave Dr. Venn's side, so the best I can do right now is crane my neck and try to see past him. It looks like a small room, about the size of a closet. There's what looks like a long metal cage hanging from the ceiling.

"Controls here," Dr. Venn rasps, pointing to a strip of dials and levers attached to the wall. "Start, stop. Monitors. Earphones and goggles in there. Very important," he says, pointing to me. "Wear both." Another cough shakes him. I can hear the liquid in his lungs with each breath. "Timer. One hour. Come back. Very important—*come back.*"

And then Madeline herself comes back, and she rushes Dr. Venn away.

Daniel and Red and I stand alone in the office. I don't know about Daniel, but I'm feeling pretty shaken.

Dr. Venn is right. He might be in the hospital for a long time. Or worse, he might never…

I can't think about that.

The door to the other room is still standing open. I shift so I can see more of the metal cage. There it is, empty and waiting.

I take a deep breath. "So."

"It's your decision," Daniel says, "but I think we should wait."

"For what? You heard him. You saw him."

"Audie, someone has died in that machine before. We don't know how to operate it."

"We can practice before I do anything."

Daniel runs a hand through his short hair. "There's

no rush, is there? Not really. Things are stable. Every-thing is good right now."

"Maybe here," I say, "but what about back home? If the time difference is still the same, Thursday morning here means Sunday night there. Halli is going to decide within about the next twelve hours to drop out of my school. She's going to start making plans. She's going to run away."

"Let her," Daniel says. "You have your own life. You're doing well here, aren't you? You could be … happy here."

I close the distance between us and wrap my arms around him. I understand what he's saying, and he might be right, if not for one important thing. One important person.

"I am happy here," I say. "I'm happy with you and Sarah and your family. And you're right—so far I'm doing okay. This is working way better than I ever hoped.

"But I love my mother," I tell him. "I can't just leave her. I can't let Halli break her heart. If I can find Halli and talk to her, tell her I'm working on the problem and not to do anything drastic, but just wait for me—I need to try. Yes, things are nice here right now. But none of this is natural. I can't pretend it is.

"Besides," I add, hoping to sound upbeat and care-free, "aren't you curious?"

"Not enough to endanger your life."

Oh, boy.

We stand here for a moment longer, locked in the warm security of our tiny little bubble in the world. But then I force myself to unlock and back away. It's so easy sometimes to do nothing. To stay comfortable with how things are, when you know in your heart you have to make a change.

"We're smart," I say, "right? We can figure out how it works. And if we can't, then I won't do it. I promise. We'll be safe."

Daniel doesn't look any more sure than I am. But finally he nods.

"Okay, then," I say, "let's go."

43

It takes us a few tries to understand how to even turn it on. But then once we do, the metal cage begins swaying with a gentle motion, back and forth, then side to side, then in a kind of random sequence that sometimes seems like a circle, but then changes course so it's never going the same way twice.

Just watching it makes me a little queasy.

Then there are the goggles Dr. Venn mentioned. The goggles are complete blackout ones: coated with a thick black film on the inside, and rimmed in thick padding so that no light can get through to my eyes from any angle. So I'm going to have to sway in the dark. That doesn't sound any better.

And last, the earphones. Once Daniel finds the controls for those, we can hear a kind of gentle ping coming out of them, followed by a kind of chime. That's not so bad.

"Here's the timer," Daniel says. "One hour, two hours—five hours maximum."

Dr. Venn said one hour, and we both agree. The truth is, if there were a setting for only ten minutes, I'd take that instead. I'm trying to act like I'm not nervous, but I'm sure Daniel can tell.

You're a brave girl.

"Okay, so I'm going to get in," I say. "Just to test it."

The cage hangs about six inches off the ground. It's easy for me to climb in, although I wonder how it was for Dr. Venn the older he got and the harder it was for him to move. I wonder when the last time was that anyone used this contraption. I hope everything still works the way it's supposed to.

There are metal straps to attach across horizontally at various spots and hold me in place from my shins up to my shoulders. They can all be adjusted for height. Another strap fits across my forehead to hold me perfectly still inside.

If I were claustrophobic, I'd be shouting for Daniel to rip off all these straps right now. It would be better if even just my arms could be free, but they're locked in, too. It gives me a feeling of true powerlessness. I feel like a metal mummy.

"All right?" Daniel asks.

I try to nod, but my head won't move much. I force myself to take normal, steady breaths.

There are sensors in all of the straps, and those are what send information back to the monitors. Daniel goes into the other room and adjusts the dials until he can see my pulse rate, my respiration, skin temperature, and the wavy line representing my brain waves.

Dr. Venn's machine might not be the most modern, sophisticated apparatus in the world, but his design still seems to work. I have to believe that.

Red has been sleeping in Dr. Venn's office this whole time, but unfortunately he decides now would a good time to wake up and come see what we're doing.

He immediately goes berserk.

"Red! Red, it's me! Look! It's okay." But it's not okay, and he knows it. He's bawling at me like the space alien I am. Daniel races to unstrap me so I can soothe the poor freaked-out dog.

I lead him back into the office and spend the time it takes to calm him down. I can't let this dog be a problem.

"We have to close the door while you're strapping me in," I say. "But you're going to have to do it fast, otherwise he won't want to be out here all alone. I don't know what he'll do to the office."

I bribe Red with a series of treats and wait until he seems fine.

I look up at Daniel and point to the other room. We go in there and quietly close the door.

I quickly step into the machine and let Daniel strap me in. He locks my head in place, then fits the earphones over it. Finally he positions the goggles so he can just slip them over my eyes.

But first he kisses me. While I can still see him. Then he lifts one of the earphones and tells me, "I love you. Come back. Don't forget that part."

I smile. "I love you, too. Don't worry. I know this will be fine."

Even though I don't know anything of the sort.

He kisses me one more time, then covers my ears and my eyes. I assume that within a second or two later, he's left the room.

A few heartbeats later, I feel the gentle sway of the machine.

Then the pings start.

Here we go.

44

I understand the swing.

It's completely disorienting. Moving this way, in no particular pattern, with all of my senses shut off —no touch, no sight, no hearing, nothing to taste or smell— I'm out of my body with remarkable speed. There's nothing to anchor me inside it.

The pings give way to a soft gong, like the sound felt-covered mallets make against a xylophone. But the instrument here is my brain. I can feel the vibrations on first the left lobe, then the right, then back and forth in some kind of song or rhythm like someone is playing a tune against the various folds of exposed brain inside my skull.

There are stars in here, bright gold against a pitch

black sky, then silver ones, and bright white, then flashes of color like red and a lucent green. But I'm seeing them on an enormous scale, not the way I would if I were just looking at them through eyes. I've spread out, the girl or the mind who is Audie Masters, and I'm composed of the same material as everything else I see, the blackness of space, the silver and red glow of stars, the vastness that lets me know I'm far, far away from where I was, and now I need to direct myself or I'll just float this way forever.

Focus and defocus. Isn't that how Dr. Venn described it? I understand what he meant. How I am right now is huge. No boundaries at all. But I can't go anywhere like this. I just *am.* If I want to move, I have to focus myself into something smaller.

Daniel's drawing pops into my mind. *Root.* Root down.

I picture myself diving like an arrow straight into a patch of fresh soil. I can smell it now, that earthy, moist mixture of vegetation and dirt, and I keep diving deeper until I find my line.

It's thick. White. Like holding on to a giant-sized bean sprout that's too big to get my whole hand around. I'm still moving. Gliding. Letting the root direct me like someone following a rope through the dark depths of an ocean.

"Halli," I think to tell it, and the glide continues, seamlessly pulling me along through the dark soil into

the fresh air of a girl's bedroom with the window open and admitting a fresh breeze.

I gently shake her awake. "Halli."

She jolts up in bed, takes a moment to believe, then hugs me so hard all the air collapses out of my chest. Then she's laughing and crying and repeating my name over and over, all at the same time.

"Audie, Audie, Audie, Audie…" It's a chant and a song, quietly under her breath. "Oh, Audie. You're here. You're alive. You're back. You don't know how happy I am to see you."

I know I was angry with her before. But I don't feel that way now. I don't think I can ever feel that way again. This is *me*. She is my blood and my sister and my other and my friend. And I nearly lost her more than once.

And she is me in the flesh. This is my old body I'm hugging so hard. If I could slip back inside it right now I would. Erase everything that's happened for the past few weeks and two other lives. Just come home now and be back in my own bed and wake up in the morning as me.

Not possible. I know. *Put it out of your head.* Halli needs a place to live, too.

"I have less than an hour," I tell her. "I'm bilocating."

"From where? Where are you?"

"Back in London. In your universe and one of your bodies."

"One of my—"

"I'll tell you as much as I can. But first I need to see my mother."

I don't know when the thought occurred to me, but somewhere along the way I knew I couldn't make the same mistake twice. Last time I talked to Halli and Professor Whitfield first, and by the time my mother came home from work and I could have seen her and hugged her, I was ripped away from my body and never saw her again.

Not this time.

"Here," Halli says. "Not like that." She gets up and hands me one of my old familiar sets of pajamas. I look down at what I'm wearing. I'm dressed like Halli Markham, of course. She's right—my mother will think it's weird. I quickly change.

Halli turns on my desk lamp and fishes a pair of scissors out of my drawer. It takes me a moment to understand.

Then I willingly turn my back to Halli and let her cut off her own beautiful hair.

She scoops it into my wastebasket and ties up the grocery bag I always keep as a liner. I know she'll hide it in the morning. It's what I would do.

"Turn around." Halli nods in approval, then guides me over to the full-length mirror on the back of my bedroom door.

We stand there side by side, looking almost like

exact replicas. I doubt my mother will notice the difference in my height and bulk. Not when she's groggy from being woken up in the middle of the night. But Halli's right—the hair would have been impossible to explain.

"I'll be back," I whisper. "Then I'll tell you everything I can."

I pad across the hall to my mother's bedroom. I quietly open the door.

The room smells like her. And there she is, a lump under the covers, a woman I haven't seen in far too long.

I ease onto the bed and scoot closer and closer until I'm just an inch or two away. "Mom?" I whisper.

"Mm?" She makes a kind of nasally, snuffling sound, then looks like she's fallen back asleep.

"I had a bad dream," I say.

"Oh, honey." She's still on the edge of dozing, but she instinctively loops her arm around me and pulls me in for a hug. "It's okay." Then she nudges me into flipping over the other way so she can pea pod me from behind. That's what she's called it since I was a little girl.

I don't need to talk to her. This is enough. To know she loves me and will take care of me, no matter what. To know I can come to her even when things are completely out of control, and just crawl into bed and let her protect me and tell me it will be all right.

My newly-cut hair brushes the tops of my shoulders. I wonder if my mom can smell the unfamiliar shampoo. I wonder if somewhere in the deep recesses of her dreaming mind she knows this girl she's hugging isn't really her daughter. Isn't really the same.

That's why I can't stay. I know it. The worst thing would be having her wake up and know in her heart I'm not me. What will her expression look like? Do I really want to face that?

Better to leave while I know I'm loved.

"Thanks, Mom," I whisper. I kiss her hand. Then I gently lift it off my arm so I can slide out from underneath.

I stand at the side of her bed for a few extra seconds. Just to remember what all of this feels like.

Then I retreat back through the door, back toward my own room, where I know there's a girl who's desperate for facts.

But first I get to have this moment for myself.

I bend at the waist, here in my hall, and press my hand over my mouth. And here in the privacy of the dark, I allow myself to grieve. Not long, just a few minutes, but I've needed this cry for a while. There's only so long you can keep going and going and thinking and thinking, and never take a moment to feel.

If this is my life, and I've lost it—

If this is my world, and I can only visit—

If I'm the one who has to tell Halli now that she'll need to make the best of it, keep lying and pretending, even if the life I lead is nothing like the one she wants—

Then yes, that's me. Yes, that's true. And standing here weeping in the dark isn't going to change that. The only thing that has any chance of making a difference is to keep going and going and thinking and thinking. I've known that all along.

I stand back up straight. Wipe off my wet eyes and cheeks. Time is ticking away.

I owe Halli an explanation.

45

I consider lying. Trying to make things sound better than they are.

But I wouldn't want her to lie to me.

"There's a lot going on," I start. "And that's an understatement."

"I think you saved my life," Halli says. "Am I right?"

I nod.

"Thank you," she says. "Obviously. But then this happened?" She gestures to me and then herself. "Is there a way to undo it?"

"That is the question." I make a decision right now not to tell her about Professor Whitfield's theory. She doesn't need to know there might not be a body for her to switch to.

"Listen," I say, "Daniel and I are working on this right now."

"Daniel?" she says with a smile. "How nice."

"Yeah." I smile back. But then I realize it's ridiculous to take a moment for that when I have a lot more important things to tell her.

"There's a professor at Oxford who's done all this himself."

"Really?" Halli asks. "He found a parallel universe?"

"And his parallel self—lots of them, actually. He and I are working on the science together right now—"

I guess I am lying after all, since Dr. Venn is out of the picture.

"—and we're going to figure out a way to fix things very, very soon."

"Good," Halli says. "No offense, but … good."

"I know you don't really like it here," I say.

"It's not bad. I really like the fact that no one knows me. That's a definite plus."

"Having had a taste of it," I say, "I know exactly what you mean. So anyway, what I need from you is to just keep doing what you're doing."

"I can't," Halli says. "It means I'd have to go to school as you tomorrow."

"You were going to do that anyway," I say.

"Not necessarily," she answers. "I've been developing backup plans."

"Well, please don't use any of them. Halli, really—

I'm going to solve this. You just need to have faith in me. And give me more time."

"When will you come back?" she asks. "Can't you just go to school yourself?"

"Maybe, but is that really how you want me to spend my time? Or would you rather I keep working with Dr. Venn and figure out a permanent solution?"

Halli pats me on the arm. "See you. Hurry now. Nice chatting with you, but ... go."

She smiles to let me know she's joking. But I know she really isn't.

"I'm on a timer," I tell her. "I have no idea what it sounds like. I'm going to stay until I hear it. This was an exploratory mission. I need to learn how to use it."

Halli leans back on my bed. "So what should we talk about? Daniel? No, Red! How is he? Is he alive? Please tell me he is."

"Alive and just as crazy as ever." I describe the fit Red threw when he saw me in the machine.

"That's how you're doing this?" Halli says. "Wow."

"Have you ever heard of Dr. Venn?" I ask. It just occurred to me she might. Dr. Venn is part of her world.

"I don't think so."

I decide I'd better tell her the truth about him. "He's ... really old. And he's sick. So it's just Daniel and me figuring out his machine on our own."

She doesn't seem concerned by that. And why would she? Halli has done risky things all her life.

I hear the edge of a sound in my mind. It's the xylophone tones again, and that makes me wonder when they went away. Have they been there this whole time, and I've just stopped hearing them?

Because the very next sound is a low-pitched ping. Followed by another one, then a higher-pitched tone, and I know it's calling for me.

"I have to go," I tell Halli. "But I'll come back. It's easy. I'll do it again soon."

I hug her quickly and then close my eyes. It seems like the thing to do.

Then I consciously choose to defocus. Let go of what I see and hear. Let go of the feeling of my bedspread against my leg. Stop living in a body that feels real.

As the pings continue, I'm back in black sky, with stars twinkling silver and gold. I am large again, weightless, made up of particles scattered in space, suspended on a blanket of black.

A voice speaks softly in my head. "Coming back now … feeling refreshed … awake and alive … coming back … and now you open your eyes."

I do.

I wait a moment, trapped inside the machine.

"Daniel?"

A moment more passes, then light floods in as Daniel pulls up the goggles. The earphones are next.

"Hi," I say, smiling widely.

"Hello," he answers quickly. "Please wait."

He continues pulling loose all the straps until I can finally climb down from the machine and into his arms.

He lifts me off my feet. He's so happy right now, it makes me laugh. Then he sets me down and laces his hands through my hair and I lift my lips to meet his.

I stop and jerk away.

"What's wrong?" Daniel asks.

I reach back to feel my hair. It's long again. Or long still. The scissors never touched it.

"It works," I say. "I bilocated. I stayed right here, didn't I?"

"The entire time," he confirms.

"Halli says hi."

Daniel smiles. "You found her."

"I did. And I got to see my mom."

A hint of a tear wants to sneak out of one eye, but I smudge it back in place.

"How do you feel?" Daniel asks.

I do a quick internal check. "Fine," I say, "except I'm *starving*." It's like I traveled all that way on foot. Every bit of my breakfast has been used up, and I'm probably starting in on last night's cookies.

"I could use a walk, too," I say. "Being trapped like that…"

"Let's go, then," Daniel says. "There are cafés everywhere. We'll feed you and you can tell me everything that happened."

Red is as happy as I am to be outside. He runs to his favorite tree to catch up on his marking, then bounces along beside us, stirring up drifts of fallen leaves.

As Daniel and I walk along, I describe the experience to him. He asks the right kinds of questions to keep me remembering more and more details.

"So you simply thought her name, and there you were."

"Yes, but it's not like I really focused hard," I say. "It's more like…" I tighten my hand into a fist for a second, then relax it back open again. "Holding it loosely. Thinking about her, but not making up any specific rules. I don't know, I'm not really making sense."

I thread my fingers through Daniel's and lean on him for a few steps. This is a perfect day: cold, dry, the sun staying out from behind the clouds. Red is done with his leaping and bounding for the moment, and walks closely enough at my side that I can reach down and pat his head whenever I want. A dog, a boyfriend, a beautiful day—Daniel's right: this life isn't bad. I could be happy here.

This probably isn't the right time to tell him I'm leaving.

46

The idea occurred to me in a flash just a few seconds ago. It was so obvious, I almost blurted it out to Daniel right away.

But I want to enjoy a little more time with him now, just like this. So for once I keep my new theory to myself.

We find a café and sit inside near one of the big windows and enjoy a mocha and a sandwich for me, tea and a sandwich for Daniel, and a bowl of water and some chunks of cheese for Red. Our server recognizes me and can't stop smiling. She even does a little curtsey when she brings us our order.

"Miss Markham," she says with shy enthusiasm, "I used to read all your field reports when I was in school.

I wanted to be just like you." She laughs uncomfortably. "But … as you can see, didn't quite get there."

I know that feeling. That feeling of not living up to Halli's example. I used to feel so inadequate next to her, too.

But I don't feel that way anymore. Maybe because I've stopped trying to be Halli, and just concentrated on being me—no matter whose body I happen to be wearing at the moment.

But since I can't exactly use that as an example, I go with something I think Halli might say. "I used to feel like I could never be like Ginny. She was so smart and brave and … well, you know."

The server nods. "Oh, yes. I wish I had a grandmother like that—everyone did. I used to pretend I was friends with both of you, and you used to take me with you on all your adventures together..." She claps her hand to her mouth. "I can't believe I just told you that."

"Why?" I say. "I think it's nice."

The server blushes deeply. "I'm sure you don't want to hear about me and my silly ideas. You have much more important things to do. I'm sorry to take up your time, Miss Markham. But … I just wanted to say we were all so sad for you when your grandmother passed. It was such a shock. I cried all day when I heard."

"Thank you." There it is again: that feeling that my feelings aren't entirely my own. Is there some thread of

Halli in me that's making me choke up right now? Or is it just that the more I've heard about Ginny, the more I feel like I know her?

"And I keep babbling!" the server says nervously. "I'm so sorry. I'll leave you two alone now. Please enjoy your lunch." She hurries away before I can say anything else.

I slouch back against my chair and blow out a breath.

Daniel leans forward and whispers, "Nicely done, Miss Markham."

"I don't know how she used to do this," I confess.

"The same way you just did."

"Come on, you saw that. I never know what to say to these people."

"You seem to be doing fine," Daniel says. "You're kind. Isn't that what anyone wants?"

He holds his palm out on top of the table and I slip my hand into his. It feels so natural and nice. Here we are, the two of us enjoying a nice quiet date on a lovely afternoon—

So I guess it's time to ruin it.

"Daniel?"

"Hm?"

"I've been thinking."

He can probably tell from the look on my face that what I'm thinking isn't necessarily romantic. He lets go of my hand and scoots his chair closer so we can have a more private conversation.

"I want to go back," I tell him.

"Back where? To Dr. Venn's office?"

"No, back further in time. I think I might have figured out how to change all this."

47

It's not a conversation I want to have in a small café where anyone might overhear. We quickly finish our lunch and head on back across campus.

"I just have to climb further down the root," I say. "Past the avalanche. Even past that Sunday when the new universe split off."

"To where, then?" Daniel asks.

"Back to when Halli was about to make her decision to stay in the Alps those extra days and keep on hiking with Karl. If I can go back to that point in time and warn her not to do it, then maybe none of this will have happened."

Daniel is quiet while he thinks that over. "You're not concerned you'd be interfering with her free will?"

"No. Because I wouldn't be inside her head trying to

take over, I'd be outside, in my own body, talking to her like we are right now. She can ignore me or take my advice—that's completely up to her."

"So let's follow that through," Daniel says. "If you tell Halli she's going to be in danger a few days hence, and she decides to hike out with Sarah and Martin and me on Sunday, then that means everything goes on as it was. Halli remains Halli 1, you remain Audie 1, and you still come visit her using your same original methods."

"Right," I say. "That's it."

"But how will you ensure you can find her at that precise moment?"

"I'll ask," I say. "I'll make it my focus. The same way I did when I just thought of her name and showed up in my bedroom. It's so much easier using Dr. Venn's machine than it was the way Olga and Christine showed me. I don't know what it is—the motion, the complete darkness, I'm not sure."

"Or it might be the tones," Daniel points out. "You said you could feel the vibration on your brain."

I stop short and grip his arm. "Oh my gosh. That's it. That's what happened to Dr. Sands. I know why he died."

I wonder if even Dr. Venn knows. I only know about it because of a story Professor Whitfield told me. I quickly repeat it to Daniel.

"Professor Whitfield developed some kind of sound

system using tonal oscillations. He said it helped the left and right lobes of the brain communicate with each other. It also allowed people to have OBEs—out of body experiences. There's a professor at Columbia who tried it, this man named Herbert Hawkins, and it freaked him out so much it completely ended his friendship with Professor Whitfield."

"How did the process work?" Daniel asks.

"Professor Whitfield would monitor the person closely while the tonal vibrations let their consciousness leave their bodies. He'd let them do it for about an hour or so, just like Dr. Venn's machine, and then he'd call them back somehow and they'd re-enter their bodies and return to normal."

"What happened to their bodies while they were gone?" Daniel asks.

"I don't really know. I mean, they were alive. They were breathing and everything. But it sounded like their bodies were just in some sort of suspended, dormant mode while their minds went off and explored other dimensions."

"And how does that relate to Dr. Sands?" Daniel asks.

"Dr. Venn said he went somewhere and forgot how to come back. What if Dr. Sands abandoned his body? How long could it keep living if his consciousness didn't come back to it? I mean, I don't know, Daniel. What happens if you just get up and leave your body like it's a pair of clothes you don't want anymore? They're still there, lying in a heap—"

"Much the way you used to vanish in front of me," Daniel points out.

"Yeah, but it's because I—the me inside here—was always with my body, and I needed to get it back to where we belonged."

I do my temple-pressing thing, but it's not really helping. This is all so huge for me right now, it feels like it might be beyond my mental capacity to keep it all straight and organized in my head. It's why I'm so glad I have Daniel to talk to about it. He's like an external hard drive for me.

"So let's return to Dr. Venn's models," Daniel says, proving his worth in organization and logic. "He told you he and the other Edgar Venn had discovered three ways of observing, and that now he knew you had discovered a fourth."

"Right," I say. "So their first way was bilocation. That's what I did this morning. My body stayed in the machine—you can verify that."

"I can. I saw you and I monitored your vitals."

"Okay, good. So while I stayed there, the machine let me create a duplicate of myself to travel to Halli. That's method one.

"Method two," I continue, "is what I did last time I was Halli, and what ended so badly for me and for the other Edgar Venn. We inserted our consciousness into someone else's minds, and then got treated like the invaders we were. Pain, agony, death. So we'll be staying away from that one."

"Then there's the third method," Daniel says. "The one in which they could watch a scene taking place and even convey suggestions to the versions of themselves they were visiting, but it was all accomplished at the mental level. The two Dr. Venns never actually appeared in the flesh."

"Right," I say. "And that's the one that sounds like what Professor Whitfield described. You send your consciousness someplace else, but your body stays behind. And you're not bilocating, because you don't create a duplicate body. You just hang around and watch, but no one can see you."

"Did your Professor Whitfield say anything about being able to communicate with anyone involved?"

"Sort of. He said Professor Hawkins had some contact with an 'entity'—I have no idea what it was, and Professor Whitfield wouldn't tell me. But he said Hawkins and the entity seemed to recognize each other and maybe even had some history together. The two of them had a pretty long conversation and Professor Hawkins ended up crying afterwards. I don't really understand what went on. Maybe it's the same as what the two Edgars did, maybe it's not."

"So which of those do you intend to use?" Daniel asks me. "To find Halli in the Alps?"

"Bilocation. Definitely. I want to talk to her face to face."

"What will you tell her?"

"The truth," I say. "I'm going to tell her everything that's gone on. She's an adventurer—she'll love to hear about it. But then she's going to have to make the right choice."

"Do you believe she will?" Daniel asks.

"I'm positive. She isn't crazy. She wants to live just as much as I do. And I'm very sure she wants to keep living as Halli Markham, not as Audie Masters."

I hug Daniel hard. Then crouch down and pet Red in such a vigorous way he barks at me and lets his tongue hang out. He can tell I'm happy. Maybe happier than I've been here so far. I feel light-hearted. So close to freedom. And itching to get back in the machine.

But there's still one thing I need to take care of.

I wrap my arms around Daniel again and look up into his eyes. "You know what this means, don't you?"

He holds me close, just the way I want him to. "Ideally," he says, "it means none of this takes place. But it also means we continue on the way we were. And that's a comforting thought."

It's a weird thing to feel sad about leaving your boyfriend in one life just so you can go back to dating him in another one. But he's not the only person I need to get back to. I'm happy I won't have to give him up just so I can be with my mom again.

When we get back to Dr. Venn's office, I can barely wait to climb back into the machine. This time it doesn't feel claustrophobic at all. I feel like I'm getting into a rocket ship, built just for me, and as soon as all systems are in place, I can take off and travel the universe.

"One hour again?" Daniel asks.

I think about that. "Let's make it two. In case anything goes wrong, and I need more time, I don't want to have to come back here and then start all over again."

It's clear from his expression that Daniel doesn't like the sound of that. "Two hours is an awfully long time. You don't know what it was like waiting for you during only one hour."

"If this works," I remind him, "you won't even remember it. It will be Thursday afternoon, and I'll already be in town along with Halli to come to your dad's birthday party tomorrow. I'll make sure that I come."

Daniel shakes his head. "I'm glad you're able to keep track of all this."

"I've had a little more practice than you have."

Before he straps me back in, we take a moment to embrace for what might be the last time in this lifetime. It's a little sad for me, but it's also what I want. I need to be Audie again. Inside and out. And Halli deserves to have her life back, too.

"Okay," I tell him. "Let's go."

He fastens the straps, adjusts my earphones, and prepares to lower the goggles over my eyes.

"See you," I say.

"See you."

Then I'm in the dark. A minute or so later I feel the gentle sway of the machine. The pinging starts. Then the soft mallets against my brain.

I defocus. I am stars and space. But there's no time to linger here. I have work to do.

I dive down into the soil. Take hold of the Mother Root. And focus on a specific moment.

"Take me to the original Halli before the decision that will cause her death."

The dark and the stars fade away as a new scene comes into view.

I'm not in the mountains. There is no snow.

Instead, sights and smells and sounds I'm not expecting. And don't recognize.

I don't feel safe right now. I don't know where I am.

So I purposely stay hidden. Stay an observer. Don't let my duplicate body take form.

There's a girl standing in a kitchen. She is barefoot and brown skinned and young—maybe around nine or ten. She has a knife in her hand.

She slices open a cloth sack that looks like it's filled with a grainy kind of flour. She scoops some of it out into a bowl. Then she mixes in water and what looks like milk and some spices.

She pours the batter onto a heated griddle. Cooks it up into four flat pancakes. Then she carries them out on a plate into another room.

There's a table in there, low to the ground, and people are sitting on pillows all around it. They're wearing colorful clothing in reds and greens and purples, made of soft gauzy fabrics with sashes draped diagonally across the women's torsos.

There are six people at the table: a woman and a man and two children, all of them with dark features and dark hair. They look like they might be from India.

No, they *are* in India, I realize. As are the other two guests at the table: Halli and Ginny Markham. And from the look of Halli, not that long ago. Maybe a year.

Halli takes two pancakes off the plate and gives them to Ginny. Then she takes the other two for herself. She says something to the girl in a language I don't understand. Then Halli and Ginny dig in.

I'm watching, but I don't believe it.

I think I'm about to see how Ginny Markham died.

48

I don't want to watch this. It takes me a moment to remember that I don't have to—I'm in charge.

So I change my focus.

"Forward," I think. "Twenty-four hours. Show me Halli."

I want to know how she's coping. I want to comfort her, if I can. Speak some words of hope in her ear. Tell her she'll be happy again. Tell her … something. I don't even know. I just know that she needs a friend right at this moment, and I'm here, and I want to help her get through this.

I'm in a bedroom. There's a mattress on the floor. Colorful wall hangings. Pretty flowers in vases.

People gathered around the bed. Sobbing. A shape

on the bed—a body—completely covered in a white sheet.

Ginny is inconsolable.

Because it's Halli who is dead.

"*NO*," I tell myself, jerking back from the scene. I can't watch this. I don't want to know.

But there's a part of me, a voice inside, asking, *"What did you expect?"*

Not this! But I must have. Didn't I ask to see the original Halli before her death? *This* is the original Halli—not the girl I met. I don't know when my Halli came to life, but it was obviously some time after this.

My head is spinning.

Meanwhile I'm deep inside the soil, hanging on to a thick white root, wondering where I should go and what I should do.

"Forward," I say. "Later."

I don't have a particular time or destination in mind, but I know I want to get away from India. Get away from the what I'm sure will be the very sad, drawn out, and very public mourning for world-renowned and much beloved teenage adventurer Halli Markham. Be someplace quiet and private where I can process what has happened to my friend.

And find out what's happened to her grandmother.

The new location takes shape. I know this place. I've been here several times before.

I recognize the celery green couch. The lavender chair. The walls completely covered in maps.

The house is empty. But there are lights on and I can smell coffee. Outside the big front windows I can see sunlight sparkling on dew. It's morning here in Colorado, in the house Halli used to share with her grandmother.

I hear a door open. I move into the kitchen where I can watch Ginny come from the separate house that she turned into a greenhouse. She's carrying a basket filled with fruit she just plucked from the trees and vines growing in there.

She doesn't see me. I'm still just a thought in the air.

I hesitate. I'm not sure I should do this. Is it selfish to want to talk to her? To find out what happened? And yes, I'll admit it, to finally meet this wonderful woman I've heard so much about?

What will she think if her granddaughter simply materializes in front of her? Will she have a heart attack? Will I kill her?

No, Ginny is strong. Even in grief or in shock, she'll be strong. And I have to know how she did it. How she survived this time, when the Halli I know is the one who lived.

I make a body. I gather my courage and walk into the kitchen. Ginny is standing at the sink washing off strawberries. She has her back to me.

I clear my throat. "Hello, Ginny."

She whips around and stares at me, wide-eyed and amazed.

And then I know in an instant I've made a terrible mistake.

49

The cry that erupts from her lips is like an animal in horrible pain. She grips the edge of the sink as she collapses to her knees. She's on all fours on the floor, her body shaking with sobs as she tries to gasp out Halli's name. "Hal … Hal …" She doesn't have enough breath. She's sobbing and shaking, and I don't know what I should do, but I know I have to do something.

I rush over to her and grasp the sides of her arms and start helping her to her feet. She hugs me so hard the breath is surprised out of my lungs. She clings to me like a drowning woman desperate to save her life. There's no doubt that these are the arms of a woman who once rowed across an ocean.

"Oh, Halli," she cries. "My child." She releases her

hold enough to lean back and look at me. She's so happy it nearly breaks my heart. She gazes at me with the kind of fierce love I always knew she must feel for her granddaughter.

It's time for me to tell her the truth.

"I'm not Halli. I'm sorry. My name is Audie. I'm from another universe. But Halli is alive. I know her. She loves you. She misses you."

Ginny bursts into fresh sobs. I don't blame her. It's a lot to take in all at once. I help her to a chair and sit in the one next to her and let her keep holding my hand. She covers her mouth with the other one and gazes at me with eyes still pouring out tears. "Please," she says shakily, "please. Please tell me it's true. Tell me my Halli's alive."

"It's true," I say. "I promise." And now I'm crying, too. It's impossible to watch this strong woman crumble without crumbling right along with her.

"Oh, sweetheart," she says. "Oh, child." She runs her hand over my long thick hair. "You look exactly like her. I never thought I'd see her again. This is the most wonderful thing you've done."

She stands up and reaches for my arm. "Come into the living room. I need to sit somewhere comfortable. You have to tell me everything."

She keeps hold of my arm as the two of us move into the next room. She's not holding me because she's frail, it's because I know she doesn't want to let go. She sits on the soft green couch and I consider taking the chair, but I know she needs me nearer. I sit down beside her and she covers us both with the white blanket folded nearby.

"You're shaking," she says.

"I know. I didn't really know what to expect. I probably should have done this differently."

Ginny laughs in a wet, phlegmy way. "How, exactly? It was going to be a shock no matter what."

But now that that initial shock is over, I'm starting to see the strong woman come back.

"Tell me who you are," she says. "Tell me how this happened. I need to know about Halli. I need to know she's all right." She tucks her legs up onto the couch and readjusts the blanket over both of us. Then she gives me her full attention. She's obviously settled in for a long, complicated chat.

Unfortunately, I don't have that kind of time.

I don't know how much of my two hours is left. Now I wish I'd asked Daniel to set it for five.

I'm going to have to go straight to the tough stuff.

"I met Halli in a universe where you're the one who died."

A strange look of happiness seems to wash over Ginny's features. Her worn, weathered face relaxes into a smile.

"Good," she says with a tremendous sigh of relief. "Then it worked."

"Have you ever had a vision?" Ginny asks me.

"I'm … not sure what you mean."

"A glimpse of the future. Of the way something might be."

I consider telling her about my experience with remote sensing. About how I saw Halli as she was about to die. But it's too long to explain. I go with a simple, "Yes."

"Then you must also know that nothing is permanent," Ginny says. "You can see what *might* happen, but sometimes you still have the chance to change it."

I've never thought of my remote sensing as a *vision,* but I definitely understand what Ginny is describing. I changed Halli's future—and mine.

"I saw her," Ginny says. "Laid out in a bedroom

where we were staying in India. She was dead. She'd eaten something contaminated. It killed her within just a few hours."

"But what about you?" I ask. "Didn't you eat it, too?"

Ginny gives me a curious look. "How do you know about that?"

"I … may have seen it. The pancakes."

"They aren't called that," Ginny says, "but yes, that's what they look like. The flour was contaminated. Halli and I were the only ones who ate it. My friend Bija threw it out the moment she realized we were sick."

"So what happened?" I ask.

"After we ate," Ginny says, "I hiked down to a quiet stretch of river where I always liked to go. Halli was going to join me later. I usually spent a few hours there in meditation every morning, but this time I started feeling sick almost right away. I began vomiting uncontrollably. My body was pouring off sweat. My gut felt like someone was tearing it open from the inside. I knew I'd eaten something deadly. And my immediate thought was that Halli had, too.

"I tried to get up, to go to her, but I didn't have the strength. I just lay there convulsing, while my mind took the journey for me.

"That's when I saw her," Ginny says. "My wonderful girl, dead. I couldn't help her. I couldn't stop it. There was nothing I could do."

Ginny pauses for a moment. The memory is obviously still painful.

"But you did help her," I say. "The Halli I know survived."

"I never had any way of knowing that," Ginny answers. "Until today." She smiles. "So maybe you can understand my reaction."

The pieces don't fit yet. I'm not hearing the whole story. And my time is ticking away.

"How did you save her?" I ask. "You obviously figured out what you could do."

Ginny shifts her weight. Sits up straighter. Looks more energized all of the sudden.

"Have you ever seen a mystic?"

"A mystic? No. I'm … not even sure I know what that is.

"There are yogis in India—very advanced yogis," Ginny says, "who can manipulate matter. Send their bodies to other places. Heal others through touch. And even heal people from a distance without ever touching them at all."

I know about the body-sending part—I'm doing it right now with bilocation. But I don't want to take the time to discuss that. I want to hear about the rest.

"I studied with one of them," Ginny says. "I watched her save a man's life. He'd been lying in bed for over a week with an infection spreading throughout his body.

One of his legs was already black from it. The doctor said he wouldn't last another night."

"So what did she do?" I ask. "How did she save him?"

"She sat beside him in deep meditation. She never even laid a hand on him. But I sat there in that same room with them, and over the course of about an hour watched all the blackness fade out of his leg. Then the rest of his skin returned to its regular healthy color. Soon enough, he opened his eyes for the first time in three days. When we came back the next morning, he was up and eating rice and drinking his tea."

"Wow."

"But what was really interesting," Ginny tells me, "was what my teacher did when she was done. She flicked her hands like she was getting rid of something disgusting off the tips of her fingers. She said the infection was like a poison. She'd drawn it all out, but now she had to get rid of it so it wouldn't hurt her."

"Is that what you did?" I ask. "You drew the poison out from Halli?"

"I didn't know how," Ginny says. "I'd only watched that one time—I'd never done it myself. I tried to imagine pulling it out of her, draining it off, but I couldn't do it for very long. I was getting sicker every minute. I hoped it was because Halli's poison was coming over to me. I could try to get rid of it later. But in the end … it didn't work. People found me passed out by the river. By the time they carried me home, my girl was dead."

"Not in the other universe," I say. "You died, Halli lived."

"How is she?" Ginny asks. "Tell me everything you can."

"I might have to leave soon," I say. "I'm in a kind of machine right now, and when it makes a sound I'll hear it and I'll have to go back. But I'll tell you everything I can until then."

Ginny settles back against the cushions again, anxious to hear whatever I might say.

But I already know one thing I won't be telling her: that she's given me a very special gift just now. A gift I can't wait to share with Halli.

Because for the past year, Halli has believed that it was her grandmother who poisoned her. That Ginny knew she was going to die, and instead of warning Halli and telling her goodbye, or even leaving her any kind of note, instead Ginny put something in Halli's food so she'd be too sick to follow and see Ginny die that day.

And what's worse about that—what's haunted Halli this whole time—is that Ginny taught her all kinds of first aid. Halli thinks she could have saved Ginny, if only she'd been given the chance.

But now I know that's not true. Both Ginny and Halli were headed for death, one way or the other. And

Ginny did what she always did: she tried to protect her granddaughter.

I hope that will finally ease Halli's mind. And I need to be able to offer her something. Because I know very well that even though she'll be ecstatic to find out that Ginny is still alive somewhere, she's going to be devastated that she wasn't the one to see her.

This might be her only consolation.

"Tell me first," Ginny says. "Is she happy?"

Apparently Ginny likes to start with the tough stuff, too.

"She's … getting there," I say. "She really misses you. I'm not going to lie."

Ginny's eyes well up. She brushes away an escaping tear and gives me a stoic nod.

"Then I have a favor to ask," she says.

"Okay."

"I need you to bring her here."

51

This time when I emerge from the machine, my legs feel wobbly and useless. Daniel releases all the straps, and then he isn't so much hugging me this time as he is holding me up.

"What's wrong?" he asks. "What's happened?"

"Just help me sit down for a second."

I sink to the floor. I don't really feel like taking the long walk to the next room. I feel weak and starving and used up. I try not to let Daniel see me shake, but I'm not doing a very good job.

"You're freezing," he says. He runs back into Dr. Venn's office and brings me back his coat and a blanket he found somewhere. He also brings a big warm dog, and Red does his job of sitting as close to me as possible and laying his head on my lap and sharing some of his heat.

"Audie, look at me. Let me see your eyes."

I do my best to focus.

"Come out here where it's warm," Daniel says. "Let me help you."

It feels like a supreme effort, but I manage to get to my feet and let him lead me back into the office and into a chair. He bundles me up in whatever extra coats and sweaters he finds hanging from a rack in the corner.

"What do you need right now?" he asks me.

"Food," I say. "Something hot. Lots of it."

Somewhere during all that fumbling with coats, he already pulled out Jake's card. He presses it in the center and orders soup, sandwiches, and tea.

My mind feels very mushy. I wish it would solidify again so I could act normally and Daniel won't have to keep looking so freaked out.

"I'm fine," I tell him. "I'll explain it all in a minute. I just need some food first."

He pulls up the other chair close to mine, and sits there massaging my hands the way we've both watched Madeline doing for Dr. Venn. It's a weird solution to what's obviously going on much higher, up in my brain, but I have to admit it feels very soothing, and it's also helping to keep me awake. If not for the constant sensation, it would be really easy to fall asleep.

After a while there's a knock on the door and Daniel jumps up to get it. Red growls as soon as he gets a whiff of Jake, and it gives Daniel a great excuse for slipping out and closing the door behind him. I'm glad Jake can't see me like this. I don't want to have to answer any extra questions.

My hand shakes as I reach for a sandwich, but I don't care because I know this is what I need. I have no idea why traveling with my mind would make my body so ravenously hungry. It's one of the questions I want to ask Dr. Venn. Along with about a hundred other ones. As soon as I'm strong enough to go.

Daniel opens the soup container and helps me eat some of it so I don't just spill it all. After about five minutes of steady eating and drinking, I'm starting to feel more normal—at least normal enough to talk. Poor Daniel has waited long enough.

"I met Ginny."

The look of shock on Daniel's face actually makes me laugh. I would have been disappointed with anything less.

And thanks to that laugh, I now find I can smile. I didn't realize how frozen my face must have seemed the whole time I've been sitting here. I must have looked like a statue.

"I saw Halli die in India, and Ginny's the one who lived."

"And you spoke to her?"

"For about the last hour, I think."

Daniel takes that in. Then rather than asking me more about Ginny, he asks about me. "Why are you so affected this time?"

"I don't know. Maybe because I went further? What did the monitors show?"

"Nothing out of the ordinary," Daniel says. "The same sort of readings as last time."

I pause to eat some more sandwich and spoon in more of the soup.

"How are you feeling now?" Daniel asks.

"Much better. Thank you." I reach for his hand.

"Warmer, too," he says. "Good. Audie, I don't think you should do it again."

"No, I won't today. I want to go see Dr. Venn—"

"I mean ever."

"Ever?"

"There's too much risk," Daniel says. "It's not worth it."

"But I have to try again," I say. "I went back to the wrong place. I still have to find Halli in the Alps."

"Why? She has a life now, you have a life—why risk losing what you have?"

Before I can argue with him, he adds, "Look at you. You're not well. You were as white as a corpse when I found you. People have died in that machine—you know it. Please. I don't want to lose you."

I lay my hand gently on his cheek and give him a

tender kiss. He deserves it. I love him. He's the best boyfriend I could ever imagine having.

And I'm going to have to tell him no.

"Let's go talk to Dr. Venn," I say. "We'll describe what happened. He'll know what to do."

"And if he doesn't?" Daniel says. "Or he's too ill to see us? How far will you go when you know it might mean your life?"

A reasonable question. One I can't blame him for asking.

"I don't know," I tell him honestly. "But today I saw things I never would have thought were possible. Do you realize I went to a universe where Halli isn't even alive anymore? That means I don't even need that connection. And if I can go there, don't you think that means I can find a universe I've already spent time in, and convince Halli to save her own life?"

"I don't care about Halli," Daniel says. "I only care about you. I can't let you sacrifice yourself for her."

"It's not just for her, it's for me. Daniel, I need to go home."

"Let *this* be your home," he says. "At least you'd be safe."

"I wasn't safe last time," I remind him. "Do you really think I can live out a nice, long life inside some other person's body?"

"Why not?" Daniel answers defiantly. "What do you think Edgar Venn has been doing?"

52

"I was going to wait until you recovered," Daniel says.

"I'm recovered." Although right now I feel as light-headed as I did when I first stumbled out of the machine. "What do you mean Edgar Venn has been doing that?"

"My sister notices more than the rest of us. She knew just from watching the films. The Edgar Venn who is living here now is not the same Dr. Venn who came here originally with the rest of the Pact members in 1946."

"How do you know?"

"Because a man who has been living with his family all their lives doesn't need to keep notes to remember the history they've had together."

Daniel reaches across Dr. Venn's desk to a stack of file folders there. "I found these in a locked drawer. He must have forgotten he left the key in it."

"Daniel! I don't think we should be snooping—"

"I was looking for information about the machine," he says. "Besides, it's better that you and I should find these than his granddaughter or someone else from his family. They might wonder why he's kept files describing their personality traits and the nicknames he has for all of them, and what memories he should know of the various experiences they've had together."

He hands me one of the files. It's marked *Elinor* on the tab. While I start scanning through some of the notes, Daniel brings up a page on his tablet.

"Here is Dr. Venn's biography. Son, George. Daughter, Elinor. Various grandchildren and great-grandchildren."

Madeline is on the list. As are nine other names. And as Daniel shows me, each one of them has their own file.

I open the one for Madeline and read the notes: *Nurse. Married to Tom. Children Edgar, Eloise, Edith.* There's a long list of other kinds of information, including *Good cook. Good listener. Hates classical music.*

I glance through some of the other files: Rachel, Richard, and Marnie—other grandchildren. Their children with various birthdates in the past five to twenty-five years. There are fewer notes on the youngest members of the family. Much thicker files for the oldest, especially Dr. Venn's son and daughter.

I look up at Daniel. "What do you think is going on?"

"I think at some point the two Edgar Venns switched lives. Or perhaps he wasn't exactly honest with us when he claimed it was the other Edgar Venn who died. It could have been the one here, and the Edgar from your universe took his place."

My mind is reeling. Daniel is forty steps ahead of me right now. I'm racing to catch up.

"I want to go talk to him," I say.

"He might be too ill," Daniel says. "Or he might be reluctant to tell the truth."

"Or maybe he left the key in that drawer on purpose," I say. "And he's tired of being the only one who knows his secret."

53

It's a strange sensation, being back in this hospital. Passing nurses and doctors I'm almost sure I've seen before.

There are two in particular I'd love to see again: Bertrise, the wonderful nurse who was always so kind to me, and Dr. Rios, who was always honest with me about what was happening with my body, and who let me see my friends even though Halli's parents and Jake tried to keep them away.

But what would I say, even if I saw either of them? *"Hi, you won't remember, but I was in here last week, and I just wanted you to know I appreciate everything you did taking care of me. Even if it didn't work in the end.*

"But look—I'm back. I'm not dead. So in case you were feeling bad about that..."

Daniel pauses in front of the room we've been told is Dr. Venn's.

"Ready?" he asks.

I nod.

I feel nervous all of the sudden. Not about the questions I need to ask, but because I'm afraid what I'll see behind this door. Has Dr. Venn gotten better since this morning, or worse?

Only one way to find out.

His eyes are closed when we come in. His skin is very, very pale. There's an oxygen mask over his nose and mouth, and I can hear puffs of air being rhythmically pumped into him like exaggerated breaths.

There's an old woman sitting in the chair beside his bed, holding his hand. I wonder if it's his wife. She smiles at us, but then startles at the sudden movement of Red leaping onto the bed. He makes himself comfortable in a space at Dr. Venn's feet. I hurry to grab him off.

"Red! I'm so sorry—"

"No, leave him," the woman says in a soft, slightly hoarse British accent. "There's nothing my father would like better."

Not his wife, his daughter. This must be Elinor.

"Hi, I'm Halli Markham. This is Daniel Everett. We're..." What should I say? *Friends of your father's? Students?*

But I don't need to worry. "Yes, I know who you are," Elinor answers.

"We're sorry to bother you," I say. "It's just … we were with your father this morning. We wanted to make sure he's all right."

I'm prepared for her to be angry, to scold me the way Madeline did. But instead Elinor says, "He's very weak, I'm afraid. My father forgets his age. But I'm not surprised he escaped his sick bed this morning. He's been very eager to speak to you. I doubt any illness could keep him away."

A nurse comes in. Not just any nurse—Madeline.

"You two," she says as soon as she sees us. "Out."

"No, dear," Elinor says, "they can stay."

"Mum, these two are the reason Granddad is here right now. I warned them not to exhaust him, but obviously they didn't listen—"

"I'm sorry," I say. "We did listen. We always tried to stop whenever he was tired—"

Elinor holds up her hand. "Both of you, that will do. Maddy, your grandfather specifically asked me to welcome them if they came to visit. I intend to honor his wish. We'll be very careful—I give you my word. But I know he would like to see them."

Madeline doesn't look the least bit happy about that. She ignores all three of us for a few minutes while she fusses with Dr. Venn's oxygen and monitors and takes his pulse. Finally she looks at her mother.

"Please don't kill my grandfather."

"I have no intention of that," Elinor says.

Madeline turns to Daniel and me. "My mother is old and frail as well."

"I'm very well today, thank you," Elinor protests.

But Madeline is still looking at Daniel and me. "I warn you, you hold two of my family members in your hands right now. Both of them are very dear to me. I'll be checking on them frequently. And mind your dog. If he jostles any of the equipment loose—"

"Maddy, come now." Elinor rises slowly from her chair and steadies herself against Madeline's arm. Then she politely escorts her daughter from the room, whispering something to her along the way. Once Madeline is gone, Elinor holds her hand out toward Daniel for a steadying arm back.

He helps her to her chair. Then she points to the other chairs stacked in a corner. "Please, sit down. I need to speak with both of you."

Daniel and I draw our chairs close to her so we can keep our voices low and not wake up Dr. Venn.

"Audie," Elinor says, "it's all right. I know who you are. My father has told me everything."

"Oh." I glance over at Daniel. He's as surprised as I am.

"But I'm the only one who knows," Elinor says, "and I'm certain he would like it to remain that way. So we'll need to take precautions."

"Of course." Although I'm not sure what precautions she means.

"When I first visited him here this morning, he asked me to give you a message. He wasn't certain you would come, but he hoped it."

"Of course we'd come," Daniel says. "We were worried."

Elinor smiles. "Thank you. One's parents obviously can't live forever, but I've always hoped to have as much time with him as possible." She reaches over to cup Dr. Venn's hand in both of her own. "He's a dear man, and I feel I've barely gotten to know him. You know who I am, don't you?"

"Yes, you're Elinor," I say. "His daughter."

"The daughter he never had," she answers. "I was never born in his other life. He has only known me here."

54

"He came for my mother," Elinor says. "She was still alive then. The two of them were able to enjoy eight more years together."

"Wait," I say, "so you knew?"

"Not always," she says. "I noticed the change, of course. Their dispositions were very different. But one wouldn't assume the true reason behind it. I didn't know the extent of my father's experiments at the time. It's something I learned of only later."

"Did your mother know?" I ask.

"Eventually. She told me she confronted him. He confessed everything." Elinor smiles. "I believe they were very happy together after that."

This is all too much for me. Daniel can see it. He's fresher than I am—he hasn't already spent today traveling to other universes and back. So he quickly steps in.

"How long ago?" he asks.

"Eighteen years," Elinor says.

"After the conference we saw," Daniel tells me.

"Yes, the conference," Elinor confirms. "I'm afraid the pressures he felt at the time took their toll. My father became reckless. He felt he had much to prove. And then his colleague Dr. Sands died…"

I'm starting to catch up. "So is it like he said?" I ask. "About the other Dr. Venn? But it was really him—your father—that it happened to. He tried to take over someone else's mind, and that's … how he died?"

"In essence," Elinor says. "Yes, I believe that's true."

"How did you find out?" Daniel asks.

"From my mother. She deteriorated very rapidly toward the end. A few days before she died, she called me into her bedroom and told me everything."

"But you said you suspected," Daniel says.

Elinor smiles. "I loved my other father. Dearly. But this one…" She's still holding Dr. Venn's hand. She lifts it to her cheek. "He was different. Warmer. Kinder.

"I didn't blame my other father," she hurries to add. "He faced so many disappointments. He was treated very harshly by the scientific community and his colleagues. I think it left him very discouraged and angry. But we all loved him—my brother and I, our children, my mother—and we would have mourned him very deeply if we'd known he died."

"But you didn't know," Daniel says.

"No," Elinor says. "He came home that night just as he did every other night. And our lives went on. Now that I look back, of course the signs were obvious. My father was suddenly so much more light-hearted and loving. He spent a great deal more time with all of us than he ever had before. He seemed to want us all around as much as possible. He especially treasured my mother. Whenever they were together, he rarely let go of her hand."

I love the image of that. The idea that a man goes off to work one day and returns home in love with his wife.

"Was his own wife still alive?" Daniel asks.

"No," Elinor says. "That was the reason, you see. She had died several years before. He had been alone for a very long time."

"So he saw a way to be with her again," I say.

"And with children and grandchildren," Elinor answers. "He didn't have any of those in his other life."

"But … there was a son," I say.

"My brother George," Elinor says. "He died over there. In the Vietnam War. He was only twenty. He never married. He had no children."

"And you were never born there," Daniel says.

"No. My parents stopped at one. Well—those

parents," she corrects herself. "I never knew that mother."

"So he didn't have anything left over there," I say. "When your real father died, he decided to take his place."

"I don't know how much of a decision it was," Elinor says. "I believe it was more of an impulse. Once he knew my father was gone—"

"He jumped over," I say.

I think about that for a moment. About the mechanism that made it possible.

"So it's the same as what happened to Dr. Sands," I say. "He left his other body behind and never came back."

"I don't know," Elinor says. "I'm not sure if even he knows for certain what happened in that life. I asked him, but he's never been curious to see. He said he's too happy here."

"Do you think anyone else has ever suspected?" Daniel asks.

"I don't know," Elinor says. "I do know it's been very difficult for him at times to pretend to be other than he is. It's one of the reasons he retreated so quickly from the public eye. He was always afraid someone would suspect the truth. Although the truth is so inconceivable, I doubt there's any real danger. In any case, he's always been very, very careful."

I think about that first conversation we had, over

the comm in Daniel's kitchen. Dr. Venn was so harsh with us, so grouchy and rude. Was that really just an act to keep strangers from getting too close? Or was that his way of imitating the Dr. Venn people remember?

"Does anyone else in your family know?" I ask.

"No," Elinor says. "When I told him I knew, he begged me not to tell any of the others, and I've abided by that. But if he … well, after he's gone one day, I might tell my children. I think they'd be proud of the extraordinary work both their grandfathers have done. And I don't wish the secret to die with me.

"My father didn't want that, either," she tells me. "That's why he asked me to speak to you if you came here today."

"Me? Why?"

"He said he left you a key."

Daniel looks at me. "The drawer."

"Yes," Elinor says. "There are details in there. Drawings. Plans. He wants you to have them."

"But … shouldn't you?" I ask. "Or someone else? I only just met him a few days ago."

Elinor shifts her hand away from her father's, and reaches for mine instead.

"You and I both know why, Audie. He said you're the one to carry on his work. I trust his judgment implicitly. I think you should, too."

"I … I don't know what to say." And it's true: my

tongue feels thick and slow, and my brain can't come up with the right answer to such a generous offer from a stranger.

I'm still feeling tongue-tied when the door opens and Madeline returns.

"Everything all right here?"

"Yes, dear," her mother answers as she releases my hand. "Thank you."

Madeline stands there for a moment, surveying the scene. She seems disappointed that Daniel and I aren't doing anything wrong.

"All right," she says. "Call me if there's any change at all."

Dr. Venn coughs.

Madeline rushes over to him. "GRANDDAD, CAN YOU HEAR ME?"

Dr. Venn coughs again and nods.

"HOW ARE YOU FEELING?"

He pulls away his oxygen mask. "Lou—" He coughs hard. "Lousy."

"LET ME GET YOU A DRINK."

Madeline raises the back of Dr. Venn's bed so he can sit up, then she fills a cup of water. She offers it to him with a straw.

He sips thirstily. Then slumps back against his pillow.

He waves the cup away. "Thank you. Fine."

He finally looks over at me and smiles. I smile back. Then he pats his daughter's hand.

"Told you they would come."

"YES, FATHER, WE'VE BEEN ENJOYING A CHAT," Elinor shouts.

"Have you?" Just that amount of talking is too much for him. He strains hard into another coughing fit, and Madeline hurries to help him. She supports him until he's done, then slips the oxygen mask back over his face.

"Enough," she tells us sternly. "You too, Mum. Enough. He needs his rest."

Dr. Venn shakes his head.

"YES, GRANDDAD. THEY CAN COME BACK LATER."

Red has inched up the bed so he can lay his head across Dr. Venn's lap. Dr. Venn reaches down with a crooked hand and pets the dog on the head.

A tear slips out of his eye. Madeline uses the edge of her sleeve to wipe it away.

"OH, GRANDDAD," she says, her own eyes looking misty. "PLEASE. DON'T BE SO STUBBORN. I'M ONLY DOING WHAT'S BEST FOR YOU."

He holds up two fingers.

"NO."

But Dr. Venn thrusts the two fingers forward.

Madeline groans. But she gives in. "TWO

MINUTES. THAT'S ALL. THEN NO MORE VISITORS TODAY."

Dr. Venn nods. And as soon as Madeline leaves, he pulls off his oxygen mask again.

"You did it?" he asks me.

"Yes. I saw Halli—"

But I realize he can't hear me. And this isn't something I'm going to shout.

Daniel takes out his tablet. He presses some setting that allows me to dictate into it. My words then show up in large letters hovering in front of Dr. Venn.

"I went two places. I saw Halli the first time. Back in my old life. And then I tried to go someplace else. But I made a mistake."

Dr. Venn reads that, then shrugs at me instead of using his voice.

I explain in as few words as possible how I tried to find Halli in one life, but ended up seeing her in another. Then watching her die.

"But then it was strange," I say. "I'm hoping you can explain it to me. I went forward in that world, even after Halli died, and I saw Ginny living without her."

Dr. Venn's forehead creases as he reads. Then he looks at me.

"How could I do that?" I ask him. "I thought I could only go places where there's a parallel version of me. How could I find Ginny?"

Dr. Venn shakes his head. He traces his finger in the air. I study the motion, but I have no idea what it means.

"Thread," Dr. Venn rasps. "Start with … thread." Then he grabs his oxygen mask again and fumbles it over his mouth. He takes long, desperate breaths. I can hear the wetness in his chest.

"Out," Madeline orders from the doorway. "Out this instant. Mum, you can stay. They have to go."

Dr. Venn looks me in the eye and nods. I don't really know what he's just told me. But I nod back as if I got it. I don't want him to be upset.

Madeline rushes Daniel and Red and me out the door. The three of us stand in the hallway together without any clear direction of what to do next.

"Did you understand that?" I ask Daniel.

"About the thread?"

"Yeah."

"I'm not sure," he says.

And with people walking by, some of them glancing curiously at Halli Markham, I know this isn't the place to talk.

"What do you think we should do?" I ask.

"Examine the contents of that drawer," Daniel says.

"That's a good idea." I pull out Jake's card from my pocket and press it. "Let's go back right now."

"Now?" he says. "It's late. You've already had a long

day. And the way you looked when you came out of the machine that second time—"

"I know," I say, "but I'm fine now. And Daniel, face it: if there are things in there that we need to ask Dr. Venn about, we should probably do it tonight.

"He might not make it until the morning."

I t's dark outside, but the Oxford campus is lit everywhere with warm white and yellow lights. Wilkinson insists on giving me his huge flashlight, even though I don't need it.

Jake isn't happy.

"I'm sure this could wait until the morning," he says.

"I'm sure it can't," I answer. "We'll be about an hour. If you two want to go get dinner or something, help yourselves."

"You're sure I can't help you," Jake says. He takes a step too close, and Red lets him know to back off. Jake is probably tired of that by now, but Red never seems bored. He's decided that's his job and he does it.

"You could bring us back some food to eat in the car on the way home," I say. "That would be great."

We're halfway across the first courtyard and well out of earshot when Daniel says, "He looks at you, you know."

"Who, Jake?"

"All the time."

I laugh. "Daniel, he's not interested in me—unless you count wanting me to hire him. Which I have no intention of doing. Besides, your sister likes him. I'm hoping they'll hit it off tomorrow night at the party."

"She'll be disappointed," Daniel says. "Because he wants you."

A dark campus is full of all sorts of dark corners. I pull Daniel into one of them and spend a few moments reminding him he has nothing to worry about.

"Come on," I say once I've proven my point, "we have work to do." I hold his hand and lead him toward Dr. Venn's office.

The light comes on automatically as soon as we walk in. I look around for a box we can use, while Daniel begins pulling out files.

We decided we'd do it this way instead of trying to read everything while we're here. Better to take it home and be able to spread it out and look at it at our leisure. When Dr. Venn is ready to come back to work —*if* he is, which I hope—we'll just box it up and bring it back.

I empty out a crate that's filled with dusty text-books. I stack them neatly in a pile. Then I start loading the file folders Daniel has been pulling out of the drawer.

I glance at some of the tabs. Not just family members' names, but also initials that don't mean anything to me. I open one up. It holds ripped out pages from books. The first page has the title *Lunar Influence on Tidal Sequences*. Another page says *Westwind Enclosures and Small Conductivity*. Neither one of those sounds promising, but I close the folder and add it to the crate anyway.

"Anything else?" Daniel asks me.

My eyes stray to the door just beyond him. We closed it when we were finished this afternoon. But open or closed, I still know what's behind it, and I'm still curious. And tempted.

I glance at the clock on the wall. I do a quick calculation. Halli is at my school right now, if she hasn't already given up and quit.

"I'd like to look in on her," I tell Daniel. "Just for a few minutes."

"There's no setting for a few minutes," he says. "The shortest is an hour."

I bite the inside of my lip. It seems a shame to be here and not take advantage of the machine. I'm feeling perfectly fine again. I've recovered from whatever happened after the last session.

Thread. Start with thread.

"Oh," I say out loud, suddenly getting it. "Follow the thread."

"Meaning what?"

"Start from a known position and I can follow it as far forward as I want. Start with Halli, end up with Ginny. Start with Halli…"

End up with me.

"It's a loop," I realize.

Daniel looks at me curiously. "What's a loop?"

"Me to Halli back to me again. I could see if I make the loop."

Daniel sighs. "Audie, unfortunately I am not inside your head right now, so you're going to have to use more words. Please tell me what you're thinking."

I give him my full attention now. "I saw a past where Halli died. I saw a present where Ginny lives. I went there and talked to her. What if what Dr. Venn was saying was that I could have followed that thread even further? Out into Ginny's future?"

"All right, what if?"

"Then why can't I do the same thing with Halli right now? Go pick up the thread of her in the present, off at school pretending to be me, and follow it further ahead to see if I really do succeed at figuring out a way to switch us back?"

Daniel shifts forward in his chair. I can see from the look on his face that he understands what I'm saying.

"You'd see whether you are back in your own body some time in the future."

"Right," I say. "Then I'd follow the thread back, and see how I did it. Be my own future self whispering in my ear about how I can make it work."

"I can't believe these are the conversations we have," Daniel says. "They're mad."

"What's crazier is that we both understand what we're talking about."

The two of us smile at each other. I really love that guy.

I glance at the clock again. It's getting late, but it's worth it.

"One hour," I say.

"One hour," Daniel agrees. "Let's get you into the machine."

56

O*nly to watch*, I remind myself. Not to bilocate. Just watch.

Halli is sitting in class, bouncing her heel rapidly against the floor. She's already looked at the clock four times in the brief time I've been watching. She's tensed up like a horse about to bolt out of a starting gate.

I wish I could tell her I'm here.

How did Dr. Venn say they did it? Not invading another person's mind, but whispering into it somehow, making suggestions, giving nudges.

"Halli, it's Audie. I have things to tell you. Important things. Can you hear me? Scratch your nose if you do."

She doesn't. But she does tug at her earlobe. Is that the same, but just a miscommunication? I have no idea.

When the bell rings Halli is up and out of her chair and out the door in record time. She shoulders my backpack and takes off across the campus, running for home.

She's going to quit school again. I can feel it.

Follow the thread ...

As much as I love watching my body running like that with such strength and abandon, that's not what I'm here for. So I imagine the scene as a rope lying on the ground. I pick it up with both hands. I start pulling myself along it, slowly at first, then in long stretches, like I'm being carried in a rapid river and just need to grab onto the rope every now and then to make sure I stay in my lane and don't get lost.

Halli climbing up a mountainside. Snow on the ground. She hears something, looks back.

She kneels down and pats her thighs. "Come on, Moose, good boy!" A black Lab puppy bounds through the snow to catch up. Halli enfolds him in her arms and kisses the side of his face half a dozen times. The puppy pants happily and chews a few strands of her hair and licks Halli on the cheek. She lets him go and hikes on. "Come on!" The puppy stretches his little legs and gallops after her, ears flopping with every step. Halli is happy.

She's not me.

I turn around and pull myself back the way I came, surprised to find I'm not fighting any kind of current.

It's as easy to travel in this direction as forward. I just pull myself along the thread.

Halli and my mother, saying goodbye. They hug. My mother is crying. Halli smiles at her, but I can see tears on her cheeks, too. She wipes them away. "Don't, Mom. I'll call you tonight. I love you!" She hugs my mom one more time, picks up the handle of her rolling luggage, and heads toward the line at airport security.

My mom watches her for a few more moments, then turns away, still crying.

I look at the girl.

Me.

I'm pretty sure that's me.

It's so tempting to try to get inside her head. See if I'm right.

But I can't put myself through that again. I have a strong instinct for survival now. I won't ever invade another person's mind again.

But I have to know.

I watch her give her ID to the security person. Watch her choke up again for a moment when she turns back to look for my mom. Then she takes her ID and the ticket back, faces forward, and continues on her way.

She is happy. She is me.

I pull myself along this thread. Just a few strong pulls—I don't want to go too far.

I'm in Professor Whitfield's lab. He's here, along

with his lab assistant Albert and some other people I don't know. I'm pointing to a drawing on a sheet of paper. We're all excited about something. Professor Whitfield asks me a question that I can't hear, but then I clearly hear my answer: "It's a secondary power source. In case the first one goes down. You don't want the person to be stuck. You always want them to be able to hear the return command."

I look over my own shoulder at the drawing we're all studying. I recognize the machine right away. I've somehow brought the plans to Professor Whitfield. We're going to make our own.

I need to keep going backward. See how I made this future. See why Halli is still there, too, hiking with a puppy in the mountains, and where the two of us split off.

"Coming back now ... feeling refreshed..."

No!

"... awake and alive ... coming back ... and now you open your eyes."

I blink in the pitch black. "NO!" I shout as I struggle against the straps holding me in. Daniel pulls away the earphones and then the goggles. Light floods into my eyes.

"What's wrong?" Daniel asks. "What happened? Audie, are you all right?"

"Please, just get me out." As soon as my arms are free I hug him. I know I'm crying, and I'm not exactly sure why. Yes, I'm frustrated, yes, I'm angry the machine pulled me away too soon, before I could find my answer.

But there's something else, something deeper than that, something my body is reacting to even if my mind doesn't understand why.

"Tell me," Daniel says, still holding me tightly. "What happened? What did you see?"

"I can do it, but I don't know how. There's a way, but I couldn't see it. I was there, but Halli was, too, and I don't know why we'd both be there at the same time—"

But then, suddenly, I do.

"Only one of us is real," I say. "The other one is a bilocation."

And I know which one is which.

There's no reason for Halli to have to pretend. That has to be her, still in my body, hiking somewhere in the snow. If she were really back in her own world, she'd be with Red. Her hair would be long. She'd look stronger and more substantial and she wouldn't be me.

But the girl at the airport? Just a projection. Not real. Enough substance to hug her mother, to pull a suitcase, to appear in Professor Whitfield's laboratory later and talk to real human beings.

But she's just an illusion. And she'll never be able to stay.

The pain in my heart tells me I'm right. I press my hand there and let out a sob.

"It's me, Daniel. I'm the mirage. I'm never going home."

57

I'm silent on the ride back to London. I hold Daniel's hand and gaze out at the lights of the city and think about where I went wrong.

We went back to the hospital, but Dr. Venn was asleep and Madeline wouldn't let us wake him. I understand—I know she just wants to protect him—but right now my mind is reeling and I don't feel I have any of the answers I need.

How did I look?

I think back to the expression on my face in both the scenes I saw. I was sad to leave my mother, but I was also excited to get on the plane. I know that. I could see that.

And what about later, in Professor Whitfield's lab? I

was smiling. I know I felt smart. I felt like I was doing important work.

Is that so bad, as a future? Even if I'm just visiting for a maximum of five hours at a time?

When I came out of the machine, back into Dr. Venn's office, the first thing I did was look up at the clock. There was no way I'd been gone for a full hour. It felt like barely fifteen minutes.

But the numbers on the clock couldn't lie. And Daniel wouldn't, either.

I wanted to go back in right away. But I also knew I shouldn't. My body was screaming for food, as usual, and when Daniel said he thought I should wait until morning, let myself rest, I knew he was right. But it didn't mean I liked it.

Jake was waiting for us outside Dr. Venn's office. I nearly ripped the bags of food out of his hands. I started eating as we walked to the car. I gave Red his portion, too. And I felt surly and mean and didn't want to talk to a soul.

Even when Daniel reached for my hand a moment ago, I was tempted to snap at him, tell him to leave me alone, tell him I needed to think.

What's happening to me?

I give his hand a squeeze, then gently pull mine away. I use it to pet the big dog lying across my lap.

Maybe that hurts Daniel's feelings, but he doesn't say anything about it. I appreciate that. I hate people who keep bugging you when it's clear you need a moment to yourself. If they'd just wait, give you time, you could get back to normal much faster than if they kept pestering you with *"What's wrong? What's wrong?"*

But Daniel lets me have my silent brooding. I'm grateful.

I keep trying to piece together everything I saw. It makes sense that I'd tell Professor Whitfield how to make the machine. If I have one in my world, and another in this one, maybe Halli and I can both go back and forth. She can come here and be herself for a while every day, or at least every now and then, if she wants to.

But would she want to? What's here for her? Her dog, sure. But is there really anything else? How is being the famous Halli Markham in this world where too many people recognize her and are in her business any better than the life I caught a brief glimpse of, hiking in the mountains somewhere with a sweet little puppy?

Halli has no incentive to switch with me, even if I can ever figure it out. I might as well face it.

The life I can see her wanting is one with Ginny again. Maybe that's something she could do with the machine. I could tell her how to find that end of the thread and follow it forward to find her grandmother.

I pinch my fingers against my eyes. I don't know anything anymore.

"Headache?" Daniel whispers. I can hear the concern in his voice. I understand why.

"No." I pull my fingers away and give him a reassuring smile. "Just tired. My brain's on overload. It's been a long day."

I'm relieved when Wilkinson finally pulls up in front of Daniel's house. I could use some more food, something hot to drink, maybe even another bubble bath so I can keep thinking in peace.

Daniel retrieves the crate filled with files from out of the trunk and starts carrying it toward his house. Red and I are about to follow when Jake lowers his window and says, "Halli, can I talk to you for a minute?"

Great, now there's this guy.

"Sure. I guess. Just a minute." I walk with Daniel and Red up to the house, then ask Daniel to take the dog inside.

"I'm worried about you," Daniel says.

"Don't be," I tell him. "I'm fine. I just need some soup and some of Sarah's cookies. I'll be in in a minute." I clasp his hand for a second, then turn around and head back to the car. I gather Daniel's coat more tightly around me then bury my hands in the pockets. It's cold out tonight.

Wilkinson is still standing outside the car, holding open the door. Jake is in the backseat waiting. I hesitate for a second, then slide in.

Jake gets right to the point. "I'm leaving in the morning."

"Oh." I wasn't expecting that. "But I thought … okay. If you have to." I was going to say something about him going to the party, but really, does that matter? People should do what they want. I don't really care. I have too many other things to think about.

Still, I'm curious. "Why?"

"Your father's going back," Jake says. "I thought I'd catch a free ride before I quit."

"Quit? Why would you do that?"

"Because this didn't work out the way I wanted it to. I think it's time to move on."

"Jake, if it's because of me—"

"It is because of you, but probably not what you think. I was serious about wanting to work for you, Halli. I think we'd make a great team. But it's pretty clear you don't want that, and the truth is, I'm tired of lying to you."

I'm guessing the next words out of his mouth are going to be about how he's been hiding his feelings for me all this time. How he's loved Halli ever since he was a kid and Ginny told him stories about her. And how now that he's met me, he's still in love with me. It's flattering, but it's not what I want. And I don't need some guy to put himself out there and confess his feelings when I'm just going to have to turn him down.

So I try to head him off. "That's really nice of you, but—"

"How is it nice of me?" he asks. "I've been doing what your parents wanted ever since I picked you up in Colorado. They had an agenda and I've been helping them. I should have said no from the very beginning. But then I doubt I would have met you."

"What are you talking about? How have you lied to me?"

"You want the whole list?" he says. "Okay. I told you you could trust Monsieur Bern. You can't. I told you not to trust Mrs. Scott. You can. I think you figured that out for yourself. I told you—"

"Wait. Hold on. Why did you lie about Mrs. Scott?" I remember it clearly: Jake telling me after the board meeting that I needed to be careful with Mrs. Scott— that she and Ginny hated each other and had been enemies for years.

I couldn't believe it. Mrs. Scott had just stood up for me against Halli's father in the board meeting. He tried to pressure everyone to vote on the purchase of my shares, but Mrs. Scott is the one who said that since I was a 49 percent shareholder, I should have as much time as I wanted to learn more about the company first. She told me how much she admired Ginny, and offered to help me in any way she could. She told me I could stay with her any time I was in London—even on short notice like when I asked her if I could come back with her the next day.

All of my instincts told me I could trust her, but Jake tried to change my mind. And then when she visited me in the hospital last week, he was so rude about throwing her out. I assumed at the time Halli's parents didn't want us talking, and now it's been confirmed.

"But we stayed with her when we first got here," I say. So obviously Jake hadn't been trying too hard.

"Against my advice," he says, "yes."

I wonder what other lies he's told. But I don't wonder enough to want to keep talking about all of this. The truth is, what Halli's parents say and do and want doesn't have anything to do with me anymore. I've got a lot bigger concerns to deal with.

Although I am curious enough about one thing. "So why have you told me so much about my parents? Like what they've been saying behind my back? Some of the time you act like you're on my side."

"I've *always* been on your side, Halli. I've just gone about it the wrong way. I was stupid. I shouldn't have cared about my job. I should have just come to you on my own. Maybe then you would have hired me."

"Maybe," I say honestly. "I don't really know. Although I still don't know what I'd hire you to do. It's not like I'm running a company the way my parents are."

"You're about to invest in a new one," he says. "I could have helped you with that."

I pinch my fingers against my eyes again. I do have a little headache, but I know it's not serious. Just too much noise, too much talking, when what I really need is some time alone.

But then one more thought occurs to me. "Why did you show my father Sarah's invitation to the party?"

Jake seems surprised by that. But he recovers quickly enough. "He wanted to leave this morning. He knew by yesterday afternoon that you weren't going to meet with any of those professors he lined up. So he gave up on you. I told him I thought you were already bored with the whole idea of being involved in the company, and that if he gave me a few more days, I could probably talk you into selling him your shares."

"You said *what*? Jake, I have no intention of—"

"I know," he says, cutting me off. "I know. I was just trying to buy more time with you. I told him it was hard to get you alone—you were always with Daniel or Sarah or your dog—but if he'd let me stay until the party, I could figure out a way to talk to you there. Then if it still didn't work, I'd fly back home."

"So then why are you leaving tomorrow?"

"Because there's no point," Jake says. "It was clear to your parents last night after I told them about the interview that you're going to do whatever you want.

They can't control you. So they might as well just wait and see what you do."

I feel a surge of pride at that. Those two people who used to intimidate me so much know that I'm too strong to boss around. I wasn't that girl just a few weeks ago. It feels great to see that through someone else's eyes.

Defiant.

"And I'm not going to be a part of it anymore," Jake says. "Although, like I said, I won't break it to them until I'm all the way back home. I may be stupid about some things, but not that."

"Jake, you don't have to quit. Not for my sake."

He shrugs. "This apprenticeship was always a means to an end: meeting you. And now I have. Like I told you before, it's been worth it. But I don't want to have to keep working for your parents on the hope that I might run into you again. You have my card. You can find me whenever you want."

Jake leans back against the seat. "So there you have it. Do what you want. I like you, Halli, I'm not going to lie about that. I know you're involved with—" He jerks his head toward the house. "But if that ever changes…"

I have to give Jake credit. He made me uncomfortable in the hospital last time with how jealous and possessive he was whenever Daniel was around—even though it was Jake I was with back then, not Daniel.

But this time, to see him being so cool and reasonable about my choosing Daniel—he doesn't know it, but he just gained a whole bunch of points with me. Now I really do wish he'd give Sarah a chance. I think I could really recommend him.

"You sure you don't want to stay for the party?" I ask. "You might meet some people you'd like."

"No, I need to head back. I'm going to have to look for another job. It might take a while."

I nod. I suppose someone else might say, *"Oh, don't worry, I'll hire you,"* but I don't want the responsibility. That's not the future I see—the future I saw. We're all on our own out here, Jake and me included. He should do whatever he wants.

"See you," I tell him. "Thanks for your help—I know you did help me sometimes. Good luck with whatever you're doing."

I'm about to open the car door when Jake takes my hand in his and lifts it up to his lips. He plants a kiss softly between my knuckles. It's a lot better than him grabbing me in front of a bunch of reporters and planting a kiss right on my lips.

I'll admit it gives me a funny feeling. He's the spitting image of Will, after all. And he's Jake Demetrios, the guy I was incredibly attracted to just a week and a lifetime ago. It's not like my skin is totally immune to that.

But my heart is.

"Take care," I tell him, then I reclaim my hand and exit the car.

I find my boyfriend sitting on the couch with his father, deep in conversation. But not so deep that he doesn't look up the moment I walk through the door.

"Everything all right?" he asks.

"Perfect. I just need to eat."

I head into the kitchen where Sarah and her mom are making what has to be the last of the party food. Red is comfortably stretched out on the rug.

"Opinion, please," Sarah says. "Nut ball A, nut ball B."

I take a bite of each. "Both."

Sarah sighs. "I thought so, too. I'll be enslaved to this kitchen until we're celebrating *my* fiftieth birthday."

"Hungry?" Francie asks me.

"Starving," I say. She reminds me a little of Elena, Will and Lydia's mom, always ready to mother me, to set out an extra plate, to make sure I feel welcome and fed and cared for.

Maybe it's not so bad that I can never go back to my old life. Maybe I can be just as happy here.

Or maybe that's the kind of lie you tell yourself when you're close to giving up.

I'm not giving up.

I thank Francie for the plate of food and head back out to the living room.

"Ready?" I ask Daniel.

There's a crate full of files waiting for us.

And maybe somewhere in there is a better answer for me.

58

I find the drawing almost right away.

It's in a file marked *Combustion Oscillation*. An interesting way to hide it. I doubt anyone would open a file like that on purpose.

"This is it," I tell Daniel. "This is the one I saw."

"This exact drawing?"

"No, a drawing I made, I think. I must have had to copy it from memory."

Looking at Dr. Venn's drawing now, I can see what a risk that presents. There are so many numbers written all over it—dimensions, ratios—I doubt I was able to remember all of them at once. I probably had to copy it in stages, memorizing as much as I could, then bilocating to Professor Whitfield's lab and writing it all down before I forgot.

"What do you think happened to the other machine?" I ask. "The Edgar Venn in my world made one, too, remember. What do you think happened to it after he died?"

"I don't know," Daniel says. "That's a good question."

"It would be so much easier if I could just tell Professor Whitfield where it was, and then he could arrange to move it to his lab."

"I don't suppose Dr. Venn would know where it is now."

"I don't think so," I say. "Elinor said he left and never went back. If it's like what happened with Dr. Sands, then somebody would have just found Edgar Venn's body dead in the machine. Maybe they'd think he had a heart attack. I doubt anyone would want to preserve something they may think killed him."

There's a knock on the door, and Sarah joins us. She's brought a resupply of cookies with her.

"No wonder you have to keep making more," I tell her. "I must have eaten half of them already."

"Biscuits are brain food," she says. "Of course you need them." She surveys the piles of folders and papers spread all around us where we're sitting on the floor. "Can I help with anything?"

"Oh!" I say, just remembering I haven't told her yet. "You were right about Dr. Venn. You did see two different men in that footage."

"Of course," she says with casual pride. "Never doubt the observational skills of a girl who can detect the false Halli Markham."

The false Halli Markham. Something about that phrase is nudging against my brain.

I close my eyes and try to capture the thought.

It has something to do with hair.

Just a little bit of concentration, and I get it. My eyes pop back open. *Yes.*

"When I saw myself tonight," I tell Daniel, "I knew it was me. It was me at the airport, then me at Professor Whitfield's lab. And both times, my hair was short—the way you cut it, Sarah. Remember?"

"Yes. Not *your* hair," she says gesturing to the ponytail I'm wearing right now, "but … your other hair."

"When I visited Halli this morning—"

"You saw her?" Sarah asks. "How is she?"

"She's great. She's fine. But when I bilocated there—I'll fill you in on all this later," I tell Sarah, "—but anyway, my hair was long and I knew if my mom woke up she'd notice. So Halli had to cut my hair. Then when I came back here, it was still long."

"So what are you thinking?" Daniel asks.

"If I'm trying to pay attention to the details and match what I see in the time loop, then that means I have shorter hair there. I doubt I'm having someone cut it over there every time I bilocate. So that means…"

I look at Sarah.

Her smile flattens out. "Oh, no. I won't. You can't."

"You have to, Sarah. Please."

"But it's *gorgeous*!" she protests. "That hair is your crown. I don't mean to hurt your feelings, but your other hair was an atrocious, piteous thing. It deserved to be cut—but this!"

"Scissors?" I ask Daniel.

He gets up to pull a pair out of his desk drawer.

"Please, I beg of you," Sarah tries one more time. "Isn't there any other way?"

"Sarah, what you don't get is that I'm *happy* about this. It means I've figured out another piece of the puzzle. So please be happy for me. And chop it off the way you did in that meadow."

"Chop it off," Sarah scoffs. "I only had a dull knife that day, if you recall. I can do something much more stylish than *chop* with a proper pair of scissors, thank you very much."

"Don't worry about stylish," I say. "Just try to make it look exactly like what you did before."

Sarah accepts the pair of scissors. I take my hair out of its ponytail and comb it loose with my fingers. It's been fun having this long, thick mane. But giving it up is a small price to pay for getting to become the girl I saw in my future.

Even if I am just a mirage.

Sarah shakes her head sadly. Then gathers up a section of hair and gets to work.

I glance over at Daniel during the process. The more Sarah cuts, the more he seems to have that same look in his eyes that Red did every time Dr. Venn held out a treat for him.

"What?" I ask.

There's just one long section left. Sarah snips it off. And now Daniel has a kind of grin I don't think I've ever seen on him.

"What's going on?" I ask him. "Does it look weird or something?" I reach back to feel the thick, blunt ends.

Now Sarah is smiling at me, too.

"What?" I ask them both.

Sarah leans forward and gives me a hug. "Hello, Audie. Nice to see you again. Now I really believe it's you." She pulls back and gives me one more appraising look. "Yes. The cousin."

"The cousin," Daniel agrees.

I have to go look at it for myself.

I hop up and cross the hall to the bathroom and shut myself inside. I feel almost shy about looking at myself. But then I stand in front of the mirror.

Hello, stranger. Welcome back. I smile at my reflection. I know that girl.

Yes, her shoulders are still broader than their at-home ones, her arms are bigger, she's a little bit taller.

But from the neck up, *Hi.*

Now I understand that silly-looking grin on Daniel's face, because I've got it, too. I can't help it. I'm just so glad to see me. After too many times of looking in the mirror and finding Halli Markham staring back, it's a relief to finally see a more recognizable me.

But there's something else: I feel like I'm finally close. I'm inching my way back to my real life, one small action at a time. Yes, maybe I'll only be able to visit as a bilocated version of myself, but at least I'll be able to consult with Professor Whitfield again. At least I've brought him the plans for the machine. Maybe in time that will lead to a permanent solution to all of this. I just have to be patient and have faith.

"Keep going," I tell the girl in the mirror. We all need a pep talk sometimes. And sometimes the best person to deliver it is the one who knows exactly what you're going through and exactly how you feel. *"I have faith in you,"* I whisper. *"You're smart and you're brave and you'll figure all of this out. Keep going, Audie. You're close."*

I splash water on my face and then blow my nose. Compose myself. I can't stand here all night just gazing at my reflection. There's too much work to do.

I return to Daniel's room and the three of us divide up the files. "I'm not sure what we're looking for," I tell Sarah, "so just keep your eye out for anything unusual. I'd like to get through all of these tonight. If Dr. Venn is ... feeling better in the morning—" I almost say *still alive,* but I don't want to even consider the alternative right now. "—then I want to be able to be able to ask him as many questions as I can before his grand-daughter kicks us out."

"And then we go back to his office?" Daniel asks me.

"Back to the machine," I confirm. "I need to see more of that future. I want to know what it is I did that got me there."

59

"Ten minutes," Madeline tells us.

Daniel and I exchange a look. He's probably thinking the same thing I am, which is that ten minutes feels like a complete luxury compared to only two. We'll try to make good use of it.

Dr. Venn is sitting up in bed. Instead of the full oxygen mask, he's only wearing the small prongs that fit in his nose. His eyes are closed. But as soon as Red leaps onto the bed, he opens them.

"Red!" He hugs his frail arms around the dog. Red does his usual therapy dog bit by lying fully stretched out next to the patient and wagging his tail in obvious delight. I remember how much I loved it when he visited me and did the same thing. I understand Dr. Venn's smile.

I hold up the microphone and earphones Daniel thought to bring back from the office last night.

"Oh, yes," Dr. Venn says. "Very good."

I plug us both into the trapezoid and gently slip the earphones over his head.

Dr. Venn clasps his fingers around my wrist. He takes a deep breath from the oxygen, then says, "I'm sorry I lied to you. About who I am."

"It's okay, Dr. Venn. I understand."

"I'm so used to keeping all my secrets," he says. "But I should have told you—you of all people, Audie. I'm very sorry."

"Really," I tell him. "It's fine."

I don't want to waste any of our precious ten minutes—probably only eight by now—with him worrying he has to apologize. I have much more important things to discuss.

Dr. Venn beats me to it.

"You asked me last night," he starts to say, but then he has to pause to cough. And even though it still sounds awful, it's still a lot better than yesterday. He clears this throat and draws in a breath before starting again. "You asked how you could see Halli's grandmother."

"Yes. Exactly. You told me to follow the thread."

He takes another deep breath, then pats the dog on the head. Red snuggles in a little closer.

"The thread holds one parallel lifetime to another,"

Dr. Venn explains. "But you can go beyond your parallel. First you need that initial connection. But even after some version of you dies, the rest of that world, and all the people you used to love, still go on until it's their natural turn to die. Edgar and I spent hours sometimes just looking around in places where other versions of us used to live. It's a wonderful way to experience history as it unfolds."

I'd love to hear more about that, but my time is ticking away. I probably only have about three minutes left.

"Dr. Venn, I saw myself last night. In my old world. I think it was just a projection of me—a bilocation— but I was showing my professor friend a copy of the drawing we found for how to construct the machine."

"Were you?" Dr. Venn asks. "Very good."

"So do you think we could do it?" I ask. "If I can bring him all the directions and the dimensions?"

"I did it," he says. "Edgar told me how to do it, and I made one of my own."

"How long did it take you?"

"About two months. Some of the materials were hard to replicate—they have specialized metals here that I had to find substitutes for."

"Is that written down anywhere?" Daniel asks.

"Not here," Dr. Venn says. "Everything was back in my old office."

I'm about to admit it's pretty unlikely we'd ever find

that, even if he gave us his old address, when Dr. Venn adds, "But I remember it all. Very clearly. *You* can write it down."

Madeline stands in the doorway. "That will do," she tells us.

"When?" I ask Dr. Venn. "Today?"

He consults his stern granddaughter. "Maddy? Can these young people come see me again this afternoon? It would do an old man good." He gives me a sly wink, but then unfortunately follows it up with a body-shaking coughing fit.

"Out," Madeline tells us as she hurries over to help him. I quickly remove the earphones from his head and pick up the rest of the equipment and tug Red off the bed by his collar. Then the three of retreat out of the room and keep on going out to the street.

My driver is there waiting for us. He's wearing a much more casual outfit than I'm used to seeing him in —for one thing, it doesn't have the company logo *OPS* embroidered over the pocket—and the car he's driving isn't the luxurious black sedan I've been riding around in while I'm here.

I was a little confused when I came out of Daniel's house this morning and found Wilkinson waiting for me just like he is right now, but by the time I reached the car I understood.

Halli's parents had removed that particular privilege. But Wilkinson showed up on his own. I'm sure if they found out, they'd fire him.

So I hired him on the spot.

It's not like I really *need* a driver. And it's a little strange to be driven around in a car that's even older than the one my mom and I share at home. But it's definitely nice to have someone on call so I don't have to waste time figuring out how to get from point A to point B. This morning, for example, from Daniel's house to the Oxford hospital to the Oxford campus. Then I'll want to reverse it all this afternoon.

"Thank you," I tell Wilkinson as he closes the door behind us.

The back seat isn't nearly as roomy. And there isn't a divider between the front and the back. But it's clean in here, and the car still drives itself while Wilkinson goes back to reading his book, and I can obviously afford to pay someone and probably treat him better than Halli's parents have been doing.

Decision made. Done. No regrets.

Daniel and Red and I cozy up on the shorter seat. I don't mind being stuck between my two boys.

And it's fine to be quiet on our way to Dr. Venn's office. Daniel and I already discussed the plan on our way out to the car. We both know what I'm going to do.

I argued for the maximum amount of time—five hours. Daniel argued for two.

"You don't know how it will affect you," he said. "You were a wreck last night. You can't deny that."

"But we brought food this time," I remind him. "I'll have a snack before I go in, then I'll eat as soon as I get out. That's really been the main problem."

What I don't want is another situation like last night where it feels like I've barely gotten started, and suddenly the voice in my earphones is calling me back. I need to have more time. I want to follow out the thread of the life I got a glimpse of, and treat what I see as a map. I want to know some of the twists and turns ahead so I can backtrack and make sure I do everything right.

So we finally agreed on a compromise: three hours in the machine.

I hope I can get a lot done in three hours.

Wilkinson stops the car in its usual place and comes around to open the door. Then he hands me his card so I can contact him whenever I want.

"It's going to be awhile," I tell him. "Probably not until after lunch. So go ahead and do whatever you want for a while."

"I'll stay in the vicinity," he tells me. Then he smiles. "It's my first day on the job, Miss Markham. I want to make a good impression."

"You already did, Wilkinson. Thanks. We'll see you in a few hours."

Red bounds ahead, stirring up yellow leaves while

he sniffs his way along our route. Daniel and I walk hand in hand. I don't care anymore if anyone sees us or stares at us or even films us for some history program. All of that seems so insignificant now. It seems so … three days ago.

"Tell me about some of the people who will be at the party tonight." I'm feeling a little nervous right now, and I could use the distraction.

Daniel squeezes my hand. "I'd rather talk about you. I'd still prefer only two hours. If all goes well, you can rest, eat, and then go again for another two hours this afternoon."

I know that sounds reasonable, but I just don't want it. My time in that world last night ended so abruptly, I can't go through that again. I need to know that I have plenty of time to explore. That I can follow the Audie thread for a while, then the Halli thread, and see if there's a point where maybe I can finally take over.

So I stick to the three hours. Decision made. Done. No regrets.

Before I go into the machine room I eat a few figs and take a few sips of water. That's about all my stomach wants to handle right now. I'm getting more nervous by the minute.

This needs to work. I need to find my way back there again. And this time I need to understand what lies in my future.

Once I'm in the machine I let Daniel attach all the

straps on my legs, but then I hug him before he can strap in my arms. I run my fingers through the sides of his short hair, and give him a reassuring kiss.

"I'll be fine. I love you. I'll see you in three hours."

"I'll be watching the monitors every minute."

One more hug, one more kiss, then it's time.

Daniel fastens the rest of the straps, including the one across my head. Then he lowers the earphones and the goggles.

And I'm off to the sound of the pings.

60

I decide to do it the way I did last night: keep hidden, watch, don't let anyone know I'm here.

I start back in my bedroom. Halli is asleep. It's around three in the morning on Tuesday here right now. I don't know if Halli ended up going back to school yesterday, or giving up and staying home.

I don't want to waste time finding out.

I reach down for the thread of this life, pick it up, and start pulling myself along.

Stop after just a few pulls.

Halli riding in a car with Daniel. No, not Daniel—this is the other one, Colin. Halli has the window down and the wind is whipping up my hair. Her eyes are closed, she's relaxed, she looks happy. Colin glances over at her and looks pretty happy himself.

That's nice for them. But too bad—I don't want them to have it. Because if they're on a road trip together, it means Halli has still run away and probably still not left my mom a note saying where she was going. I can't let her do that.

I turn and start pulling in the other direction.

Halli standing at the base of a cliff. She has a harness around her waist and she's holding a rope and looking up. I look up, too. There's a young woman crawling up a long sheer wall. Halli shouts out, "That's right, April, keep going! You've got it!" The climber smiles grimly to herself, then moves her left hand into the tiniest of cracks. Steadies herself. Moves a foot. Then next hand.

Nope.

I keep searching for the right length of thread. Go back just a little further, stop.

Halli pulling herself along the railing of a boat. Rain is lashing against her face. She hurries to secure some rope pulled taut against a tarp. A man inside the cabin of the boat shouts out instructions. Halli nods and keeps working along the railing to the next lump of equipment covered in a tarp.

This makes no sense.

I thought I was pulling myself backward, not forward, but maybe I've lost my sense of direction. Like a drowning person underwater who doesn't understand which way is up. All of these scenes have to be what happens after Halli leaves here. Obviously none of them happened before.

Unless …

I stop exactly where I am, with Halli still on a boat in a storm.

Am I looking at a different past?

Is this retro-causation? Has the Halli who became me rewritten her own version of my life before that, and become someone I'm not? Someone I never was?

Maybe the scenes I saw yesterday were just a few in a whole variety of possibilities. And somehow in the past twelve or fourteen hours, these new possibilities I'm looking at right now have become the more probable ones.

Maybe I'm too late. Maybe I've already lost my opportunity.

"Audie?"

I hear the word and look up. I'm back in my room, and Halli is sitting upright in bed, whispering into the dark. "Audie, are you here?"

I am now. I make myself a body. And stand in front of my bed.

"Hi!" Halli whispers. "Are you here for a while? Do you have time to talk?"

My mind is still reeling. I don't understand what I just saw.

But talking sounds like a good idea.

Halli leaps out of bed and gets dressed, and the two of us sneak out of the house into the cold dark night.

I've been mostly silent so far, because I don't know what to say. I've lost the threads I found yesterday. Is that future gone?

"Tell me what happened today," I say. Maybe that's where the change took place. Something Halli did created a new future, and my other one is lost.

Circumstance and choices. This is free will in action. Halli has every right to live her life—even her life as me—whatever way she wants.

Even if it ruins what might have been a happy future for me.

Halli describes her day. From leaving class when I saw her, to going for a long run, to talking to Professor Whitfield and Albert that afternoon. I don't remember every detail of the Monday she spent last time, but that all sounds about the same so far.

"Did you go back to school in the afternoon?" I ask her. "Talk to the counselor about graduating early?"

"No."

"So no one told you I could graduate early if I passed algebra?"

"What?" Halli says. "No."

Great. Now I have no idea what's going to happen.

We walk along my old neighborhood street in silence while I think.

"What do you want?" I ask Halli.

"What do you mean?"

"I mean, if you could go forward from right now, what would you want to see happen?"

"Obviously I'd like to go back," she says. "Switch places with you."

"But what if we can never do that?" I ask. "What would you do with a life here?"

Halli considers that for a moment. "I suppose I'd start over. Go back to doing what I know. Maybe find a job guiding in the mountains someplace. Or … I don't really know. I haven't thought about it much. The truth is I've been waiting for you and Professor Whitfield to sort this all out."

"Halli …" I don't know what I'm allowed to say. I don't know if there are any rules. I know I'm not supposed to interfere with someone's own free will, but this has to be different—I'm outside her head, not in it. We're just talking. I'm just giving her information.

So I give her information. "Let me tell you what I saw."

I describe all the scenes I viewed last night. Tell her about the machine, and bilocation, and the two Dr. Venns. Tell her what Dr. Venn told me this morning, about being able to replicate the machine here in my world.

Tell her I couldn't find any of that again tonight. Describe the different scenes I saw instead.

"What do you think that means?" Halli asks.

"I don't know. Except I think it all has to be your choice. I don't get to come in here and say, *'Hey, pick this future, I like this one best.'* You get to decide where you go from here."

"But in the future you saw last night," Halli says, "you were there, too."

"A bilocated version of me, yes."

"And you're not in the other future you saw tonight?"

"Not so far."

Halli stops walking and turns to me. "Let's just say that's the future now. We're both stuck with it. What would happen to you back in my life?"

I let out a breath. "Well, it's interesting. I think I've at least changed enough that I'm not going to end up dying in the hospital from some sort of brain eruption. I've been busy the last few days. I've made quite a few changes in the life of Halli Markham."

I fill her in on all of it: the lie about going to Oxford, my interactions with her parents, the research I've been doing with Sarah and Daniel, the whole situation with Jake, the hiring of my first employee.

And finally the offer to become an investor in Francie and Sam's history studio.

I feel a little weird telling her about that one. It's her money, after all. Maybe she won't like me spending it however I want.

But Halli loves it. "That must have made my parents crazy."

I smile. "Pretty close."

"How much did you invest?"

"I haven't done any of it yet. We're still underage, so it's going to have to go through your trustee, Monsieur Bern—"

Halli scoffs. "Him? I wouldn't trust him with one icie of mine, let alone millions. I'll just wait until I'm eighteen. It's only a few more months. Then I'll spend my money however I want.

"Besides," she says, "I think Ginny would get a kick out of that. After all those years of the two of us being filmed wherever we went, to instead be a part owner of one of those companies? I think she'd love it. Especially if it's History 14. They've done some of the most amazing stories—Ginny and I always loved to watch them together. It was a great idea, Audie. Thank you. That sounds like a lot of fun."

I realize the two of us have been standing here talking as if we've already switched places. As if Halli is about to step in and take over her life from where I left off. As if it's already a done deal.

But right now it's all just wishful thinking.

And her comment about History 14 reminds me that I have something else to tell her—something that she's going to wonder why I didn't tell her the second I saw her. It's just that there's been so much else going on in my mind every minute since I got here, it's hard to remember which to talk about first.

"Halli, there's something else."

I start slowly. Explain it the way Professor Lacksmith described it to Daniel: that all the parallel versions of us are connected to the same Mother Root, and we can find all the other ones if we just explore down the line.

And then I tell her what Dr. Venn said this morning: that once we find that connection, we can even go further, beyond our own parallel, and see what happens in the future even after that version of us is gone.

"I did that," I say. "I found one of the versions of us who died, and I kept going to see what happened next."

"Who was it?" Halli asks.

"You."

I tell her what I saw. Everything about her death. All the way up to seeing her body laid out on a bed, with Ginny grieving nearby.

"Then I followed Ginny forward," I say. "And I found her."

"You *what?*"

"I sat with her. I talked to her. She told me how she saved your life."

"But … wait a minute," Halli says. She's breathing harder now, clearly under stress. "You *saw* her? But …

how? And what do you mean she saved me? You just said I died."

"You did," I say, "in her world. But you lived in the one where I met you. Ginny sacrificed herself so you could live. She took in the poison, drew it out of you. But she never knew that it worked. She always thought it must have failed—I mean she saw you, dead. So for the past year she's been living all alone in that same house where you were, just as sad and lonely as you've been without her. And then one day I just showed up out of the blue, and she practically lost it. She thought for sure I was you."

Halli covers her face with her hands. The shock has finally set in. She's quietly crying now and murmuring, *"No, no, no … I can't believe this."*

"Halli, she was really happy. I can't tell you how happy she is. To know that you're alive? And I told her I'd tell you I found her. That … maybe I'd even try to bring you to her one day—"

Halli's hand flashes out and grips my arm—hard. She's so quick and fierce I yelp in surprise.

"You have to take me to her," Halli says. "Can you do it right now? What do I have to do?"

"It's not that simple," I tell her. "I'm just learning. I only just started this yesterday. You have to give me a little more time—"

"Audie, please." Tears spring from her eyes again. *"Please.* If I've ever asked you for anything before, I'm sorry. Because this is all I'll ever want from you for the rest of my life. Please take me to her. I want to talk to her. I want to see her again. Please!"

I don't know what to say. I've never seen Halli this emotional before—this raw. I don't think I've ever even seen her cry. She's usually so tough, so stoic, but this pain is obviously as deep for her as it was for Ginny. Of course I want to help them however I can.

And I tell Halli that. "But you have to be patient. I'm not sure how all of this works yet."

"But you've come here twice now," Halli says. "You know how. Isn't there some way we can just trade places now? And then you can tell me how to find Ginny from there?"

"I need to sit down." I sink onto the nearest curb. Then I cross my arms over my knees and let my head rest there. This is all too much. I need to think. And think fast.

I can see the faint light of dawn on the horizon. My time must be running out.

I think about telling her what Professor Whitfield said—that I can come back into my old body, but Halli can't switch into mine because she was never in it to begin with, so it won't recognize her. That she has no place to go.

But as I sit here in the waning darkness beside the body that used to be mine, I wonder if Professor Whitfield might have been wrong.

Because even though Dr. Venn split into two different versions when he signed the Manhattan Pact, the original Edgar Venn was never in that second body. The new Dr. Venn just went forward in a new universe, continuing with his own different life.

Yet when that second Dr. Venn died, the original Edgar Venn saw his opportunity. He was able to move right in.

So why can't that work for us?

"Coming back now..."

"Halli, I have to go."

"Why? Not yet!"

"Feeling refreshed..."

"I'll come back."

"When?"

"As soon as I can. Today—"

"... now you open your eyes."

I blink in the blackness behind the goggles. Soon light filters into my eyes.

Then I feel the strong arms of my boyfriend as he helps me out of the machine.

Then, much to my surprise, I start crying.

"Audie? What is it?"

I can't tell him. Not yet. I'll pretend I'm just hungry. Or tired. Or something else having to do with the machine.

I'm not ready to tell him yet that if I'm right about everything, this might be our last day together.

Instead I wipe away my tears and kiss him. "I need food. Then I'll tell you what I saw."

I won't be like Halli. I won't leave without saying goodbye. I can't do that to Daniel, or to me.

"Did you see your future again?" Daniel asks me.

I don't know how to answer that. Because the future I'm looking at right now is one I haven't made yet. I don't know how it will turn out.

"I saw other possibilities," I tell him, and that much is true. But I won't add the rest:

Possibilities where Audie Masters is a girl adventurer who's probably never read a physics book in her life. Wouldn't know there are parallel universes, wouldn't know how to find them.

Which also means she'd never meet and fall in love with a guy named Daniel Everett. None of this history would ever happen.

"We need to get back to the hospital," I tell Daniel. "I need to ask Dr. Venn some questions."

"About the materials for the machine," he says.

"Right." And something else equally important.

I'm leaving today if I can.

Dr. Venn can tell me how.

It's time Halli took this life back.

Even if it means I'll have to give it up.

61

I think I finally understand math.

The numbers have always intimidated me. There's a right answer or there's a wrong one. A teacher writes some numbers on the board or corrects them on your test, and you see right there whether you understand the proofs and the problems or you don't.

And I never have. Before now.

But now I see that math is just a series of steps. Small, logical steps. You take them one by one and don't worry about the outcome as you go. The answer will come. It might surprise you, it might not be at all what you expected, but you know that it will be right. Because you didn't skip anything. You started at the beginning and you followed it through. You never gave up until the answer was finally there. The equation is complete. Then you can stand back and look at it as a whole and think, *Yes, I know that's right.*

On the ride back to the hospital, I'm already starting to see all the pieces. The equation is falling into place: Dr. Sands dying in the machine. Where did he go? Does it really matter? The point is he journeyed somewhere else and either forgot or decided never to come back.

The Dr. Venn in London invaded another person's mind, and he died, too.

Creating an opening for a very lonely man who wanted to live out the rest of his years with a wife and family he no longer had.

I understand the steps for me. If I'm going to have any hope at all of moving back into my old body, Halli is going to have to leave it first. I can't take over while she's still in there, or my body will reject me. I'll be right back where I was last time.

And it's the same for Halli and this body: I have to leave before she gets here.

So how can we make that happen? How do I make sure we both have a body to come home to?

It's the entanglement. It has to be. The question is how to use it.

I remember what we both looked like, those wave forms of us, on the screen in Professor Whitfield's lab. He had Albert draw an outline around the two separate blobs of light that were Halli and me. She was there in the room with me, even though her body had never been there before. And even though my body was away at that moment visiting her in her own universe. Somehow the two of us were still together in that most basic, quantum way.

And that's why I think this could work.

Wilkinson drops us off, and Daniel and Red and I return to Dr. Venn's room. Madeline isn't standing guard at the moment, but Elinor is inside. She sees us and holds her finger up to her lips. Even though without his earphones and amplifier, Dr. Venn wouldn't hear us unless we shouted.

"How is he?" I ask.

"Sleeping," Elinor says. "But better. Already much better."

Red hops up to resume his rightful place. Dr. Venn opens his drowsy eyes. He gives the dog a brief pat, focuses on Daniel and me and smiles, then closes his eyes again.

That's no good.

"He told us to come back this afternoon," I tell Elinor. "He wanted to tell us some things. When do you think he might be awake?"

"Not for a few hours, I hope. They've given him something to settle his chest. I'm afraid he slept poorly during the night."

"Oh. Okay." I bite the edge of my lip. I look at

Daniel, but all he has to offer is a shrug. I guess we'll have to come back later.

Elinor reaches into the purse at her side and pulls out a brown rectangular envelope. "He wrote you this," she says, handing it to me. "Or more accurately, I wrote it. My father dictated. I believe that's why he's so exhausted right now."

I pull out a set of folded papers. The first two pages include a long list of materials and an even longer set of instructions. After that, there's a letter.

"I hope that provides you what you need," Elinor says. "He was most concerned to help you."

I quickly scan through the letter. Then back up and read it more carefully. Then finally I hand it to Daniel. We can talk about it later. Right now I need to pay attention to someone else.

I gaze at the old man lying peacefully in the bed. I don't know if he's right, what he said before: that the reason he got to live so long was so he could meet me.

But I know I'm incredibly grateful that he did. Otherwise I might never know how to go back.

I tell Elinor thank you, then reach over to squeeze Dr. Venn's hand. I don't know if he can feel it, but it's all I can think to do. I'd like to see him again some day, but I don't know if I ever will. "Will you tell him I said thank you?" I ask Elinor. "From the bottom of my heart?"

"Of course I will, my dear."

I clutch the envelope tightly as the three of us walk back through the hospital, out to the car. What I hold is a gift. It means I'll be able to build a machine in my world. Which means, I hope, that I'll be able to come back and visit here. Bilocate just like Edgar Venn did. Any time he wanted.

"Where to now, Miss?" Wilkinson asks me.

"Back to the college," I say. "But first, can you find me another cash machine?"

"Au—" Daniel catches himself. "Halli, you don't have to do that."

"I'll tell you later," I whisper to Daniel. Because the money isn't just for him.

I have an employee now, and I'd like to give him a bonus. If Halli becomes his employer by later today, she can pay him from that point on. But he's been a good driver for me—loyal and kind. And it would make me feel good to reward that.

I'd also like to hand Daniel one more heap of cash. Tell him it's for the party. Tell him it's for the studio. Tell him he can't say no.

As the car starts up, I shift even closer to Daniel and he wraps his arm around my shoulders.

"I love you," I tell him, and he says it back, and that's all I wanted to hear.

Then I open Dr. Venn's letter again. And read what he wanted to say.

62

Dear Audie,

Thank you.

A teacher's worth is measured by how much he can give to his students, and for years I've given very little. I learned from Edgar's experience to keep silent. Because of his other accomplishments in science, he expected his colleagues to be respectful, if not enthusiastic, about his other discoveries. Instead he was met with doubt at best, but more often ridicule. It changed him in ways I did not want to change. So I kept my discoveries to myself.

But now I can tell you what I've learned: that a rising tide lifts all boats. Edgar and I visited countless other men and women tied to the same threads that we were. What we saw was that when one triumphed, we all did. When one despaired, we all did. Haven't you ever felt suddenly sad or *happy for no apparent reason? It's a ripple down the cord. Somewhere, one of you is learning something all of you will benefit from knowing. It might be a hard lesson or a joyful one. But what each of us does matters to all.*

Never doubt that one life, your life, is precious. What you think about is important. What you feel is vital. The shy, homebound widow is as essential as the great politician or famous humanitarian who seems to make such a difference in the world. We all matter. We are all learning. And what we learn, we add to the whole. You have seen that for yourself.

You told me you feel different now. Bolder. Stronger. I told you it's because there are strands of Halli in you. That is true, but only in part.

The greater truth is that you are awake to your life. You pay attention. You think and feel and act. You love, you fear, you search. You try. That is all anyone ever needs to do. What Edgar and I found was that each and every one of us is here on purpose. Our purpose is to be exactly and only the person we are. Our individual experience is what we have to offer to the whole. Then when one of us learns kindness, we all learn. When one of us learns courage, we're all a little braver. Do you see what I mean? Every life is important. We are all like explorers sent out into the world to bring back great discoveries of what it means to be this type of human or that.

You and I have taken it further than most by actually inhabiting another's life. I have been immensely happy with my choice. I love my family more than any accomplishment or possession or anything else in any world. I know that is also why you want to go home.

Here is the secret: defocus. Let go of the form. Allow yourself to move beyond molecules and return to pure energy. Completely abandon ship.

It isn't death. Edgar didn't die. He lost the boundaries of his form. One day soon I will, too. Then I'll return to the whole and send out new explorers, some of whom will contain strands of me. If I ever see you again, we can talk about this further. But I'm growing tired.

Set the machine for one hour. Then let go. You'll know what it is when you feel it. You won't be afraid.

Thank you, Audie, for the gift of allowing me to be a teacher again. It has been an honor to meet such a brave and intelligent girl. I know you will do great and wonderful things with your life. You already have, simply by living as you are every single day.

With great affection and regard,
Edgar Venn

63

I let Daniel read the letter on purpose. My subtle way of preparing him.

But now I can't put off talking about it any longer. "Daniel…"

"I know."

I look up at him as we walk back across the campus. He gathers me in closer, putting his arm around me as we stroll step in step.

I'm not in that much of a hurry. Neither is he.

"Once we build the machine where I am," I say, "I'll be able to bilocate here whenever I want."

"That's good," he says. "It's something."

"Don't be sad. I seem to recall you saying you wanted the old Audie back."

"I've grown to love this one, too," Daniel answers. "It's hard to let you go."

"Don't." I clear my throat to fight off a cry. "This time was *so* much better than before. Thank you for figuring out who I really am. Otherwise I would have missed all this. And now, if this works, we'll just be apart for a little while. It won't be so bad."

I'm trying to convince myself as much as him.

As we approach Dr. Venn's office, I see a small form sitting in front of his door.

I'm not the only one who sees him.

"Red!" But it's too late. He chases off Lewis the schnauzer, who shows remarkable speed for a dog that pudgy. Red trots back to Daniel and me looking very proud.

It's probably just as well that Lewis moves on. I don't know when Dr. Venn is coming back—if at all. The poor little dog needs to alter his route.

Daniel and Red and I enter the office and Daniel removes his coat. I take mine off, too, and hand it to him.

"Thanks for letting me borrow this. I'll probably need it again in a few months. Will you hang onto it for me until then?"

Daniel's answer is to swoop me into an embrace and a long farewell kiss. It's fifty times better than the one we shared in the Alps the first time we said goodbye. If he keeps this up, I'll want to leave him every day.

I almost tell him that, but I don't think he's in the mood to joke.

"So what happens now?" Daniel asks.

"Ideally? In about an hour you go in that room and help Halli out of the machine. You give her some food. You fill her in on some of the details, like the name of her driver and your parents' names…" I just remembered. "And you introduce her around a party tonight. She'll like having the company. I think she's probably been alone for too long."

"And what will you do, Audie Masters? How will spend your night?"

"Getting takeout with my mom. Sitting on the couch under a quilt with her and watching something stupid on TV."

I can feel the moisture welling in my eyes, both at the thought of that and of what I'm leaving.

"Tell Sarah I said goodbye, okay? Tell her she's smart and fun, and I adore her and I appreciate everything she did. I'll tell Halli she should keep her on as an apprentice. I'm sure there'll be plenty for her to do."

And now for my last faithful friend.

I crouch down in front of Red and fluff up the sides of his neck. I kiss the side of his nose. "Thanks, Red. I love you. You've been a great dog for me. But now your real girl is coming home! I know how much you'll like that. Thanks for letting me be your girl for a while. You made every day of mine better."

I can't do it. I can't be strong. I stand back up, crying, and lean into Daniel's chest so he can hold me while I let it out.

"I'm not going away forever," I remind us both. "Just for now." I stand back up straight and wipe my eyes. "And hey, it might not even work. We might be going through this whole thing again tomorrow."

"Anytime, anywhere," Daniel tells me.

"Okay, deal."

The best thing to do is just do it. I walk into the other room and climb into the machine. Daniel secures all the straps, then pauses as usual before putting my goggles and the earphones on.

"Be safe," he tells me. "If it at all seems dangerous…"

"I will. It'll be fine."

He kisses me once, then finishes the preparation. And then I know he's gone.

I let out one more quiet sob, then tell myself, *"Okay. That's it. We have to go."*

Soon I hear the pings. Then the gong. Then feel the soft xylophone mallets playing against my brain. There are stars now, bright gold, then silver and white and red.

I'm the stars, I'm the darkness, I'm the boundless vastness of space. I'm no one in particular, just a gathering of energy and heat, aiming for one particular spot on the map.

There's a girl there, quietly moving around my

room, unpacking all the clothes she'd put away in bags, thinking she might have to be in that life for a while. But now she knows I'm coming home. And she's going home, too. And she wants things to be nice for me.

"Halli."

Whether she heard me with her ears or just felt me in her head, she obviously knows I'm here. She goes to my bed, props up the pillow, then sits there quietly stilling her mind.

She was always so much better at meditation than I was. Thank goodness. She doesn't need the machine for this. Ginny taught her how to do it early on—who knows, maybe for exactly a moment like this. Maybe Ginny had her own time loop, and a future Ginny warned her what Halli would need.

However it happened, it turns out Halli and I are both perfectly suited to be exactly the girls we are. We couldn't know that when we met, but there must have been future versions of us sending back waves saying, *"Yes, this one. This one will be your friend."*

Why are we entangled? I have no idea. I only know what I saw with my eyes. Halli and I are tied together somehow, and it's a mystery I intend to solve.

That and about five hundred other ones that have come up in the last month alone.

She's left my body now. I can feel her. Moving up the branch to meet me. Then she passes and keeps going, and it's my turn to take her place.

It's not like waking from a dream. I'm not startled, I don't gasp—it's nothing dramatic like that. I just stretch myself into all the corners and curves of my body, and wait for it to fill in like a wave seeping into the sand.

It's funny, but I'm sad—I'm not going to lie about that. I thought I'd feel so thrilled to be back. But it's like I've just returned from a very long trip, and I'm not ready for real life quite yet.

I stand up. Test my legs. Stretch my arms out to my sides and up above my head. Yes, this body fits me. It's like putting on worn-in jeans. I stand in front of the mirror and wait for the reality of my reflection to sink in.

"There," I whisper, because there is finally my smile. I give myself a little wave. I used to think I was so dorky when I did that. But I'm not. I know better than that now.

It's late morning here. My mom must be at work. That means I'll have the next several hours free.

I go to my desk and open my laptop. It takes me a moment to remember what to do. But this is technology I can actually work. I press all the right buttons, click the right links, and pretty soon I hear the sound of a phone ringing over the speaker.

There's a tired, unshaven face looking back at me. "Hi, Halli. Any news?"

"Hi, Professor. It's Audie. And yes, I have quite a bit of news."

64

<u>Three months later.</u>

I was wrong.

About a lot of things, I'm sure, but about a few of them in particular.

"Shame on you, Audie Masters," Sarah told me the first time I saw her again. Then she hugged the stuffing out of me, gave me another stern glare, then hugged me once more. "Welcome back, you scoundrel. Leaving me without a word."

"I told Daniel to tell you—"

"As if he could ever do it justice! *'Audie says goodbye,'* she imitates in her most boring voice. "Do you know how I cried for you? And how do you think that looked to Halli Markham? *'Oh, hello, Halli. Bwahhh!'* Very cheery welcome, indeed."

Two and a half months is a long time to be away. If Dr. Venn built his own machine in only two months, all by himself, then I'm really impressed. It took Professor Whitfield and me and his whole team the extra half-month, even with all of us working around the clock. Since I couldn't go get any of the information myself without my own machine, Halli used Dr. Venn's machine to keep making trips and bringing us more details on the design. That was her drawing I saw the professor and me looking at that day.

I brought Professor Whitfield another project, too. A certain hydro-catalytic process that can convert a simple cup of water into enough energy to fly a jet or power a fleet of cars. If you modify all their engines first. I tried to remember as much as I could from that meeting I had with Mr. Chilton at Halli's parents' London headquarters.

I felt a little weird about it in the beginning, but then I realized it isn't that different from modern scientists looking at Leonardo da Vinci's old designs and deciding to make some of his machines. My idea just happens to be something I learned from some scientists in a parallel universe. It would be like meeting an alien race and checking out their space pods and then trying to duplicate their designs back on Earth.

Besides, it's all in a good cause. Not only will it make my own world a better place by solving our energy needs, it will also help a certain small college in the Colorado mountains. I figure if it could make billionaires out of Halli's parents and Ginny, then it can help fund some new equipment and buildings for the labs run by Professor Whitfield and his colleagues.

You might say I have a vested interest, since I'm a freshman in the physics department here now.

Which means I finally passed high school algebra.

Through a combination of finally getting over my fear of it, plus trying out some of the techniques I saw Halli use when she was studying to take the test, I even managed to get better than a passing grade. No one was more surprised than my mom. I know she hoped to have me home with her for a whole other semester, but I had too much work to do. I moved up here right after Christmas.

And I was wrong about something else.

"Come on, Moose, good boy! Let's go!"

This is me walking up a hill, toward the trees just beyond the college. Me calling to my little black Lab puppy, who's bounding through the snow with his ears flopping, racing to try to keep up. Me scooping him into my arms and kissing him all over his face. Me, the girl who's happy. Me who's found her way.

I'm not the only one.

When I was done saying hello to Sarah and Daniel

again—with the promise to Daniel that I'd talk to him later in private—Halli and Red and I took a walk up to the third floor of the History 14 studio. I love my little Moose, but I'll never get tired of seeing Red. He's the one who convinced me I needed a dog of my own back in my other life.

"How's Ginny?" I ask.

"Great as ever. I swear, it never gets old. Every time I visit her now she still acts like it's the biggest miracle."

"Probably because it is," I point out.

"Halli?"

Red answers with a low growl. We turn to find Jake hurrying up the stairs. He tosses Red a treat, and the dog lets him approach. I always knew Jake was smooth.

He gives me a smile. "Hi, Audie." As far as he and the staff here are concerned, I'm the long-lost cousin. When Halli first introduced me around, she told Jake if he ever heard anything about me, he should squash it. "She doesn't exist. Especially to my parents."

"Got it."

We told Francie and Sam the truth. Once they got over their initial excitement, they immediately wanted us to do a special program for History 14. But Halli and I made it clear that we're both done living our lives in public for a while. Probably a long while. We're also not going to be seen together anywhere outside the studio. If I want to go somewhere in her world, she'll stay out of sight.

"Sorry to interrupt," Jake says, "but I thought you'd want to take this. It's Sensorio."

He hands Halli a small tablet with a man's face frozen above it.

"I'll just be a minute," she tells me. Then she unfreezes the face and starts talking to it in Italian.

She's been living with Mrs. Scott for the past few months. I think working with Daniel's family *and* living with them was a little too much. I haven't heard that Red gets along with the yippy dogs any better than he did before, but Mrs. Scott has a huge house, so everyone probably has their own space. I want to visit there as Halli one day, just to see her again.

I open the door to the room where Daniel and I once hid so I could try to contact Halli. At the time there was just a big gel-filled chair in here. Now it's set up as my own private office for whenever I want to visit.

There are three file cabinets where I keep all of Dr. Venn's papers. He asked Elinor to give them to me after he died. Along with the machine that's currently hanging in a locked room down the hall.

Every time I come here, I reread his letter. It's not something I can bring back with me, so I can only enjoy it here.

I open one of the drawers and pull the letter out of its folder. And skip to my favorite parts:

Never doubt that one life, your life, is precious. What you think about is important. What you feel is vital.

We all matter. We are all learning. And what we learn, we add to the whole. You have seen that for yourself.

You are awake to your life. You pay attention. You think and feel and act. You love, you fear, you search. You try.

That is all anyone ever needs to do.

Mena's first week of high school?
DISASTER
But things are about to evolve...

**Riley is an expert with dogs.
With people? Not at all.
But maybe her dogs can help her
finally find her own pack.**

It's like your own long chat with Halli and Audie.

SPECIAL CODE FOR PARALLELOGRAM READERS

Treat yourself to a soft, comfy, custom-made T-shirt designed by Robin Brande herself, inspired by the *Parallelogram* series and her other books! You can see all of them at robinbrande.com/collec tions/t-shirts.

And here's a secret just for you: Use the discount code **AUDIE10** at checkout to get **10% off any items in the store**. That means books, T-shirts, hoodies, mugs—whatever! Go ahead and treat yourself. And high-five, book lover.

Ginny Markham's Motto

Embrace your nerd

Sleep-Read-Repeat

BOOK LOVERS
ARE THE BEST
I CHOOSE THE
BOOKISH LIFE

About the Author

Award-winning author Robin Brande is a former trial attorney, black belt in martial arts, Reiki Master, and wilderness medic. She writes in multiple genres, including young adult, mystery, fantasy, and science fiction.

She is also a designer and maker whose work celebrates the bookish life.

You will find all of her many books and designs at:
RobinBrande.com